TH RESIDENT

Francis Cottam lives in Kingston-upon-Thames. After a career in men's magazines, he is now a full-time novelist.

THE RESIDENT

FRANCIS COTTAM

Published by Arrow Books in association with Hammer 2011

4 6 8 10 9 7 5

First published in Great Britain in 2011 by
Arrow Books in association with Hammer
Random House, 20 Vauxhall Bridge Road,
London SW1V 2SA

www.randomhouse.co.uk

Addresses for companies within The Random House Group Limited can be
found at: www.randomhouse.co.uk/offices.htm

The Random House Group Limited Reg. No. 954009

A CIP catalogue record for this book
is available from the British Library

ISBN 9780099556251

The Random House Group Limited supports the Forest Stewardship
Council® (FSC®), the leading international forest-certification organisation. Our
books carrying the FSC label are printed on FSC®-certified paper. FSC is the only
forest-certification scheme supported by the leading environmental organisations,
including Greenpeace. Our paper procurement policy can be found at
www.randomhouse.co.uk/environment

Typeset by SX Composing DTP, Rayleigh, Essex
Printed and bound by CPI Group (UK) Ltd, Croydon, CR0 4YY

Prologue

Crouched in the darkness, he could hear his own breath quickening as he watched the scene in front of him. He knew what was coming next; he'd seen it countless times before, but it never failed to excite him.

She undid her bra, and he stared avidly at her pert little breasts, until, as she pulled down her panties, his attention was drawn to the downy pelt of hair between her legs. Lowering herself into the bathtub she began to soap her breasts; the white suds were astonishing in contrast against the dark buds of her nipples. She was humming, and his head was filled with the sound of her soft voice, the splash of the water and the buzz of excitement in his ears that was growing louder and louder. He shuddered as a thrill of shock so sudden and great it was almost seismic ran through him.

Suddenly a hand gripped his neck with the rough implacable strength of a workbench vice. The shock of the attack and a sudden overwhelming sense of shame, made him lose control of his bowels. The foul stench made him gag, as the grip on his neck tightened.

A voice murmured intimately against his ear. 'We

should leave now. We should go before the respectable people on the other side of the wall detect the stink of a pervert's shit.'

One

Juliet Devereau arrived home shattered and bruised – literally – from her day at work. Even though ER could be volatile at the best of times, it was rare for a doctor to be injured on the job. Drunk patients were unpredictable, their relatives sometimes worse, but the staff at Williamsburg hospital were protected by security and cameras; so she'd never expected the blow when it came.

Standing shakily outside her front door, Juliet fumbled in her pocket for the key. She felt pretty nauseous, to tell the truth. She was dizzy and her head pounded with dull, rhythmic hammer blows and there was the bitter taste of bile at the back of her throat. She thought she might feel better if she gave in to the strong temptation to puke.

She would do that when she got inside. The home she shared with her husband, Jack, was a neat, half-timbered house in the suburbs outside New York. It had a small manicured front garden with a bright green lawn, painted picket fence and twin rows of neatly planted perennials. A puddle of vomit would do nothing to enhance its general appeal.

Juliet took a couple of deep breaths; the trick was to

try to concentrate her gaze on a single object until it gained clarity. She stared at their house number, seven, described in a brass figure screwed to their door. It didn't work; the brass reflected the sunlight from behind her back into her eyes in a way that made her wince. She blinked and steadied her door key using both hands and finally it scraped and slid into the slot.

Juliet thought back over the past few hours. Who would have thought such a sick guy could pack such a punch? He'd weighed at least three hundred pounds and the bits of him that weren't bone and sinew were all muscle. He had come in running a high fever, complaining that he was hot and sick and that he felt floppy and listless.

'Jesus,' he said, 'the lights in here are bright. It's hurting my eyes.' He shaded them with one enormous, trembling hand. 'Could I trouble one of you people for a drink? I'd kill for a glass of water.'

He was displaying the classic symptoms of viral meningitis. He had taken ill at the gym and had staggered into the hospital under his own steam. But shortly after he arrived, he started to lapse in and out of consciousness. It took four burly orderlies to get him onto the gurney.

'I'm going to give him a muscle relaxant,' Juliet said, filling a syringe from a clear ampoule she had taken from the drugs cabinet.

One of the nurses frowned. 'Why not just turn him on his front and go for the lumbar puncture now?' she said.

It was a fair question; you had to be quick in the treatment of meningitis and the analysis from the lumbar puncture would let them know exactly what they were dealing with. But the situation was complicated by the patient's physique.

'Look at him. He's rigid with pain,' Juliet pointed out. 'The guy has to be a body builder. This is steroid-fed muscle and there's a strong likelihood the needle will break before we extract any spinal fluid. It's a tricky procedure at the best of times. Tissue this dense won't puncture easily. His neck has to measure more than twenty inches and we need a clean sample, not a broken probe. What we really need to do before we do anything else is to take some of the tension out of him. We need to soften him up.'

The patient was lying on his back, his chest rising and falling frantically, his face glossy with sweat. Juliet pulled back the sleeve of the gown they had put him in and cleaned an area of skin with a swab of disinfected cotton wool. The guy had little body fat and veins bunched like the lines of a railroad junction from the inside of the wrist up. Juliet popped the syringe point into a track just below the joint of his arm. The drug she was administering was quick-acting. In minutes, his muscles would relax and he would be ideally prepped for the procedure they had planned. She depressed the plunger steadily with her thumb.

It might have been a defensive reflex or it might simply have been a nervous spasm, but the patient's free arm jerked suddenly up from the gurney and the club of his fist collided with a sickening crack against her left temple.

'Jesus, Juliet . . .' The shocked gasp of the nurse beside

her was the last thing she heard as blackness washed over her.

She came to lying on the floor with worried faces around her. 'Juliet, are you OK? Can you get up?' the nurse said.

'I'm all right.' Juliet put a shaky hand to her face; the skin was tight and puffy on her cheekbone. 'How is he?' She looked up briefly, but the bright light of the ER room caused stars to explode in her head. 'He's right,' she said, hearing her own slurred voice in ringing ears. 'The lights in here are painfully bright.'

'Don't worry about him right now, he's being seen to. Come on, let's get you lying down.' One of the nurses lifted Juliet gently from the floor.

'Seriously, guys, I'm fine. Just a bit shaken. You go back to him, I'll just go and sit down.'

'Oh no you don't. You're probably concussed, I'm taking you to Holstrom.'

There was nothing Juliet could say, even if the blood in her mouth hadn't made talking unpleasant. She grimaced as her tongue discovered a loosened molar. The area around her left eye was swelling rapidly, so that she winced with pain when she blinked; she'd have an ugly purplish circle of bruising to the socket tomorrow, but her range of facial movement was relatively unimpaired and the pain was not sufficiently intense so at least he had not broken any of her bones. Juliet was thankful for small mercies.

Holstrom examined her himself. Her supervisor was regarded with something like awe among the junior house doctors, and there wasn't much that escaped his notice. He gently but thoroughly studied her injuries.

'You have a mild concussion, Juliet.'

It wasn't in Juliet's nature to accept defeat, and no matter how much she respected Holstrom, she wasn't about to accept it now, despite the pain in her head. 'I don't think I do.'

'You're contradicting me?'

'Probably a bad idea,' she said. 'In career terms.'

He chuckled. *Maybe I'm concussed after all*, she thought. She wouldn't ordinarily have the nerve to crack so wise with her boss. Normally she would have exercised greater caution.

'Go home,' he said. 'Rest. Sleep.'

The treatment of concussion was tedious in the extreme: television wasn't allowed; reading was forbidden. The idea was to sit in a darkened room and vegetate until you healed. 'A couple of Demerol and I'll be fine,' she said, trying to butch it out.

He shook his head, he wouldn't budge. No surprise really, he ran a frontline resource with rigid efficiency, he couldn't risk dazed staff treating their emergency admissions.

'The hospital will pay your cab fare home. I would send you in an ambulance, but that's a little ostentatious, don't you think? Wouldn't wish to set the neighbours' curtains a-twitching.

'Keep us informed about your recuperation but on no account rush back. I know how conscientious you are but that would be self-defeating, Juliet. You have suffered a severe blow to the head. Allow yourself the time you'd give anyone else to recover fully. Try treating yourself with the same compassion you show your patients.'

She smiled at him. She was very fortunate; she could not imagine a kinder boss, nor one for whom she could have more personal admiration or professional respect. 'I'll do my best not to throw up on the cab ride home,' she said, finally admitting that her boss was right.

Stepping through the front door, the first thing in there she noticed was the smell of perfume. But then it was probably a weird symptom of the concussion. The brain was complex, knocked off-kilter it could run riot with sensory impressions.

But the moment she closed the door behind her, she instinctively looked up the stairs. Had she heard a noise from up there? Yes, she had. It hadn't been the hammer thud of her heartbeat through her concussed head and neither had it been the ringing that still afflicted her ears. It had been something caught and suppressed, a gasp or sob and it hadn't been Jack's, had it? It had been girlish, female. Silently taking the first step up the thickly carpeted flight, Juliet thought that it had sounded sexual in character.

She knew she was wrong. She had to be wrong. Yet she climbed the stairs silently, holding her breath, fear clutched her stomach. Goose bumps were rising on her skin, coarsening it, she saw, in the light coming in through the open curtains on the landing above. All was silent up there now. But it seemed a fraught, concealing silence; someone hiding or lurking rather than being innocently absent from the home she shared with her husband.

She was completely unprepared for the sight that met her as she opened the bedroom door. Her first thought was that the blow to the head had affected her more than she had thought, and had triggered this lurid hallucination.

They hadn't heard her. They weren't lying looking sheepishly back at her when she pushed open the bedroom door and exposed them. Nor were they dressing hastily in clothes discarded carelessly about the bedroom. They were in the act, quite oblivious, her husband's muscular back arched in pleasure. All Juliet could see of the woman was her knees gripping his waist and her splayed hair streaked and tawny against the pillow behind her husband.

She looked away from them, flinching, touching the swelling around her eye with tentative fingers. And she looked back. Even when they sensed her presence and Jack paused in his rutting thrusts; even when the woman looked around his shoulder at Juliet with a start of surprise, she did not really believe it could be happening.

Somehow she managed to stagger down the stairs, though how she managed that without her legs buckling she had no idea. She was wondering what to do, flapping like an injured bird, hopeful and incredulous, when Jack turned her by the shoulder and stood before her naked.

She looked down and saw the wet coils of his pubic hair, slickened and matted with sex. She smelt the musky raw reek of it beneath the accents of the perfume that permeated the house. Her stomach heaved: she could no longer repress the nausea that had threatened to overwhelm her since the attack. Pushing past Jack she rushed to the bathroom.

When she emerged, teary-eyed and shaken, her husband was waiting for her, wrapped in a robe now, the physical evidence of what he'd done hidden. The smell muted slightly.

'It's adultery, Jack,' she said. She heard herself slur out the words. Her mouth was swollen inside.

He nodded. There were tears in his eyes, but he remained silent. But what could he have said? The woman he'd been fucking was still in their room.

'In our home, Jack. In our bed. How could you?'

He just looked at her. She could see that he had already regained something of himself. He was a self-possessed man in most situations and even now, his composure was coming back to him. He said, 'What's happened to your face?'

She touched the side of her damaged eye with her hand. She felt the swelling there and the sore heat of it. 'It's nothing.' She could feel the tears coming. 'What have you done to me?'

She was overcome with the irresistible urge to flee. She couldn't bear him to see her like this. She was utterly broken by his betrayal, but she didn't want him to know how completely destroyed she felt. Not with him standing there smelling of sex with another woman, and the woman in question upstairs, listening to them, no doubt taking some sort of perverse satisfaction in being involved in this tawdry little drama. So Juliet left.

Their lawn sprinkler was on. A little rainbow of colour shivered through it as it showered the cut grass in the late August sunshine. Jack had remembered to switch it on. He had possessed the presence of mind to carry out that mundane chore on the day he had fucked someone else in their bed. It suggested to her that he had done this more than once. Of course he had; it was a part of his routine, like turning on the sprinkler and checking his email and sending her the witty text messages that made her smile in the precious moments of relaxation that punctuated her frenetic shifts at the hospital.

She smiled grimly, what were the odds of her catching him on the first occasion of his infidelity to her? Astronomical, she supposed. His betrayal of her was probably as mundane to him as a trip to the supermarket. Get up. Eat breakfast. Kiss your departing wife goodbye as she leaves for work. Write your novelist's quota of words for the day. Fuck the pretty blonde from the tennis club. He had probably been doing it for months. Maybe he had done it from the very start of their marriage and just never bothered, despite their vows, to stop.

She almost turned around and went back into the house. It was instinct, of course. It was what you did in times of trouble: you yearned for home and the consoling arms of the one you loved. But there was no consolation there; only treachery and humiliation. Her husband had proved himself a deceitful stranger. She could no longer call this place a home.

Where would she go? What would she do? To whom would she turn? She moved her loosened molar with the tip of her tongue and wondered whether she might lose it. But what was the loss of a tooth? She had just lost a marriage.

Sobbing, she limped to the end of the block, fumbling in her pocket for her cell phone and called Sydney. Sydney wasn't just a colleague, she was Juliet's best friend. They shared the same occupation and the same boss and the same sometimes insane demands on their time and professional skills.

Despite the sluggish speed at which her mind was working, Juliet was processing what she had just experienced. It was a failure and humiliation that she'd prefer to keep private. But right now she didn't have the strength to do that; she needed love and sympathy and Sydney was the one person in the world most willing and likely to be able to comfort her.

She got voicemail. She garbled a message out between sobs. 'I just caught Jack fucking a trophy blonde. They were in our home. They were in our bed.'

She wiped tears from her eyes and kept on walking. She had no destination in mind, she just knew she had to get as far away from what she had just witnessed as she could.

Her cell phone began to vibrate.

'Hon?'

'Sydney. Thank God.'

'Tell me it isn't true, Jules.'

'I only wish I could.'

'Get over to our place, now. Go there immediately.'

'You're on the late shift.'

'And you know I won't finish for a couple of hours. But I'll call Mike and she will be there. He's not perfect, but it's better than walking the streets. You'll stay with us tonight. You'll stay with us for as long as you want to.'

'It's only three o'clock, Sydney. Mike can't just walk out of the office.'

'He's the boss there, babe. Of course he can. He's the man in charge. And you know perfectly well he'll do whatever I tell him to.'

There was a bad moment a few seconds after Juliet broke the connection when she almost stumbled into a woman on the sidewalk wheeling a stroller while she shepherded a small boy on a toy scooter. Juliet mumbled an apology. The woman smiled at her cheerfully. *She looks happy*, Juliet thought. She looked like she was living the life Juliet had been expecting to live one day. Until now.

Christ, Juliet. Pull yourself together. Before she got a cab to take her to Mike and Sydney's brownstone miles away, she needed to compose herself. No cab driver would pick up someone looking the way she did right now. Swollen face, black eye, uncontrollable sobbing. They'd whizz right by her, refusing to be dragged into whatever trouble she was running away from.

Mike knew. Juliet saw the pity and compassion in his eyes when he opened the door to her. She took in the familiar stocky shape of him and noticed that in his slightly careless, ramshackle way he had spilled something, probably a forkful of a hasty lunch that had left a stain dried on his shirtfront.

Good old Mike, Sydney's husband of five years, the father of the child shortly to be born to them, a man who tripped over shoelaces he had forgotten to tie and was apt to dip his shirt cuffs in the sauce at dinner. A shrewd and successful mess of a man who loved his wife and was honest and true and totally dependable.

He tried, with an almost comic lack of success, to hide his shock at her battered appearance. Then he opened his arms to her and said, 'Juliet, you poor honey.' And she hugged him back gratefully and started to cry again, afraid this time that she might never be able to stop.

Two

For days after the discovery, Juliet was numb. Infidelity was the stuff of magazine features and trashy television shows, not for one moment during her time with Jack did it occur to her that it would apply to them. They were too much in love, the perfect couple. She had planned her life and her career with the utmost care, and to have it overturned in an instant was shattering.

'I don't think I understand the rules any more, Sydney.' Juliet was huddled in the corner of the sofa, while Sydney stretched out on the other with her feet resting on the arms, hands stroking her bump.

'What rules, hon?' Ever-sympathetic, Juliet was amazed Sydney still had the patience to listen to her.

'The rules that tell you how to spot that your husband is screwing around. Shouldn't I have guessed what he was doing? I mean, loads of women get these feelings when their husbands cheat, don't they? They see it in the way they behave, or the way they dress, or even the way they get their hair cut. So why didn't I spot it? How come I didn't smell that woman's vile perfume on him? How could I have missed it? Maybe I just wasn't there enough to notice. I should have spent more time at home, taken more interest in his work.'

'Come on, Juliet. You think it's OK for him to go off and sleep with someone else because he's not getting enough attention from you? You think he needs to be treated like a child?'

'I don't know, Syd. But I wasn't around much. But then, maybe that wasn't it. Maybe it was just that he was bored of me. Maybe *I'm* boring? I haven't even read his books, I don't go to art exhibitions. I mean, men don't cheat on interesting women, do they?'

Sydney rolled her eyes. 'Ain't that the truth? I mean, take Sandra Bullock for example,' she yawned extravagantly. 'And that Hillary Clinton, have you ever tried having a conversation with her? Boring as hell. Come on, Jules, you know you're talking crap. Jack's a fool, and you're an intelligent, successful, beautiful woman.'

Juliet smiled sadly. 'That wasn't enough, though, was it? And I really should have seen it, Syd. I should have noticed Jack was unhappy and that woman was sniffing around. I should have made him want me, not her.'

'OK, enough, Jules. Stop beating yourself up. This is your grieving time, but *do not* blame yourself for something he did.'

'I know you're right, but I thought he was my soulmate, the love of my life.' Juliet fought back the ever-present tears before slapping her hand down hard on the arm of the sofa. 'God, I hate being like this. It's pathetic. Do me a favour. Next time I get like this just give me a kick.' Juliet switched on a determinedly bright smile. 'Anyway, I can't hang around here for much longer. You and Mike need to make the most of your last few weeks of peace before life changes for ever. The last thing you need is me crying in the corner every time you turn around. From tomorrow I am going to walk the streets of New York until I find the apartment of my dreams.'

Three days later, Jack called. Juliet was filling out an accident report at a desk at the hospital when the call came. Her eye was a mess by then, a pulpy riot of purple and blue that screamed domestic violence to anyone unacquainted with the facts. She was not concussed any more, though, which was a blessing because work was something she could lose herself in. Holstrom had been wary about taking her back but amenable. The challenge of finding a permanent home loomed like an unconquerable mountain at the back of her mind. For the moment, she was keeping it there.

She felt her cell phone vibrate in her pocket, took it out and saw the familiar number light up the display. She did not take the call. She did not, she realised with a sick pang in the pit of her stomach, despite her brave words to Sydney, have the strength at that precise moment to hear his voice.

He called again later that afternoon, as she drank coffee which had no flavour and ate a sandwich curiously devoid of taste in the hospital canteen. It was quiet and the canteen lacked its usual metallic clamour of background noise. She walked out just the same, finding an empty room off the corridor outside in which to answer the phone in private. She felt strangely guilty for taking the call.

'Leave me alone, Jack. You've done enough to upset me. Just leave me in peace.'

'I didn't think you cared.'

'What? What did you just say?'

'I didn't think you cared.'

'Oh, Jesus. Come on.'

'I really didn't think you cared about me. About us.'

'So, what, Jack? You thought you may as well fuck someone else instead of bothering to talk to me? You think that's an excuse for breaking your vows? Breaking us? Breaking me?' Juliet hated herself, but she couldn't stop the sob that echoed off the walls.

'Jules, I'm sorry. I know I was wrong. I knew it as I was doing it. I'll never forgive myself for hurting you like this.' Jack sounded genuine, but she wasn't sure she'd ever be able to trust anything he said again.

'Poor you, Jack. That must be so hard for you. God, what were you *thinking*? And with the Tennis Club Blonde? It's such a fucking cliché. And for your information, I don't care. Not any more.' The hand holding the cell phone was shaking, but at least her voice was steady. She had that under control. To herself, despite what she felt, she sounded reasonably composed.

'I would never have done it if I'd known you still had feelings for me,' he said. 'I only realised I mattered to you when I saw the look on your face at the house. I saw your pain. I will never forgive myself, Juliet, for inflicting that on you.'

'You're blaming me for your infidelity? That's bullshit. Seriously, I can't listen to this. It makes me sick to hear you pretending to be sorry. Because it's clear you're the one who didn't care. Not about our marriage, and certainly not about the vows you swore when you took me as your wife.'

'She means nothing to me.'

'I'm grateful to her. If I hadn't surprised you two together I might have spent years being cheated on. I owe her one.'

'Juliet —'

But the conversation was going nowhere. Juliet pressed the button on her phone, terminating the call. She went back into the canteen and her sandwich. She had no appetite, but she needed the food to keep going. She bit into the sandwich and chewed cautiously, noticing with relief that her gum seemed to be tightening its grip around her loosened molar again.

During those early days of separation, in moments of weakness, Juliet would fantasise that this was a nightmare. That at any moment she would wake and find Jack sprawled beside her, tousled and gorgeous in sleep. Sometimes she even believed it, and went around the whole day waiting to wake up. Not caring what was happening because none of it felt real. Sometimes she feared her grip on reality was tenuous and that the pain of what had occurred, if she did confront it fully, would propel her towards breakdown.

Thank God for her job. If she'd been in a less demanding profession, one that enabled her to drift off into her own world for hours at a time, she was sure she'd have lost it. Working flat-out on the front line of the medical profession meant that people depended on her every day, and if her concentration slipped for a moment it could be the difference between saving a life and losing one. But outside the hospital, without the adrenalin pumping through her, the life or death decisions, and the sheer exhilaration she sometimes felt when she performed well, life felt out of control. She had nowhere to live, no husband, no future outside her career. The breakdown of her marriage meant she had failed in one of her self-imposed life tests, and she could not think how to put it right. And she missed Jack. All the time.

A fortnight passed. Then a fortnight almost imperceptibly became a month. At the end of that month, she agreed to a meeting with the lawyer Jack had engaged to help him deal with some of the administrative aspects of his commercial success, because although Juliet hadn't managed to read one of his novels, there were plenty of others who had, and their numbers were increasing.

As the only subjects Juliet had left to discuss with Jack concerned divorce and property, she couldn't quite understand what his lawyer, who specialised in copyright, could have to say, but she met with Philip Beal because she wanted to keep things as amicable as possible. She really couldn't handle any more animosity in her life.

They met for lunch at an expensive restaurant; their table was on a terrace with a panoramic view. The lunch was on Philip. Or at least, Philip was picking up the check. Juliet assumed that Jack was actually paying and as she studied the menu, she experienced a moment of nostalgia for the time when she and Jack had met as struggling students and had gone happily Dutch on their modest evenings out together. They had been cheap, those occasions. And they had been intensely romantic and they were gone for ever, and leaving only bitterness in their wake.

'He wants you to have the house,' Philip said once they had dispensed with the small talk.

'I don't want it, I couldn't live there now, Philip. He must know that. You would know it too if—'

'I am aware of what happened,' Philip said. He coloured. 'Of the circumstances in which you became aware of his infidelity, I mean.'

'I never want to see the house again. I have to move on with my life. I won't return to the suburbs.'

'Done with the commute?'

'Done with the claustrophobia. And I seem to have developed an allergy to country clubs. Unless it's just an allergy to their blonder members,' Juliet said sardonically.

Philip's colour deepened. Obviously Jack *had* told him everything. The facts did not paint him in a favourable light. He could only have related them truthfully to his lawyer in an effort to try to achieve something. 'What does he want, Philip?'

'He wants reconciliation.'

'Then he's deluded.'

'He still has very strong feelings for you.'

'Evidently not strong enough.'

'He won't just give up.'

'And he won't succeed. So we have a stalemate, don't we?'

'I have the keys to the house in my pocket. He has moved out. He hopes to earn the right to move back in. In the meantime, he has asked me to give the keys to you.'

Juliet laughed bitterly. 'So the house is a bribe?'

Philip shrugged. 'A gesture,' he said.

'Tell him to sell it. When he eventually succeeds in doing so, we'll divide the proceeds equally.'

'He knows he's the one at fault.'

'So?'

'He feels he should be the one to lose out, as it were. The one to pay the penalty.'

'He *is* paying the penalty, Philip. He's losing out on me.'

The words sounded a lot braver than she felt and she pondered them on her way back to her temporary home, a room not much bigger than a closet in Sydney and Mike's apartment. They had originally had a spacious guest room there. But that had now been decorated as a combined bedroom/playroom for the baby. The birth was only weeks away and Juliet felt the imposition of her own presence in the apartment increasing by the day.

Sydney and Mike were wonderful and generous and never made her feel unwelcome, but the impending birth and their excitement sometimes left her feeling lonelier than ever. The pressure to go was implicit in every soft toy and item of infant clothing the couple shopped for. It was only right that they enjoyed the adventure of parenthood in the privacy of a home shared only with their new daughter.

'I'll find a place to live tomorrow,' she said to Sydney when she got back from her lunch with Philip Beal, just before she left for her night shift at the hospital.

Sydney smiled at Juliet, putting her hand on her growing bump and said, 'Just like that?'

'I know. It's likely to be a struggle.'

'It's life and death, hon. Set your heart on anywhere specific?'

'I'm done with the 'burbs. I want to live in Brooklyn.'

'Then it's not life and death. It's far worse.'

'I'll find a place. I'll have to.'

Sydney was silent for a long moment. Then she said, 'I think you will feel better when you do.'

'It will be a relief,' Juliet said.

'Are we so difficult to live with?'

'You've been sweethearts, both of you, I'll always be grateful. And you know that. But I really need to find somewhere of my own.'

'Security?' Sydney said.

Juliet shook her head. 'Closure,' she said.

Three

On the way to the hospital that evening, she stopped to buy a coffee at a small bodega outside the elevated subway station where she caught her train to work, as she had every day since she'd moved back into the city. She was preoccupied with the magnitude of the task facing her when she finished her shift. She really did intend to find a place to live. Whatever it took, she would look until the deal was done and she had the keys to the door in her hand.

It was raining and she didn't even notice the chaos of Brooklyn around her. The screech of cars braking abruptly, voices shouting above the traffic noise in the effort to be heard and music blaring in a harsh cacophony of competing rhythms washed over her. She was so lost in her own thoughts that she barely noticed two police officers sipping their own coffees as she slipped out of the bodega. She had walked only a few feet further on when a staccato burst of gunfire exploded twice in her ears from the direction of the place she had just left. Screams broke out around her, and she turned in shock, as a figure – male, young, Latin-American – blundered past the two cops and ran for an alley, reaching into his jacket before wheeling about and taking aim at the cops with what she assumed must be a handgun.

The blue steel of the raised weapon glimmered in the rain and neon. There was a moment when everything seemed as still and expectant as a frozen movie frame. Then the moment was shattered by a bright muzzle-flash from the mouth of the handgun and the loud, lethal pop of a bullet's release.

Juliet hit the wet pavement, taking cover from stray shots as the impact of a bullet exploded against a wall close by. The reek of cordite was suddenly strong in the air, overlaying the hot smell of spilled coffee. Shouts broke out around her as the shooter turned and ran. The cops ran in pursuit towards the mouth of the alley, their rain capes flapping and unwieldy, grunting out breathless calls for back-up into their radios, the heavy chrome of police issue weapons brandished dully in their fists.

Juliet rose to her feet shakily, her coffee forgotten. She gazed around her in disbelief, only dimly aware of the blare of sirens growing louder from several different directions and lights flashing as the approaching patrol cars swatted a path through the gridlock. She'd only ever had to deal with the aftermath of violence before, and that was alarming enough. Gunshot victims could be hurt without knowing it. They sometimes bled to death unaware that they'd been hit. She checked to see that she had not been wounded by a stray shot or exploding brick fragment. She was fine, unscathed; the only damage she'd sustained was a bit of street debris from the sidewalk that she brushed from the front of her wet coat. Thanking God that it hadn't been worse, she hurried to the hospital. She had no doubt that she'd soon discover whether anyone had been hurt.

It wasn't long before Juliet learned that the cops had got their man. She recognised the patient wheeled into the emergency room later that night. The details on the clipboard she was handed told her that his name was Carlos Leon, aged eighteen, and he had gaping gunshot wounds to his neck and chest.

'Punctured left ventricle and lacerated esophagus,' she said, in expert assessment of the victim's wounds. 'Prep OR 3 stat.' Her voice was commanding, authoritative. This was her domain. She was in the one place where she always knew exactly what to do.

Juliet performed the surgery immediately. She removed the bullets from her patient's chest and neck, stemmed the bleeding and stabilised his breathing in a surgical marathon that only saw her drop her bloodied scrubs into a waste bin after dawn had come up. She sat down exhausted but satisfied. Carlos would recover from the damage done to him.

Juliet heard Dr Holstrom's voice above her. 'A zone three carotid GSW? I'm starting to suspect you're a glory hound.'

She looked up. There was humour in her boss's eyes as well as in his tone. She smiled. 'Just happened to be there,' she said.

'Your colleagues will be jealous,' Holstrom said. 'Your shift ended three hours ago. Please: go home and get some rest.'

He made the proposition sound so simple. To her it was anything but. As far as she knew, her supervisor was unaware that her life had taken the traumatic turn it had. She had deliberately kept news of her domestic difficulties from him. She didn't want him to start thinking she was more of a liability than an asset. It was not in her nature to look for excuses to fail. She always strove for excellence.

She took the elevator down to the ground floor of Williamsburg hospital feeling less certain with each foot she travelled away from the ER department, her work, her sanctuary. The automatic doors opened on to the fresh air and endless vista of a vast dawn. She felt very small in it, totally insignificant, a tiny detail suddenly forgotten by a careless world.

Where do I go from here? Juliet wondered. After the chaos and excitement of the hospital she felt utterly alone, and the thought of finding a place to live seemed far harder than saving the life of the gunshot victim. She walked through the raw morning until she saw a news vendor. Buying a copy of the *New York Times* she turned straight to the property section, searching through the rental listings with something like desperation in her eyes.

Juliet loved the city just as intensely as she sometimes hated it. New York inspired her every bit as much as it intimidated her. But there was nowhere else where her skills would be put to the same relentless day in and day out examination as they were here.

She had not been tempted for a single moment by the jangle of the keys carried in Philip Beal's pocket. Her old home was a place synonymous now with heartache and indignity. She didn't think she'd ever be able to even look at the house again without the smell of that woman's perfume and the vision of a naked Jack, still sweaty from his exertions, coming back to haunt her. Just the thought of it now made her feel sick in a way that the blood gushing from Carlos's wounds could never do. No, no matter what it took she would find an apartment and start a new life. Prove to herself and Jack that she was not a woman that could be destroyed so easily.

Hours later, in the hallway of a seedy run-down building, however, she was not so sure. The search for an affordable place was relentlessly grim and totally exhausting. A nice little place in the suburbs was starting to take on an alarming attraction. Sighing, she squinted up at the narrow tenement stairs. Only five flights, she thought wearily, as she trudged upwards.

'You must be Juliet.'

She looked up. Her to-go coffee was tepid and undrinkable in one fist. In her other hand her copy of the *New York Times* was smeared and tattered. On the stairs above her was the bright-eyed and deflatingly over-eager sales agent she had spoken to on her cell earlier. 'Yes,' she said.

Juliet was still out of breath from the climb when she entered the apartment. The room was about the size of an elevator compartment, but nevertheless the realtor looked very pleased with herself. However, so cramped was the space they shared the two of them felt some-what like a crowd to Juliet.

'Which way is the bedroom?'

In a triumphant tone, the agent said, '*This* is your bedroom.' She reached across and pulled down a Murphy bed from its recess in the wall. Then, from the facing wall, she pulled down a table. 'And your dining room, your kitchen and study,' she said. 'It's real New York living. And as a bonus, the view is amazing.'

Juliet waited for another of the conjuring tricks that had made furniture materialise from nothing. She was feeling somewhat confused because the room, to her, appeared windowless. Perhaps the realtor would produce a sledgehammer and improvise one? But she did not. Instead, she pushed a chair towards Juliet and gestured above them, about eight feet high, where what looked to Juliet like a gun slit, allowed in a measly wedge of light.

'Go ahead,' the agent said.

Juliet climbed on to the chair. She stood on tiptoe and stretched her neck and was just able to glimpse the vista beyond the narrow rectangle of glass. The agent had not lied, she saw. The view was indeed amazing. 'It is a good view . . .'

'Interested?'

Juliet stared incredulously around her. Was the woman serious? She jumped down from the chair. She felt as if she was in one of those TV shows where people are secretly filmed becoming more and more indignant in a farcical situation as they're goaded by someone straight-faced and relentless.

The Murphy bed snapped shut with a suddenness that startled both of them.

'No,' Juliet said, as calmly as she could. 'I really don't think that I am. Interested, I mean.'

'Would you mind telling me why?'

Juliet thought about the question. 'I just have the fear somewhere as airy and spacious as this might trigger my agoraphobia,' she said.

'There is no need for sarcasm.' The realtor's fake smile and manufactured goodwill vanished

'I think there is,' Juliet said. 'I think there is a compelling need. You have completely wasted my time.'

Juliet stomped out of the building. *Jesus, do people actually live in these places?* She thought back to the stream of apartments she'd seen. There'd been a basement apartment so damp she could visualise the mildew creeping across the fabric of her clothes as they hung in the bedroom closet. Then there was a place so thoroughly infested by roaches that the stuff used to kill them had left a sticky residue on every surface and a smell like rotting mackerel was miasmic in every room. In one property, she'd had to use the lavatory and when she'd pressed the flush button, pipes sang in the ceiling above her head like some demented, metallic choir. It took fifteen minutes for the noise to stop but in truth, she had made her mind up after ten.

A large loft space shown her by her fifth or sixth agent of the day (Juliet was starting to lose count) appeared promising at first glance. It was spacious and airy and light-filled. It was in a part of Brooklyn with coffee shops, a bakery and an authentic and traditional corner delicatessen. In the middle of the main room, a man was teaching a little boy how to play guitar. Juliet thought it strange to be showing the property before the existing tenants had even packed up their things.

The agent showing the property said, 'Rashid only holds his classes during the day, from around nine until six. And every other Saturday. The rest of the time is yours.'

Abruptly and deafeningly, the acoustic strumming of the guitar became electric, the blare of sound from the amplifier practically blew the two women out of the room. They retreated into the relative quiet of the hallway.

'I don't get it,' Juliet said.

'It's a shared space,' the realtor said, as though explaining things to a dull-minded child. 'I've found it works quite well for working professionals with long hours. And you did say you were a doctor.'

Juliet was too nonplussed to respond.

The agent said, 'It's only six thousand a month.'

Juliet kept her eyes fixed through the open doorway on the talentless pupil making ugly noises with an off-key guitar. Maybe he was tone deaf. Maybe Rashid was tone deaf and had taught him to play that way and it wasn't his fault. She concentrated on the tableau of boy and tutor at the airy centre of the loft and tried with all her will not to lose hope completely.

Four

Home as a concept mattered more to Juliet perhaps than it did to most people. The child of hippies, she had grown up in a shifting, nomadic commune of trailers and camper vans and had been taught to believe that property was something from which enlightened people learned to liberate themselves.

She had never learned. To her, the rootless, shiftless nature of her early life was not free and easy but shameful and enervating. To fixed communities, the people of the commune to which her parents belonged were little better than itinerants; the hippie equivalent of the freight-hopping hoboes of the Dust Bowl Depression era. Radical ideology cut little ice with people who thought you might trash what you didn't steal and despoil the land before you skulked away to inflict your presence on another pretty township.

She had been solitary by circumstance and inclination in the way that ambitious and single-minded people often are, but her brains and determination had set her free. She had got through med school and begun to practise at the sharp end of urban medicine in the most demanding and volatile metropolis in the world.

Jack had completed the dream. A career, a steady

home, someone to love her exclusively. They'd even bought a dog, Amelie. Everything she'd ever wanted had been right there in the palm of her hand. But obviously it wasn't enough for Jack. The dressing might have been perfect, but it was all a sham; he'd wanted more. It was a depressing conclusion, but she could think of no other explanation for what Jack had done.

She shook her head. She couldn't keep descending into gloom like this. Life went on. You just had to adjust to the changes and come out fighting. That's all there was to it. There was time to go to one more address before returning, sleepless, to the hospital and her next shift at work, but before she did, she needed some food to see her through the next few hours.

She found a café so deeply recessed in its gloomy interior it was almost cave-like where she ate a salt beef sandwich and gulped a mug of coffee. From where she sat, through the rectangle of the café frontage, the street was framed like a cinema screen and the traffic hurtling across it was vivid and picturesque, glossy and bright in the falling rain, a colourful world divorced from her problems.

Reluctantly, she heaved herself up from her table. She was exhausted and much of her recent resolution seemed to have drained away, like fuel from a holed tank. She had to carry on, but she knew she was running on empty. She needed a pep talk before she got too mired in self-pity. Picking up her phone she called Sydney.

'Hey, Jules, how's it going? You found the perfect apartment yet?'

'Oh yeah, Syd. You know how I've always wanted one of those beds that pulls down from the walls? I've found just the place. With a spectacular view. It's just so cute.'

'Uh huh. Sounds great, hon. Is that sarcasm I hear? So was there anything else?'

'You would not believe what I've seen today. I mean, do people really live in places like this?'

Juliet told her about the apartments she'd seen so far. Sydney found it hilarious.

'That's just priceless. Seriously. OK, forget about them now, Jules. This next one is the one for you. I can just feel it. Not much longer and you'll be standing in the apartment of your dreams. And if not, well, you know you can stay with us for as long as you want.'

Juliet hung up feeling much better. She just had to stay positive. With Sydney's words ringing in her ears she approached the next building in a better frame of mind. The building was old, she observed as she approached it; built, she thought, at the turn of the previous century, its façade stolidly indifferent to the battering to which time and the elements had treated it. It was a tall building for the time of its construction and its ground-floor windows were sullenly blanked by sets of dusty brown blinds. Rain stains smeared the glass. The shadows were deepening in a dark creep through the streets.

She looked at her watch. The real estate agent was late. *Terrific*, she thought. It seemed she no longer qualified for even the most basic courtesies. Still, it was a sellers' market, demand in New York was monstrously in excess of supply; she expected that a proud tenant would soon be unpacking treasured belongings in the elevator size space with the gun-slit view. Realtors did not need to be courteous when their clients were almost always people sharing Juliet's desperate need for a place to call their own.

The front door of the building was open a chink and when Juliet tested it, it widened a fraction further, expanding the line of gloom between the edge of the door and the jamb. She took a step forward and pushed the door properly. It opened with a heavy whoosh on to a dark vestibule. She stepped in tentatively and the click of her leather heels told her it was floored in marble. Classy, was her immediate thought, an impression solidified by the weight of the door as she closed it behind her and the cool smells of stone and oiled wood and the sheer stillness of the quiet building interior.

The apartment she was there to see was on the first floor. There was an elevator, but she climbed the stairs. As her eyes adjusted to the lack of light, she saw that the bronze stair rail was thin, almost spidery, and cold beneath her touch. She expected the stairs to creak with age but under their covering of patterned carpeting, she realised that they too were hewn from stone.

The door to the apartment she was there to view was not locked. It moaned slightly on hinges grown stiff with lack of use when she opened it. The interior was shuttered, dark. She walked across the bare boards of the floor and opened the blinds over the windows. Bars of wan autumnal light smeared the floorboards, illuminating a single naked bulb hanging from a high ceiling and the faded hues of ancient, cheerless wallpaper. From somewhere, there was the persistent dripping of a faucet, the cold splash of a single drop of water hitting the stone of a sink, as if to emphasise the silence and stillness of the place.

It was a dismal prospect, but the worst aspect of the apartment was the smell, subtle but persistent, something between boiled cabbage and flowers rotting in a vase. For a moment Juliet couldn't move. Her instincts were telling her to run, gooseflesh tingled along her arms and up the back of her neck. Her breath caught. There was something malevolent in the room. Then, slowly, rationality returned and she shook her head impatiently. She was being stupid. She was a doctor for God's sake, not prone to being affected by feelings and atmosphere. Her mind didn't work that way. She was logical and reasoned and acted only when she had proof, and there was no tangible threat in the room. But despite these thoughts, she could not stop shivering and the creeping feeling of terror and helplessness would not go away.

The door behind her swung open suddenly and Juliet squealed and jumped. She'd never made such a ridiculous sound in her life. Her face reddened in embarrassment. The doorway framed a man, middle-aged, florid-faced, a yellow rose vivid on the lapel of his broadly chalk-striped three-piece suit.

'Miss Devereau,' he said, 'My apologies for being late. The day has stacked badly for me.' He shrugged. 'It happens. I'm sorry. I am Mr de Silva.'

His voice was so thickly Brooklynite, it was like listening to someone from another time. Like the building itself, she thought, except not like the building at all, because she could see that he was nice. He was a dapper, courteous man who clearly earned his living respectably.

He raised his eyebrows and made a show of glancing around the room they were in. 'All it needs,' he said, 'is a little love.'

Juliet smiled at him. She felt better now someone was with her, but she still wanted to get out of the building as fast as she could. But he was entitled to know why. 'What it needs,' she said, 'is absolution. I can't provide that.'

He opened his arms. 'You couldn't like it here?'

'Not in a million years.'

'Are you a psychic, Miss Devereau?'

'No, I'm not. But something bad happened here.'

He shrugged. 'If it did, it was an awfully long time ago.'

'It left a residue,' Juliet said. She could hardly believe she would even think something like this, let alone say the words out loud. 'I can smell it. I can feel it. What was it?'

The man was carrying an umbrella. It was furled but dry. It was raining persistently outside and had he carried the umbrella there its fabric now would be wet, dripping onto the floor from its point. He wore no raincoat and the shoulders of his suit coat were dry. His hair had been groomed with some old-fashioned pomade. There was no rain gathered between the carefully combed strands. He had not come here from outside the building.

'You aren't a realtor.'

'No,' he said. 'I'm a landlord.'

'And something bad happened here.'

'Bad things happened everywhere. The city has lived through some turbulent times.'

'It doesn't linger in most places,' Juliet said. 'It is lingering here, though.'

'What is?'

'Despair,' she said after a moment's hesitation. 'It's like a silent, deafening scream. It's like the walls are screaming. It's intolerable. What happened here?'

'Does it matter?'

'I don't suppose it does. But I would still like to know it isn't just a neurotic woman's imagination getting the better of her.'

The man smiled, sadly. He glanced down at the polished toecaps of his shoes. He was the sort of man, she thought, who would indulge the ritual of a daily shine on the street. He would know the shoeshine boy by name and tip generously. He said, 'I do not believe you to be in the slightest bit neurotic. Quite the opposite, in fact.'

'Then tell me.'

'Someone bad once stayed here, Miss Devereau. It was a long time ago, back in the days of prohibition and the mob, years before your grandparents were born, thirty years before I was born myself. He was a professional killer from Palermo. His name was Giuseppe Forno. His specialty was the garrotte.'

'I see.'

The landlord walked over to the window. He rubbed a finger across a blind slat and it came away so thick with dust that Juliet could see it from the other side of the room. He rubbed it away absently with the pad of his thumb.

'And you expected me to rent the place.'

'Some people sense it and some people don't. Most don't. Those that do are in the minority. I am sorry for having inflicted this experience upon you and having wasted your time.'

It seemed to Juliet that the dripping faucet in a room beyond them had grown louder. But surely this was something she was just imagining. Its cold and percussive splash onto porcelain assaulted her ears, almost like a rebuke. She shook her head. What her ears were insisting to her was impossible.

'Only the minority sense the killer's presence yet the dust suggests you haven't let the place for years. Why is that?' she asked.

He smiled at her again. The smile was both rueful and honest. 'I suppose the reason is because I don't like to come here. Perhaps because I sense it so strongly myself,' he said.

Five

The landlord saw her out of the building. Once beyond the apartment door, Juliet felt fine again. She had never felt anything like that contagious dread before and hoped she never would again.

She travelled on the subway to the hospital, trying not to think about the futility of her day, trying not to calculate how long it was since she had actually slept.

On her break she googled the Palermo killer, Giuseppe Forno, intrigued to find out more about the man whose chill presence she had felt in the apartment she had seen late in the afternoon. She discovered that he had worked for one of the major Sicilian crime families and she wondered whether the building she had visited had been bought on the proceeds of organised crime. Gangsters were a dapper breed, weren't they? The landlord's style might have been inherited from ancestors who had earned their living with dirtier hands than his.

Forno had been a prolific killer, she learned, an expert with the garrotte, as the landlord had said. Conscience seemed to have caught up with him in the end, though. He had hanged himself in a closet using suspender elastic knotted to a coat hook; his suicide took place in the apartment she had just viewed. What distinguished his death from those of his victims was that his had been by choice.

Sydney poked her head through the curtained-off cubicle where Juliet was doing her brief, sinister study. She twisted into the space, fatigue on her features and her hands pressed to the small of her back, visibly feeling the weight of her bump. Soon she'd be too pregnant to work.

'So how was it? Was it the place of your dreams?'

Juliet gave her an affectionate smile. 'You are not going to believe what happened.' She turned back to the computer. 'See this charming picture?'

Sydney looked at the screen. There was a photograph of Forno on his mortuary slab, the bruising on his neck plain to see. He looked serene in death. He had met his maker freshly shaven, with his dark moustache trimmed and waxed at its tips.

'Gross. What's that all about? You're not looking up ways of getting revenge on Jack, are you?'

Juliet laughed. 'Yeah, right. Although, now you mention it, being arrested for a crime of passion would at least solve my accommodation problem. No, I viewed an apartment today. It had a ghoulish history. I sensed something.'

Sydney stretched and looked above and beyond her, out at the buildings glistening through the wet pane in the rainy night.

'Really? Was the apartment nice, though?'

'Don't you think that's strange?'

Sydney yawned. 'Not at all,' she said. 'New York is a

city full of ghosts. The past breaks through into the present all the time. It's part of what I love about the place. It has a history and a soul.'

Juliet nodded. 'Yeah I know what you mean. But ghosts? I mean, to me death is a pretty emphatic conclusion to life, don't you think? You've seen it too, Syd, when the spark goes out of people it goes out totally. I've never really thought about an afterlife, but it doesn't seem likely to me.'

'So what do you think that feeling you had in the apartment was?'

Juliet paused. 'The best word to describe Giuseppe Forno's empty apartment would truthfully be haunted.'

'Juliet Devereau, are you saying you believe in ghosts? I'm shocked.'

'I didn't say I believe in ghosts, I said I thought the apartment was haunted.'

'Same difference. Anyway, I take it you won't be moving in then. Which means you won't be busy unpacking next week so you can come to an art gallery opening with me.'

Juliet looked uncertain. 'I'm not really in the mood for socialising yet.'

'Come on, you need to get out on the town again, reconnect with people. At least say you'll think about it.'

'OK, I'll think about it. I owe you after you cheered me up this afternoon. And for everything else you're doing for me. I don't know what I'd do without you, Syd. You seem to be one of the only friends I have left. I'm discovering that you don't just lose a husband after a breakup.'

'That's right. You owe me. It'll be fun.'

Juliet had meant what she'd said. She really did not feel like socialising. It was the last thing she wanted to do, with her shattered confidence and withered self-esteem. Homeless and heartbroken, she was not in the state of mind for mingling among Manhattan's cultural elite. She might, apart from anything, run into one of Jack's friends or publishing world contacts and her predicament would be obvious to them. She was not just metaphorically bruised; Juliet was emotionally naked and the scars were there for everyone to see.

'You might meet someone nice,' Sydney was saying. 'A date with someone handsome and refined would do you the world of good.'

'I was with someone handsome and refined,' Juliet said. 'It did not work out. In fact, it could hardly have worked out any worse.'

'Precisely my point,' Sydney said. 'You need it proven to you that all men are not duplicitous rogues.'

'You mean faithless bastards.'

Sydney laughed and bent and kissed Juliet on the cheek. 'That's better,' she said, 'that's much more like the old you, with the old spirit. And the sailor's vocabulary.'

Despite herself, Juliet smiled. The smile may have looked weary but it felt good on her face. 'I'll give the opening some thought,' she said. But she did not really mean it.

'They'll be queuing for your cell phone number,' Sydney said. 'You are a very attractive woman.'

But not attractive enough, Juliet thought. Not for Jack, anyway.

The rest of her shift was mired in blood and gauze and suction and suture, the casualties from both sides of a gang fight, the latest episode in a long and deadly turf war. They were brought in by heavily armed police, their wrists bound by plastic cuffs, and sat, stinking of cigarettes and testosterone, flaunting the wounds like badges of courage on their scrawny, tattooed physiques and spitting insults and threats as they were sewn back together.

Juliet was used to the damage inflicted on the body by guns and knives. The days when those injuries could shock her were long gone. She worked and then when the work was done she dumped her scrubs and grabbed a coffee.

She was sipping the hot liquid, unclipping her tied-back hair with her free hand when Dr Holstrom appeared and asked could she spare him a moment.

She didn't like the sound of this. It was barely twenty-four hours since he had complimented her warmly on the quality of her work. He was a compassionate and fair boss, but sparing with his praise and she entered his office fairly sure that she had done nothing so soon to earn more of it.

'Sit down, Juliet,' he said.

She sat. He perched on the edge of his desk. She wondered if someone had made a complaint about her. Malpractice suits were a sad fact of medical life, a constant threat when life-and-death decisions had to be made literally in seconds.

'You're tired,' Holstrom said.

'Do I act tired?'

'No, in the sense that you have not yet made any appreciable mistakes. But you will, inevitably, because tired people do. Loss of concentration is the first symptom of fatigue. You do not need me to tell you that.'

She looked up at him. He had the patrician air of a distinguished middle-aged man of Scandinavian extraction, immaculately attired under his white coat, his tie knot a perfect triangle of patterned silk, his hair scrupulously styled and combed. He had an austere, stern air that he was able to dispel simply by smiling.

'I know there has been some recent trouble in your private life.'

Juliet nodded. Hospitals were alert to the spread of infection but gossip thrived, unhindered.

'Relationships fail. It is a sad fact of life,' Holstrom said.

Juliet nodded again. She would not discuss her own circumstances in the platitudes people generally resorted to. They barely scratched the surface of how she actually felt. Anyway, heartbreak and tiredness were different things and it was clear her boss had more to say on the subject than he had so far; she was there to listen rather than to plead her case.

'Sydney will be taking maternity leave soon. We'll be losing a valuable staff member to be replaced by someone neither tested nor tried. From a purely selfish point of view, I need you at your considerable best. Sleeping on a colleague's sofa, however accommodating that colleague, is bad for your health and worse for your spirit. You need to find a place to live,

Juliet. Right now, finding a proper home should be the biggest single priority in your life.'

'It is,' she said, truthfully. It was just that saying it was a great deal easier than achieving it.

'Good luck,' he said.

'There doesn't seem to be a great deal of that about.'

'You're probably in no state to take an audit of your own attributes,' he said. 'But a neutral judge would consider you very lucky indeed. You have brains and charm and beauty. You have a rare talent for your profession. It might be difficult just now to consider the positives in your life, but you would be well advised to try.'

'Thank you,' she said. She rose, shook his hand and left his office. Her mind was full of dissonant guitar and Murphy beds and a mobster on a mortuary slab.

She needed a run to clear her mind. She had always run. She had run since she was a little girl. She craved the exercise and the endorphin rush and the vivid drama of the streets through which she ran, always at the limit of her physical capability. But running would be running away. It would not find her a place to call home.

Walking past the bulletin board outside the bank of elevators as she left the hospital, she stopped in the vain hope that someone had an apartment to rent. But there was nothing. Sighing she turned away and almost missed it. A note pinned to the board that had not been there when she had begun her shift. Apartment for Rent, it read, unbelievably, with an address beneath scrawled in biro; a modest, almost apologetic note, done on the reverse side of a card advertising a taxi company. But there was nothing apologetic about the address. Juliet worked out the location in the map of her mind and calculated that the building must have a view of Brooklyn Bridge. It seemed too good to be true.

Six

There was the bridge and there was the building, lying literally in the shadow of the fabled iron construction spanning the East River. The building itself was old and stately and simply stunning to look upon. Juliet extended a finger to ring the doorbell, noticing with displeasure that there was a slight tremor to her hand. She was shaking with trepidation. She felt in her heart that this was her last chance. There was no logic to the feeling. It was very strong, nevertheless. It had the power of instinct about it.

Nobody responded. She rang again and waited, but again nothing happened. Her shoulders slumped. She was reminded of Holstrom's warning about fatigue. Her nerves were stretched, frayed. Resilient as she was, for the first time Juliet wondered how far she was from reaching breaking point.

But then she noticed that the door itself was slightly ajar. At its foot, she saw a small cardboard sign that must have been pinned to and fallen from it. She tilted her head to read the words on the card. They read: Apartment for Rent: Ninth Floor.

Juliet pushed the door open and went through, closing it behind her, gasping with surprise and pleasure as she looked around an impeccably kept foyer with a spiral staircase rising through it. She took in the detail; the marble and wood and smoothly sanded Portland stone, the perfectly tinted tiles and the polished balustrade. The building was like some architectural tribute to austere good taste. It was handsome, perfectly proportioned, beautifully maintained.

Loud voices in Portuguese from behind one of the doors above her reminded her that for all its grace and understated opulence, this was an apartment building, a place in which people she already considered very lucky to do so, lived out their daily lives.

Her eyes moved to the Deco splendour of the antique elevator. Its interior was more spacious than the Murphy-bed garret with the gun-slit window. She stepped in and pressed the button for the ninth floor. The elevator rose with a sumptuous slowness in stately progression through the floors. When it reached the ninth it paused to settle and then dropped into place with a thud that startled Juliet, then the doors sprung open with a suddenness that seemed almost violent.

Leaving the elevator, she heard a loud whining sound reverberating through the hallway. It seemed logical to head for the source of the noise. She entered a door to see a man on all fours, meticulously sanding the hard-wood floor at the centre of a gigantic and completely empty living room. Feeling slightly timid but attempting to speak loudly enough to be heard she said, 'Hello . . .?'

There was no response. The sander whirled and whined. Wood dust in a fine cloud rose around the kneeling figure. She spoke again, louder this time, but as she couldn't hear herself, she doubted he'd notice. As a last resort she turned and knocked with knuckle-bruising force on the door. The man switched off the sander and turned to face her, his features concealed by goggles and a white protective mask. He just knelt there and stared.

'Um . . . there's a rental here?'

He pulled the mask away from his mouth to speak. 'Yeah. It's not ready yet.'

'Could I see it?'

'You're looking at it.'

His voice was gruff, not with aggression, but in the compensatory way that in Juliet's experience, concealed shyness. His manner was rougher than the floor he was smoothing. But he was a welcome contrast to the ferocious cheer and svelte tailoring of the average realtor. He began to peel the abrasive circle of sand-paper from the power tool in his hands, getting to his feet, putting it away.

Juliet looked around. The apartment was gorgeous, immaculately kept, fifteen-foot ceilings above plastered walls of flawless smoothness. 'Oh,' she said, making the necessary mental calculation. 'I can't afford this.'

She turned to leave.

With his back to her, coiling the power cable that fed the sander, the man said, 'It's thirty-eight.'

She paused. She thought she must have misheard him. 'What?'

'Thirty-eight. The place is thirty-eight.'

'Thousand?'

He did turn then and so did she. They faced each other across the wide expanse of wooded floor, an expression on his face that told her he might think her an idiot for the figure she had just mentioned. 'Hundred,' he said. He approached her. 'It's thirty-eight hundred.' He took off his goggles. Underneath them, he wore glasses. The lenses of his glasses were spattered with paint.

Juliet said, 'What's the catch? Are you putting a nightclub in on the first floor?

'Utilities are separate,' he said, ignoring her question.

He walked further into the interior of the apartment, through a hallway that, following him, Juliet saw led to a bedroom. 'It takes a lot to heat a place like this,' he said. 'So expect Con Ed to sock it to you in the winter.'

'Right,' Juliet said, 'right.'

Suddenly her heart was beating at double its normal rate. She had barely taken in what he had said about the probable cost of heating the place. Her mind was on a rent she could afford for a living space that was positively palatial compared to what she had seen over recent days. She felt as though a burden was being lifted she had almost been unaware of the true weight of, until this joyful moment of relief in escaping it.

She approached the bedroom window, taking in the epic view beyond the glass: the East River flowed beneath the Brooklyn Bridge and beyond, the Manhattan skyline rose uneven and majestic in the brightening day. It was mesmerising.

'This is the best view in the building,' the man said.

'Are you the super?'

'I own it.'

'Oh, right.' Juliet wondered if she should apologise for her lack of tact and the assumption that had prompted it. She looked at him through more objective eyes. He had a salt and pepper beard under eyes of vivid green, she noticed; they were magnetic, attractive, even.

'My family bought this place in the forties,' he said. 'And to answer your question, no nightclub downstairs. That wouldn't be my style at all. I'm kind of allergic to crowds. I'm gonna start restoring some of the apartments 'cause some of the tenants have finally moved out. But until I'm done, it could get a little crazy with the noise during the day. And I figured even a pain-in-the-ass tenant would keep his – or her – mouth shut at that price.'

Juliet said, 'I'm not a pain in the ass.'

He smiled slightly at that. 'My name is Max.'

'I'm Juliet.' They shook hands. The gesture seemed awkward, formal, Max wiping wood dust from his palm before offering it. She liked the way his grip was strong and dry. From what she could tell he seemed capable, dependable, the sort of man who had the physical strength necessary to tackle manual work without any twenty-first-century whimpering. She guessed he was roughly the same age she was, but there was something old-fashioned about him. Perhaps a more accurate word would be traditional.

'After a twenty-hour shift, I typically go comatose for eight hours,' she mentioned.

'Twenty hours?'

'I'm an ER doctor.' She did not try to disguise the pride in her voice; she'd been qualified for years now, but it still gave her a thrill.

Max took off his glasses and wiped the paint off the lenses. Juliet saw that his eyes really were an arresting shade of green. But he avoided looking straight at her.

'There are a few things about the place. Cell phones don't get the best reception. That bothers some people.'

'Not me. I'll get a landline.'

At that moment a deep rumble vibrated through the building. It thrummed through her feet, startling Juliet.

'And the F Line,' Max said.

'Jesus . . .'

He walked into the bathroom. She followed him. The rumble of the train beneath them continued, then faded and was gone. 'It's a maintenance track that runs under the building,' he explained. 'Usually it's used at night. You might not think so, but you do get used to it. And then one day you find that you don't even hear it at all.'

He turned and she was right on his heels. She thought that this invasion of his personal space might have irritated him when she saw the look on his face, but she really could not help herself. She was eager. In fact, she was desperate.

'I'll need your social security number and three references.'

'I can get you all of that, plus records of my taxes for the last five years if you want.'

Max hesitated. He appeared to come to a decision; she could see it in the relaxed way his shoulders dropped.

He blinked and smiled slightly and she could hear it in the gentler tone of his voice. 'I prefer no pets.'

'Of course.'

'The heaters are of a certain vintage. They bang in the morning. Loudly.'

'I like loud heaters.'

Max put his hand into his pocket and pulled out the key and dropped it into Juliet's palm. Her fingers closed around it. The metal was cold and solid and heavy and real in her grip. A surge of pure relief engulfed her.

Just like that, she thought, *easy.*

Just like that.

Seven

Juliet went back to Sydney and Mike's place clutching the key to the new apartment in her right hand like a priceless relic. It was a tool, obviously, a useful, practical item, one of the necessities of life. It was also a little brass metaphor, wasn't it? It was the device that would unlock the route to the rest of her life.

Sydney and Mike were both out when she returned. It was unbearable. For the first time in ages she had good news and there was no one to share it with. She paced impatiently, waiting for one of them to get back.

Syd got back first, holding a hand up as Juliet came rushing into the hall and running straight to the toilet. 'Sorry, Jules,' she called through the door. 'You know how it is. My bladder has been squeezed down to the size of a peanut. I'll be with you in a minute.'

Juliet went and made some coffee for something to do. She had two steaming cups ready by the time Syd finally came into the living room and slumped onto the sofa, groaning as she dragged her shoes off her swollen feet.

'You want to soak those?' Juliet was suddenly too excited to tell her.

'No. I want to know what's put that look on your face.'

Juliet grinned. 'Nothing much. I just found an apartment overlooking Brooklyn Bridge today. Great views, huge rooms, freshly decorated . . .'

'Right, and how much?'

'Oh, thirty-eight hundred,' Juliet replied airily

Syd sat forward. 'You have got to be kidding me.'

Juliet pulled the key out of her pocket and waved it enticingly in front of Syd.

'Nope. See this? This little object is the key to the rest of my life. You are not going to *believe* this apartment, Syd. It's totally insane.'

Mike insisted on dinner at a place in SoHo with a jazz pianist and a young Italian chef fast making a hot name for his new restaurant. The food was delicious but Juliet felt so stunned and excited by her success in finding the perfect home that she could barely eat. She could not bring herself to drink much, either. She felt drunk already on the intoxicating thrill of her triumph in finding her apartment.

Sydney said, 'When do you move in?'

'Max says a week.'

Mike raised an eyebrow. 'Max?'

'Maybe less if he gets through the re-wiring tomorrow.'

'He's going for a total refurb?'

'The place is decorated to a really high specification, Mike. You would not believe the floors and ceilings and the detail of the plasterwork. I think he just wants to do a job in keeping with what's already there.'

'Makes sense if he owns the building,' Mike said. 'Chunk of real estate like that, the guy must be worth a fortune.'

'Millions,' Sydney said.

'You wouldn't know it to look at him,' Juliet said.

Sydney pulled a face. 'Dog meat?'

Juliet laughed. It was the first time she could remember having done so since before her separation from Jack. It felt good, liberating. 'No airs and graces is what I mean,' she said. 'I mean his demeanour. He affects this surly, blue-collar persona. I don't think it's necessarily the real him. I get the impression he's quite shy and reserved. He has these startling green eyes.'

'One of those still-waters-run-deep types,' Sydney said. 'They can be rewarding if you're prepared to put the necessary effort in. They can also be a slog. You have to concentrate so hard with them. Personally I prefer shallow, superficial men who wear their hearts on their sleeves because their feeble intellect doesn't really provide them with the luxury of a choice.'

'Thank you, darling,' Mike said. 'I love you too.'

Juliet said, 'Romancing my landlord is the last thing on my mind. I could have hugged him, though, when he dropped the key into my hand.'

'Power,' Mike said. 'It's an aphrodisiac. At least, that's what I'm told. I wouldn't know, because I've never had any.' He winked at his wife and then refilled their glasses and proposed a toast to Juliet, her new home and her golden future.

There was a lull after that. The pianist on the podium,

bathed by a single spotlight, played something with a spry, syncopated rhythm. The tune was familiar to Juliet, but she could not have put a name to it.

She was aware of the clatter of cutlery on expensive plates and the chatter and laughter of people enjoying themselves. For the first time in what felt like ages, she realised she was looking at life beyond the hospital as something more than just a condition to be endured.

She was excited and unsure about the direction events might take. Liberation and independence and adventure beckoned. She was still young. She was healthy and attractive. Suddenly happiness was a possibility again.

Juliet moved her stuff into her new apartment four days later. Max had finished his work a couple of days ahead of schedule. Her heart might still be in limbo but her belongings would no longer be in storage and that would be a blessing. Actually, there wasn't much in the way of belongings to move. The ordeal of dividing the spoils between herself and Jack had not seemed worth the possessions she had accrued as a consequence.

She was not someone really very hung up on material things; antique vases moved her no more than did the latest designer chairs. But she needed somewhere to lay her head and the space she had rented was vast and would require some furnishings just so that it did not look empty. Anyway, Juliet thought that she deserved some home comforts. God knows she'd earned them after the last few weeks.

It was just her luck, though, that she seemed to have

hired the removal man from hell. Everything she owned occupied no more than a third of the capacity of his truck. Cardboard boxes were neatly piled. A standard lamp and a refrigerator and a spotless new double-bed mattress were secured by grey tape to wooden ribs along the sides of the vehicle. The man pulled a loading ramp out of the rear, pushed a dolly in her face and checked his watch. 'I gotta be uptown in exactly a hundred minutes, so you got sixty to get this shit out of my truck or I gotta charge you another day.'

Juliet looked at him in disbelief. 'Take a deep breath. I don't want you to strain yourself talking.'

He ignored her sarcasm and returned to the driver's cab where he sat back and pointedly opened his newspaper.

Juliet swore softly to herself and looked up at the sky. It was overcast but the clouds were light, benign. Rain looked unlikely, which was something, when everything she had to her name was about to be dumped on the sidewalk.

'You hired the only moving man in New York who doesn't actually move the furniture?'

Juliet recognised the voice behind her: Max. She turned round to see him. As he was when they first met, he was covered in plaster and wood dust and spattered with paint. He was a picture of practical competence and, she hoped, certainly able to help.

'I could really use a hand here,' she said.

'Evidently.'

'Are you very busy?'

He appraised the hill of stuff obstructing the sidewalk

in bubble-wrap and brown paper and adhesive tape. 'If I wasn't, I'm about to be,' he said, smiling at her.

Item by item, they brought the furniture from the sidewalk to the apartment on the ninth floor. Juliet couldn't help feeling that there was something quite intimate about the procedure, as if in handling her possessions, this man she did not really know was familiarising himself with her. That couldn't really be the case, she knew. He knew nothing about the history of what she owned and the circumstances in which these things had been used. Still, she couldn't shake the sense that he was learning things about her that she would not have chosen to reveal.

Last, they moved the new mattress to her bed. The aperture of the elevator was much smaller than its interior space and the mattress would not fit through it. There was no alternative but to haul it nine flights up the stairs. Juliet guided while Max followed below bearing the bulk of the weight. The mattress was a good one. Its fabric and springs were substantial and heavy. Sleep was precious to Juliet, a commodity she was prepared to invest in.

On the eighth-floor landing, Juliet called down, 'You OK?'

'No, but it's only one more flight.'

Tightening her grip on their burden, Juliet lifted her head and suddenly, two steps away, at the top of the flight and far too close, an elderly man stood peering intently into her upturned face. She was aware of white hair and wrinkles and the intense gaze of bloodshot, baggy eyes. Startled, she gasped and the mattress slid from her grip, banged and slithered and almost toppled over Max, who was wrestling now below her with the whole of its unwieldy weight. Juliet grabbed her end and they set it down gratefully for a rest.

'I'm so sorry,' Juliet called down to Max.

He looked up and past her to the elderly figure on the landing at the top of the flight. 'It's not your fault,' he said. He blew out air, exasperated. Then he said, 'This is my grandfather. August, Juliet. Juliet, August.'

Juliet looked up at the old man and said, rather redundantly she thought, 'I'm the new tenant.'

'You got pets?'

His voice sounded gruff. And not just with age. 'No,' she said.

'Are you loud?'

The question was so baldly put that Juliet could not help but giggle. 'No,' she said. 'Not at all.'

August looked probingly into Juliet's face. She thought that he was probably about eighty years old, tall and gaunt and with the frailness of old age, but with a strong mental energy, an emotional alertness that came off him like heat.

He said, 'I'm sorry I scared you.'

He stretched out his hand to her and she shook it, surprised at the strength of his grip. It was much stronger than she would have expected. He looked glaringly past her down at his grandson but he did not say anything further. Max said, 'Ready?' and they began to haul the mattress the thankfully short distance to her apartment and the bedroom where it would lie.

*

They were both sweating when they finally made it inside the apartment. Juliet looked at her small huddle of belongings, shrunk even further by the palatial scale of her enormous living room. The apartment still seemed empty. It would look different when she had unpacked and arranged the contents of the boxes. It might never be exactly homely; the dimensions of the place were too extravagant for that, but Juliet didn't think her new address needed to look cosy to be her home. To her, it seemed perfect.

Max was looking at the pile of boxes against the far wall. 'You travel light,' he said.

Juliet exhaled. She dabbed at her moist forehead with the cuff of her shirtsleeve. 'I needed a new start. So I had to get rid of a lot. I would have liked to saw the bed in half and burn it, but I need a place to sleep at night.'

In the charged, silent aftermath of her own words, she realised that she had said far too much. She added, 'I'm not quick at forgiving.'

'Well,' Max said, 'I think new starts are good.'

Juliet smiled. She had left him with little alternative but to say that to enable an escape from the mutual embarrassment that her gushing admission had provoked.

She was certain she would not have been so forthcoming were it not for her gratitude to the man. He'd been her saviour, first in renting her the apartment, and then again when he'd rescued her belongings from the sidewalk and helped her move in.

In his dusty clothes and paint-spattered spectacles he did not look much like a knight on a white charger, but there was a sense in which he had galloped to her rescue, wasn't there? And there was something winningly self-deprecating about him. After the betrayal her husband's vanity had led to, there was something attractive about the modesty which seemed to characterise Max.

Eight

Juliet was determined to enjoy her first night in her new home. She decided to begin it with a cleansing, scalding-hot shower. The vaguely adventurous feeling she had experienced in the restaurant with Sydney and Mike had clarified into something more purposeful. She wanted to properly settle in, to restore her emotional stamina and rebuild her self-esteem to the point at which she would be able to deal with what had happened to her and see herself as someone more than just the victim of a sexual betrayal.

Sydney was right, after all, she mused, studying her naked body in the full-length mirror on the bathroom wall. She was, by any objective measure, physically attractive. She had a good mind and a good job and a cheery disposition, in normal circumstances. The business with Jack had bruised her; it had not turned her into a man hater.

She was still musing on this, lathering her body under the showerhead with a sort of luxurious guilt, when the mirror on the wall inches in front of her began to tremble, almost imperceptibly. She put out her hand and touched the steamy glass. She was not imagining it. She could feel it shivering against her fingertips. She

64

could see the tremor running through it as her blurred reflection jittered, though under the showerhead, her body had become motionless. Suddenly, the mirror shook violently in its frame. Juliet noticed with a calm detachment that was almost cold, that if she screamed, no one would hear her.

She tried to control her breathing, to make sense of what she was seeing. Water gurgled down the drain with a groan that sounded almost human. And the entire building started to rumble as a subway train roared and juddered along underneath it.

She turned off the shower and hopped dripping to the towel rail, grabbing a big bath towel and throwing it around her shoulders. Shivering with shock, she ran into her living room and switched on the radio. She suddenly and urgently needed something mundane to help grip her mind and harness her imagination before it skittered out of control.

She punched buttons until she got a weather station and listened to talk of anti-cyclones and isobars until she was dry and had stopped shaking. The voice on the weather station talked blithely on about the chance of early snowfalls on the East Coast. It didn't help; shock and surprise had made her feel very vulnerable.

She rang Sydney on her cell phone. She got Mike.

'She's in the bathroom, puking,' Mike said. 'Morning sickness.'

'It's evening, Mike.'

'Go figure,' he replied.

She closed her eyes. The voice on the end of the

phone, with its deadpan humour and grouchy humanity reassured her.

'How you settling in?'

'Early days,' she said. 'When I am settled, I want you guys to be my first dinner guests.'

'We'd be delighted,' Mike said. 'Though my instinct for diplomacy tells me it might be better not to raise the subject of food with Syd until tomorrow.'

'Bye, Mike.'

'Is there a message?'

'What?'

'Did you call Syd for a reason, or was it just a girl thing?'

'No,' Juliet said, 'no message.'

She went to bed that night scared. Despite her crash course in radio meteorology, and the grounding exchange with Sydney's sweet and lovely husband, her fright in the bathroom had left her feeling raw and jumpy and frayed her nerves. She slept eventually but her sleep was shallow and restless. Even so, it wasn't the shadow flitting through the apartment living room that woke her.

But something did. Her eyes flew open and a sense that something wasn't right in her new space washed over her. She lay still for a moment. This was not at all the same as the feeling of sinister melancholy she had felt days earlier in the dreary apartment where a mob executioner had ended his life. It was a sense of not being alone and more than that, stronger, of being observed and perhaps even studied.

She sat up. 'Is there someone there?' she called out.

Silence.

'I know someone's there. Answer me. Don't approach me. I have a can of mace.'

Silence. But a silence that was charged. It seemed oddly watchful.

Juliet cleared her throat with a cough. The cough sounded very loud to her. 'If you do not show yourself, I will call nine one one.'

Nothing. Just more of that silence that felt somehow like scrutiny. An image impinged on her mind. It was of the old man, August, silent and staring at nothing, standing just beyond the doorway of her bedroom, in her hallway, where she could neither see him nor hear his shallow breathing. His bloodshot eyes were wide and spittle glistened in the darkness on his white beard where he had drooled with secret excitement.

Juliet shuddered, even as she knew she was being ridiculous. Her apartment had a secure lock on a substantial door and her landlord's grandfather was a harmless old man who would be fast asleep in his bed by now. So why was the sense of menace she felt so tangible?

She did not think the feeling she was experiencing had been prompted by a dream. For when she sat up with a start in bed, beyond its foot she saw a faint light glowing dimly under her bedroom door from the hallway. Her gaze focused on the light. When she could ignore its anomalous presence no longer, she stole across the floor and opened the door and walked into the hallway.

Her front door must be ajar. She was sure of it. Where

else could that subtle spread of light leaking into her home have come from? She went to close it, past the opening to her living room, where at the edge of her vision a dark figure stood still in the gloom as though poised and waiting, and when she turned to look fully at it, ominously returned her gaze.

Juliet was frozen with fear, unable to blink, much less to breathe or move a limb. Sheer effort of determined will forced her to raise her arm from her side and switch on a light. Brightness erupted overhead, filling the room, blinding her momentarily with light, so that now she did blink, involuntarily, and when her eyes adjusted, there was no one there.

She turned her head towards the front door. It was firmly closed. She approached and pushed it and found that it was indeed locked and secure. Just a shadow, she thought, the figure in the room behind her. Just a shadow cast by the bridge outside. It was first-night paranoia. That was all. A moment of small-hours spookiness provoked by the earlier incident with the bathroom mirror.

Jesus, Juliet, get it together. You're a doctor not some neurotic bundle of nerves.

But she couldn't stop the overwhelming feeling that someone was out there, loitering, lurking. She was sure of it. Someone with malevolent intent and a cunning gift for concealment was toying sadistically with her. Her intuition told her that this was more than first-night jitters.

Her heart leapt into her throat when she heard something outside in the hallway. Her body tensed, ready to flee, then relaxed as she realised that it was the elevator doors, opening or closing.

She put her eye to the peephole. At first there was nothing. Then she saw the reassuringly solid form of Max, walking by with bags of groceries, the mundane aftermath of a late-night shopping trip. She felt relieved that his apartment was on the same floor as hers. He was a man of simple and straightforward routine. He began to whistle. He whistled softly because it was late, she supposed. She recognised the tune. It was a song made famous all over the world by Frank Sinatra: 'Strangers in the Night'.

The sound faded as Max approached his own door and behind hers, Juliet indulged a secret smile.

She had exaggerated his mystery deliberately over the restaurant dinner shared with Sydney and Mike. She had made him more enigmatic than he was just to entertain them. What he actually was, was one of those what-you-see-is-what-you-get types. She felt qualified to judge. Her husband, with his interior life and his writer's ego, had been exactly the opposite.

Juliet breathed a sigh of relief and rested her head against the wood of the door, reaching up to the light switch to return her apartment to darkness. Her fingers hesitated. Her hand fell. She walked back towards her bed, determined to sleep and feeling more secure. Yet despite that determination she left the light burning through the remainder of the night.

Nine

The following morning Juliet opened her refrigerator door, her stomach rumbling with hunger, to find only a four pack of beer, perfectly chilled but hardly appropriate for breakfast and not exactly nourishing either. Her kitchen cupboards contained only a solitary can of baked beans. She opened it and spooned them down cold. She thought of Max the previous evening, groceries held in his sturdy grip, sober and sensible on her landing through the spyhole of her door. She imagined that his breakfast would be somewhat more organised and satisfying.

She was still thinking of Max on the subway ride to the hospital. His presence outside her apartment really had been a comfort in the night, the difference between being able to get to sleep and fleeing the darkness that her freaked-out state had allowed to assume disproportionately sinister dimensions.

Her intuition told her that he was a decent man. The rent he had set was a more than fair consolation for the upheaval caused by ongoing work to the fabric of the building. He had helped her move her stuff in without hesitation. It was reassuring that her landlord was a man on whom she could rely.

Trust, fidelity, betrayal: these were even more important concepts to her now. She had a strong moral instinct which had certainly not been passed down from her parents. And that moral sense was all she had now. Her mom and dad were dead; she had no siblings. She was alone in the world and God knew she had never felt it more intensely than when she saw Jack's naked back arched over a stranger.

Her parents had believed in the hippie concept of free love. In their rackety way they had practised it. Or her father had; her mother had always seemed to be left holding grimly on to the theory. They had possessed no religious faith and had regarded marriage as a bourgeois conceit. She supposed they had loved one another, probably loved her too in their vague and distracted way, but they had not been very conscientious as parents.

Heart trouble had taken her mother and her father had followed not long after with complications arising from diabetes. They had shared a drug habit they had regarded as recreational, but which Juliet now understood was more likely a chronic addiction. Since hippies did not really hit the gym, they had done no physical exercise. No doubt her own fastidiousness, like her morals, were in reaction to her parents' laxity in that department. She ran hard and habitually. She had never so much as puffed on a cigarette. Her only vice was a cold beer or a glass of wine, and she could not remember having been drunk since the night she discovered she had passed her final round of exams at med school.

Had that been the fundamental problem in her

relationship with Jack? Did he think she was a killjoy? Jack had been entitled to a little fun in his life, hadn't he? It had not been Juliet's job to provide it, but maybe her inhibited way of living had frustrated him.

There certainly hadn't been any problems in the bedroom. Their lovemaking had been wild, intense, abandoned, right until the last occasion she had ever slept with him.

The thought provoked a small, involuntary sob, which she suppressed quickly, no one cried on the subway. But there was a hollow feeling in her belly as she reminisced about Jack, remembering how they had first come to meet one another, that the cold baked beans of her makeshift breakfast did nothing to diminish.

It had been in the history section of the New York Public Library. She had been researching an essay on virology and epidemiology in relation to the Black Death. She'd had a student caffeine habit back then. So did the guy studying in the carrel next to hers and their breaks always seemed to coincide. Jack later confessed that this was not a coincidence at all. But the confession came six months after they were married, too late to have any real impact on the way events played out.

He was very good-looking with the physique of an athlete but an intellect the average college jock could only dream about. They chatted easily, a novelty for her because Juliet was quite shy with strangers. He told her that he was an aspiring writer, researching a novel he planned to set in the early 1920s. He knew quite a lot about the period because he had majored in modern history, but he did not know enough for the easy voice of authorial authority he was aiming for in his story.

'You have to write truthfully. It doesn't need to be the actual truth, but it has to be convincing,' he explained.

'I get what you're saying.'

'You have to be familiar with the world you're describing, Juliet. More than familiar, intimate.'

It was the first time he had ever used her name in conversation. It made her feel warm, the sound of it shaped by his mouth and said in his voice.

'Aren't you writers supposed to use your imagination, Jack?'

'I'm not a writer. Not yet.'

'But you will be. You're clever and determined.'

'You channel your imagination. You use it, but in a disciplined way.'

Juliet had nodded, she hoped sagely. She had no appetite at all for reading fiction. All the books she read were factual and most of them were medical text books. This seemed to delight Jack. The contrast between their tastes and their backgrounds, their life experience and their enthusiasms, only seemed to highlight, as they began tentatively to date, the things they were able to share. Together, they were the embodiment of that old cliché about the attraction of opposites.

For a while, after she qualified to practise medicine and he got his first book deal, she was sure that they were soulmates. They had been best friends and passionate lovers; she'd trusted in him completely, confiding in him, sharing what was most secret about herself. He was familiar with her innermost dreams and aspirations and why wouldn't he be, when most of them involved him.

She could not identify the moment at which she now realised they had begun to grow apart. Juliet could not have named the month, or even the season of subtle estrangement. But with the clarity of hindsight, when she thought without the blur of emotion about it, things had begun to go wrong about a year before the August afternoon when she surprised him in bed with the Tennis Club Blonde.

The TCB was a piece of work; a bored, independently wealthy woman about four years older than Juliet, sexually predatory, something of a joke really because her glamour was of the pantomimic, *Baywatch* sort. There was nothing subtle about her. She was all kitten heels and platinum locks and leopard-print catsuits.

She was actually a very good tennis player. But that hadn't really been the point. The point had been that she was an avid reader of fiction and a true fan of Jack's books. She was clever, despite the vampy wardrobe and the full make-up, and sashayed about the place like a happy object of lust, and she was someone Jack could have a serious conversation with about literature.

They had not been discussing fiction when Juliet caught them. They had not been discussing anything. The only sounds they were capable of voicing just then were of the breathless, grunted sort.

Juliet could not suppress the vision that came to her then, as she swayed along to the movement of the train, of them coupling on her own marital bed like a caricature of lust fulfilled. She could picture her own face, swollen and surprised at the door when they turned together to see her there. She could remember the perfume the TCB had worn, with its lemony top and base-notes of patchouli.

How had Jack hoped to get rid of a smell as potently strong as that? How on earth had he been doing so, and for how long? He must have been secretly laundering the sheets. She hadn't thought him that cunning or duplicitous. Slyness and premeditated deceit just weren't Jack at all. But until the moment of her discovery, she had never thought Jack would ever cheat on her.

That revelation, that she hadn't known her husband at all, shook her to the core, even more than the adultery. Was it ever possible to truly know someone else?

Ten

Her shift, when she got to the hospital, was fairly uneventful, they often were during the day.

The ER was a subtly different place during the day. There were more victims of auto and domestic mishaps and fewer victims of deliberate damage such as shooting or stabbing. Crime was more common at night, when darkness helped conceal and drink helped provoke it.

But throughout the day Juliet could not shake the sensation that she was being watched. The observation was subtle and un-intrusive, but it was definitely taking place, she concluded after a couple of hours of work.

The thought almost made her smile. Last night she'd felt that she was under covert surveillance in her new home and now she was sure she was being spied on at work. It made her think of the old joke, *I'm not paranoid, I just know everyone's out to get me.* Was there a condition or syndrome where people felt they were being watched all the time? Had she suddenly fallen victim to it?

She mentioned it to Sydney on her break. 'Do you ever feel you are being secretly observed?' she asked.

Sydney blew out a breath. Her cheeks wore crimson patches the size of apples. Work was more of an effort as her stomach expanded.

'People don't do much secret observing of women in the late-stage of pregnancy, hon. They tend instead to gawp openly and make inappropriate comments. I'm thinking of charging a dollar every time someone asks can they touch my bump. Why do you ask?'

'Just a feeling I had last night. And this morning, to tell you the truth.'

Sydney chewed this comment over. She said, 'You think Jack has maybe hired a private detective?'

Juliet laughed. 'Don't be ridiculous.'

The notion was absurd. But then a couple of months earlier she would have thought the notion of Jack screwing around absurd.

'Divorce does strange things to people,' Sydney said. 'The prospect of losing possessions they have toiled to acquire makes some people very bitter and hostile. That said, I can't quite see it either. It's too cloak and dagger. Too melodramatic. It would be like something from a trashy novel.'

'And Jack doesn't write those.'

'No,' Sydney said. 'He very definitely doesn't.'

Sydney had read both of Jack's books, to Juliet's knowledge. She had read the second because she had been so impressed by the first. That was two more of Jack's books than Juliet had read. But now was not the time to confess the fact to her friend.

'No, I think Holstrom's probably asked one of the senior house people to keep an eye on me. I mean, it's normal when you're on probation, but I proved myself ages ago.'

'He just cares for you, Juliet. And worries about you. And he doesn't want you making any mistakes that could cost you your career. You should be flattered that he cares.'

'Well, it makes me mad, especially as he doesn't have to worry about me any more. I won't be crying into some patient's gaping wound any time soon now I've found my apartment. If my cheating ex-husband should turn up, however, he really would have something to worry about.'

Juliet stalked back to work. She needed a run. Nothing else would help her get rid of the churning fury in her stomach. But she would tell Holstrom that she had found a safe and comfortable and permanent place to live. That should at least give her some satisfaction. Finding her apartment had been little more than a very lucky break, but her boss would see it as the solid achievement of someone dogged and well organised.

The question of Jack's betrayal, the mystery of it, nagged at her all day. At lunchtime she ate a huge bowl of pasta in the hospital cafeteria to fuel her later run. Was it boredom? Was it simply lust? She could not understand it because she could not pinpoint in her mind or heart the moment at which her husband had decided to stop treating her with the respect and devotion a wife deserved. At what point had he decided to renege on his marriage vows? She did not know the answer and the question was like an itch it was beyond her reach to scratch.

She missed him. It was a pitiful admission to make, but there it was. It infuriated her that she could be so competent and cool in her profession, she could make life-or-death decisions as a matter of course, and yet, she missed the man who had humiliated her and broken her heart. And though she'd admit it to no one, not even Sydney, every time her phone rang she wanted it to be him, begging her for forgiveness.

Later that evening, she entered her apartment feeling just a little trepidation, reminded by the long shadows of the encroaching evening of the events and suspicions of the previous night. She was just lacing her running shoes when her phone rang.

It was Jack, and she hesitated before she took the call.

'I want to see you,' he said.

Yes, she missed him, but pride and anger made her stubborn. 'I'm busy.'

'I need to see you.'

'Have your lawyer arrange a meeting. I'll bring mine.'

'I've offered you the house.'

'And I'm supposed to live there? With a sign screwed to the front door saying "Strictly No Admittance to Tennis Club Blondes"?'

'The offer was made sincerely.'

'And crassly. And with strings attached. I don't want you in my life, Jack. I've moved on in mine.'

'Just hear what I have to say.'

'No.'

'Juliet, please.'

'What? What exactly, Jack?'

'I miss you.'

'You miss me.'

'Yes. I do. Terribly. Unbearably.'

'Yes. Well. You should have thought of that. But then self-obsessed people rarely consider the consequences of their actions. It's why they usually end up leading solitary lives.' She could hear her own voice begin to break as she concluded this sentence. She did not want Jack to hear her start to sob. She stayed silent with the cell phone in one trembling fist, trying as hard as she could to discipline her breathing.

'Please,' he said eventually. 'Please, please let me see you.'

'No,' she said.

He stayed on the line. She could hear him breathing. He did not say anything more though, and she closed her eyes and bit down on her lip and after a few seconds of silence, she broke the connection.

Juliet ran as she knew she would, at the lung-bursting limit of her own endurance. She ran through the wet glitter of the early evening streets, through the rowdy, gaudy tableau that was Brooklyn at dusk in the autumnal rain, enjoying every muscle jarring yard.

Her phone rang again as she sprinted along a dirt path on the waterfront. She glanced down to see who it was who had called and saw that it was Jack again. She felt stronger now than she had earlier, more disciplined, steelier willed. She ignored the call.

By the time she got back to her apartment building

she was utterly spent. She did not have the energy after her run to climb the steps to the ninth floor. She took the elevator, still panting, the sweat drying on her warm skin, her heart thumping rhythmically, feeling good. Jack would call again. Persistence was a necessary element of penitence. And if he didn't call again, so what? If he wasn't truly sorry for what he had done, he definitely wasn't worthy of her.

Someone had left a gift basket outside her door. Wine bottles were cradled in it against CDs, toiletries, a fluffy hand-towel rolled and tied in a ribbon, fruit carefully packaged in tinted cellophane, a box of chocolates. A card was attached. It read: 'Welcome to the building.'

It was a sweet gesture, but also odd. There was an assumption of intimacy about some of the items it contained. There was a sense in which it breached her privacy a little. It was thoughtful; it was also rather presumptuous. She picked it up and carried it into her apartment.

Later, at the start of an evening that was blissfully uneventful, she opened a bottle of the wine and drank two glasses, listening to one of the CDs, a Gershwin collection with Bernstein on piano that wasn't really her thing but suited the grandeur of her night view towards Manhattan. The wine was really very good. For a while she just stood and sipped and savoured her view. Jack did not call again. And she did not pace the floor waiting for him to do so.

When Juliet returned from the hospital the following afternoon, Max was on the stairs above the vestibule, talking to a man in a fashionably tailored suit. She could hear their conversation and paused to listen. It wasn't any of her business, but she was becoming intrigued about her landlord. She felt that there was much more to him than met the eye.

Max spoke, his voice emphatic. 'I want to use the original plans. I'd do it myself, but I need drawings for the city.'

Juliet inferred from that that the man in the stylish suit was an architect. He said, 'There are significant dead spaces here and along these walls. There's a lot more we could do to maximise your property's potential. Knock them down, open up the space—'

'We'll stick to the plans,' Max said. 'My grandfather wants to keep it that way.'

The architect began to descend the stairs. He said, 'I'll call you on Monday with a bid.'

'Thanks,' Max said, as Juliet climbed the stairs to where he stood.

'Hi.' She couldn't explain why, but there was an awkwardness in her greeting, something she'd never felt before. Somehow the gift basket had destroyed the ease she'd felt with him until now.

'Hi.' He seemed to sense her mood and held back.

'About to start to make a lot of noise?'

'After I get the city's approval. Lots of dots and crosses to do around here.'

It was the reason she had climbed the stairs to talk to him but now that the moment had come, Juliet hesitated, before saying, 'Thank you.'

'Hmmm?' Max looked totally nonplussed.

It had already been an awkward moment, before her expression of gratitude, but she felt compelled to persist. 'For the gift basket,' she said. 'It was incredibly sweet. Really generous.'

Max cocked his head. He looked as though he didn't know what she was talking about. She was evidently making no sense to him at all.

'Outside my door? Yesterday?'

The look of confusion remained on his face a moment longer and then it lifted as he smiled and said, 'Ahhh.'

'So, thank you.'

'It wasn't me.'

'Then who was it?'

'I've no idea.'

The grandfather, she thought then. August had delivered the gift. Who else could it have been? It was the sort of courtly welcoming gesture a man of his generation would perform. He was too old, surely, to have meant the gift flirtatiously. It had been a present as innocent and thoughtful as it was kind.

'I think I can guess who left the basket,' she said, smiling at Max. 'I've worked it out the way detectives do, by the process of elimination.'

'Impressive. I admire your deductive skills.'

She smiled. 'I use them on patients. All the time.'

'I'm glad they're put to productive use.'

'I must go and thank him.'

She began to climb the remainder of the stairs to the old man's apartment. It was a long climb, which would not hinder her because her legs and lungs were strong from all the exercise she did. But Max overtook her and stood in her way.

'Now is not ideal,' he said.

'Oh?'

'My grandfather is not robust. He tires easily. He has good days and bad days. Today is a bad day. Tomorrow might be better.'

'What's a good time to catch him?'

'I'll see he gets to bed early and make sure he takes his medication. This time tomorrow will probably be fine.'

'Great,' she said. 'Tomorrow it is.'

Eleven

Twenty-four hours later Juliet knocked on August's door. As though vigilant to the unlikely possibility of visitors, he answered it promptly. She stood facing him.

'There you are,' he said.

'Here I am indeed. It's overwhelmingly thoughtful, the gift.'

'I simply put myself in your shoes.'

'You did what?'

'I thought what would I want, as a woman, alone? A new apartment. New neighbours. I'd want familiarity. A glass of wine. Some music. Bath salts, laundry detergent, a bath plug.'

Juliet had to suppress a giggle. There was something so inappropriate about this octogenarian man discussing laundry detergent, as though he might as well have gone the whole hog and bought her sanitary towels and extra-strength deodorant.

The whistle of a kettle sounded shrilly behind him. 'Tea? With whisky.'

He grabbed her forearm and began to usher her into his apartment.

'Oh . . . I can't,' she said. But his grip, as she had

earlier discovered, was strong. His momentum guided her in.

'I don't get much company.' He busied himself making the tea.

Juliet took a look around as he did so. The place was so crowded with stuff it was more an emporium than a home. Actually, it was more like a junk shop. Several decades' worth of artefacts and souvenirs and keep-sakes cluttered the place completely. Every shelf seemed filled with bric-a-brac. And it was dirty; grime and dust and stains layered surfaces and soft furnishing fabrics like the spread of decay.

August handed her a cup of tea. The china of the cup was tortoiseshell with tannin and the lip of it was grubbily chipped.

There was a stale, sour taint to the air in there, which combined with the grime made August's apartment creepy and claustrophobic; Juliet wanted to escape it as quickly as courtesy would allow. 'I've really got to go,' she said. She hoped the look on her face as she said the words would be somewhere between an apology and a plea. She really did have to get out of there as fast as possible.

August lurched forward with the whisky bottle he held. He poured a slug of it into Juliet's cup. 'Consider it tea to-go,' he said. His voice was guttural with phlegm.

She remembered her vision of him, the secret vigil of staring in the darkness beyond her door; the glistening drool. 'OK,' she conceded, taking the cup.

Juliet brought the drink August had given her back to

her apartment and poured it down the kitchen sink. She felt ungrateful doing so, but she had paid lip-service to politeness; it was too early in the day for hard liquor and besides, she did not like the taste of whisky. And anyway, she was far too fastidious to drink from so dirty a vessel as the chipped cup.

Her apartment did not just seem nakedly empty after the one she had just left, it seemed almost unnaturally quiet. There had been a radio blaring in the old man's living room, competing voices debating some issue so emotive they sounded close to hysteria. It had been very loud. He was probably deaf, the reason he tended to bellow out his words.

I don't get much company.

Had it been him? Had he been her elusive peeper of two nights ago, watching her, silent and still, while she suspected a presence she had not been able to prove to herself was there? She thought about the broken veined cheeks above his straggly beard and the carious teeth exposed in his grin. It was not a charitable way to think. A man couldn't help it if age and perhaps loneliness had contrived over the years to give him a sinister appearance. But he was creepy-looking and there had been something desperate about his urgent desire to have her stay and share his time and space and the contents of his whisky bottle.

Max was cautious around him. She had picked up on that straight away. Maybe there was something about the old man's character or behaviour that his grandson found distasteful. There was something austere, she felt, about Max and his values. Age and blood would not justify to him actions or impulses in the older man he thought deviant, or worse, perverse.

But this was just speculation. She looked at the chipped mug, empty now, in which she had been served the laced tea. And the sight of it, grubby and damaged, but probably blameless, made her shudder.

The following evening was the night of the opening. Juliet had no intention of going. She had performed a long and demanding emergency operation throughout the afternoon and was exhausted. Physically and mentally, she felt spent. She sat on a bench and wearily removed her surgical mask, wondering whether she was still on Holstrom's unofficial probation. Her phone buzzed in her breast pocket but she ignored it. She knew who the call was from – Jack – and she was in no condition to speak to him right now.

Sydney ambushed her, right there at the end of her shift. 'Heard you had a long one,' she said.

'Insane day,' Juliet confirmed.

'Mike can't make tonight, he's putting a deal together with a ten p.m. deadline so Corey is catching up on her culture instead.'

Corey was a colleague they both liked. She was fun.

'It's a shame Mike can't take you, Syd.'

'He needs his self-esteem,' she said. 'He needs the drama of conference calls and urgent cut-off points in his life. They make him feel important. A man who can't be trusted at the dinner table without wearing a bib has to find some way to compensate for that.'

Juliet laughed. 'I don't know how he puts up with you,' she said.

'Want to come?'

'I think I'm just going to go home and get to bed early,' Juliet said.

'OK, Grandma.'

Juliet did not respond to the jibe. Sydney just looked at her, a look Juliet avoided returning.

'You've got to stop thinking about him,' Sydney said, eventually.

Juliet sighed. She tried to smile up at Sydney but did not look at her directly and could achieve nothing more jovial than a twist of her lips. 'The love of my life cheated on me,' she said. 'In my own bed. Every time I look at myself, I see someone who wasn't enough.'

'Don't say that.'

'I don't know if I want him dead or I want to marry him all over again.'

Sydney was quiet for so long, that eventually the silence forced Juliet to meet her friend's eye. She saw obvious concern on Syd's face.

'It's an art opening,' Sydney said eventually. 'It won't kill you.'

'You won't leave me alone until I agree to come, will you?'

'Nope.'

'OK, then. I'll come. Just give me a bit of time to go home to shower and change.'

Sydney grinned. 'You take your time, Jules. I want you to look your best.'

*

Back at the apartment, Juliet ran a bath. She needed to get rid of the tension in her muscles that a long surgery always produced. She stripped off her clothes, then stood and examined herself in the mirror's image, barely a foot away from the glass. She was too pale; she needed a holiday. Apart from that, she could not find much to complain about. Quickly she got into the bath, feeling the warm water do its job, before getting out and pulling on her smart dress and jewellery, putting her hair up, spraying on perfume. She felt odd. Like a child putting on her mother's clothes, and it made Juliet realise that she was really out of practice at grown up, sophisticated socialising. She had a lot of rust to shed and didn't feel like shedding it at all.

She checked herself in the bathroom mirror in the moment before she was due to leave. She had put on a clingy black dress and she wanted to make sure that the lines of her underwear did not show. She didn't look too bad, all things considered. Then she grabbed her coat, hurrying because she had made herself slightly late.

The gallery opening was one of those touchy-feely, interactive events meant to demystify art and make it seem unstuffy rather than elitist. Children milled around in happy family groups. Juliet mingled holding a cheese square on a stick, self-consciously alone in a crowd, trying and failing miserably to have a good time and knowing absolutely that attending had been the wrong thing to do.

She looked at her happily pregnant friend chatting to acquaintances. She watched Corey flirt and thought about Mike closing his deal and his devotion to his expectant wife. A little girl with a painted face covered another little girl with lipstick kisses to a smattering of delighted applause and laughter. Juliet rehearsed in her head the excuses that would allow her to leave before the event really got going. The number of couples there, their shows of contentedness and public intimacy was more than she thought she could take.

The song playing at that moment through the concealed speakers of the gallery was the Michael Bublé version of the classic jazz ballad, 'Feeling Good'. It had been one of their favourites, one of the songs on Michael Bublé's album Juliet and Jack had listened to together on the balcony of his apartment while the city lights twinkled at dusk around them and they shared shots of tequila in their carefree, loving courtship. Hearing the song made Juliet feel bereft. She had been comfortable at events like this one in Jack's company, because he had an easy, cosmopolitan self-assurance that made him fit seamlessly into any social situation, regardless of how glitzy or stuck-up or sophisticated it was. He could mingle effortlessly and had a knack for small talk she did not share. It had been easy being half of a couple and it had been fun. She missed that confidence he had given her. Worse, she missed him.

She was backing off from a conversation in which she wanted to take no part, debating with herself whether a glass of champagne would enhance or sabotage her social skills, when someone bumped into her.

'Watch it,' Juliet said.

The someone she had collided with turned around.

He wore a look of surprise on his face. She thought her expression probably mirrored it. It was Max.

'Hey.'

'Hey yourself.'

Except that a different Max stood before her. This version was neither dust-covered nor paint-spattered; his beard had been trimmed and he looked altogether smoother and better-groomed. He wore a well-cut jacket and open-neck shirt and looked downright handsome, she thought, with those vivid green eyes unclouded by lenses. He seemed relaxed and urbane with a glass of beer in his hand. He certainly looked to her to be more at ease and at home than she felt at that moment.

Juliet sensed someone sidle up alongside her. It was Sydney. 'Who's this?' she smiled.

'This is Max.'

Sydney beamed.

Quietly, intimately, Juliet leant towards Max. She put a hand on his shoulder and said, 'I hardly recognised you, outside the building.'

'You too.'

'The guy from Juliet's apartment building?' Sydney asked Max brightly.

Juliet thought too brightly. To Max she said, 'This is Sydney. We work together, and I was staying with her when I was looking for somewhere to live, so I told her all about you.'

Sydney turned to Max. 'So, nice night, wouldn't you say?'

'It most certainly is,' Max agreed, nodding. He rocked

on his heels. He took a sip of his beer. Juliet had not seen him like this before. He seemed at ease, confident, almost a different man to the taciturn workaholic she had met in his apartment building.

He said, 'Sometimes it seems all I ever do is work. Twenty-four-seven. So, I decided I wanted to stop, come out, feel Brooklyn. You know . . .'

'Why don't you join us for a drink?' Sydney said.

'Oh, thanks,' Max said. 'That's very kind of you, but I'm good.'

Juliet had her eyes on Max. 'Maybe you could walk me home,' she said.

'Sure.'

Sydney kissed Juliet goodbye. 'He's cute,' she whispered, with a confidential squeeze of Juliet's hand.

The early evening was fine and mild as they walked through the New York streets. Juliet had too much on her mind to talk. Max was easy company in the silence; quiet rather than taciturn or tongue-tied, someone who spoke when he had something to communicate, she thought, appreciatively. And Sydney was right. Objectively, away from the dust and clamour of the building he was renovating, tailored and groomed, he really was cute.

'You're an unusual man in some ways, Max,' she offered eventually.

'Really?'

'You seem sort of . . . solitary,' she said. It was the subtlest way she could think of, to try to find out whether he was unattached. She didn't even know for sure whether he was straight or gay.

'August worries about me,' he said. 'People from his generation were already married with ten children by the time they got to my age.'

Juliet thought about the tea and whisky clutter of August's apartment; about the innocent intimacy of her gift package. 'He is a unique kind of guy, isn't he?'

'You could say that. Unique. Difficult. Given to eccentricity. Temperamental. A pain in the ass, would be another way to characterise him.'

'Is he OK?'

Max walked beside her, head bowed, eyes focused on his feet, pausing before he answered her. 'Until six months ago, he and I were partners in the building. We fixed everything together, made all the decisions collectively. Then he suffered a stroke.'

'And your parents?'

The question inflicted a pained look on Max's features. He said, 'I don't talk about that much. My parents both died when I was very young.'

'I'm so sorry.'

Max stopped. 'My father died instantly. According to my grandfather my mother was in surgery for six hours before the doctor came out and told him they couldn't save her.'

Juliet could read the damage this memory caused him in the pain on Max's face. He was wounded, she thought. But he was wounded because he was sensitive. He was truthful, a sweet man. 'I've been there,' she said. 'I've been that doctor before, delivering that awful news.'

'But you have also saved lives.'

'Sometimes.'

Max smiled. 'And your parents?' he said, his tone lighter, a deliberate changing of subject.

'My parents? Kind of after-the-fact hippies.'

'So you were the black sheep of the family.'

'For me, rebellion was going to med school. Free love sucked, as far as I could see. My parents were shiftless, rootless people. I never knew what a stable home was, not until Jack and I moved in together.'

There. She had said it. She had said her husband's name.

'Jack,' Max said, softly.

'My ex,' Juliet said. 'He was attracted to me and my ambitions, but when it came down to it, he wanted me at home with an apron, cooking dinner and having babies, instead of out stitching people together, so he found someone else.'

She didn't really know if this was true. She thought it plausible. Something had come between her and Jack, forcing them apart. The TCB had not been the cause of what had gone wrong, she had been a consequence. Whether it was true or not, it made Max smile softly, to himself. She thought there was a shared wavelength, an attraction between them.

Max said, 'I thought hippy kids had weird names.'

Juliet blushed and rolled her eyes.

He laughed. 'You do, don't you? What's your real name?'

'Juliet is my real name.'

'What's your middle name?'

The blush on Juliet's cheeks deepened. 'No way.'

Across the street, some kids were playing on a fire escape. They were igniting bits of paper and watching them flare into life in the dusky half-light. They would flame up and rise in fierce orange flight and then dim to red and descend, disappearing as ash as they fragmented in the breeze towards the ground. It was an old game, a simple pastime, guileless and beautiful in its brief, incandescent magic.

Max followed Juliet's gaze. Then they both looked through a window further up the building, at a family having dinner, old and young people together in the shared, messy joy of domestic harmony.

Juliet said, 'When I was little, I used to walk around the neighbourhood at night. Not my neighbourhood, obviously, I never had one, but the settled homes wherever we'd fetched up. I'd look into windows. At families around televisions. You know, brothers, sisters, parents, talking, eating . . . I couldn't touch them.'

Max looked fascinated by this admission. Juliet felt the need to qualify what she had just confessed. 'I mean I knew I couldn't be part of a family. But I could imagine in my mind that I was.'

He nodded.

'Bliss,' she said after another moment's silence. She was in a confessional mood.

'Bliss?'

'Yup.'

It took him a moment. Then he got it. 'God, I'm sorry,' he said. 'I think it a very good thing that you dropped your middle name.'

'I told you they were hippies.'

'Deliberate humiliation was probably the furthest thing from their minds.'

'I'm sure.'

'I mean, hippies and sadism don't really go hand in hand.'

'Not generally.'

They had reached their building, and walked into the elevator. They exited on their floor and Juliet took out her key and unlocked her door and then turned to Max. 'Thanks,' she said. She felt shy. But the shyness was a reaction to what she was suddenly aware she was about to do. She leant in and kissed Max on the cheek and closed her eyes and inhaled his scent. Her lips moved towards his mouth and he recoiled.

'I'm sorry,' Juliet said, opening her eyes. 'God, I'm an idiot.'

'No,' he said. 'Don't be sorry.'

'It's a bad idea. You're right. Of course it's a bad idea.'

'No,' Max said, 'I didn't mean it that way. I really didn't.'

'I'm confused, out of practice,' Juliet said. 'I'm reading the wrong signals.'

'You're not, really.'

She bit down on her lip. She smiled at him, sadly. Whatever the truth was about their instincts and impulses, their crossed wires would not be straightened out tonight. The moment had gone. The evening had begun well and offered intriguing promise and had then very suddenly unravelled in clumsiness and embarrassment. Juliet entered her apartment and closed the door behind her leaving Max in the corridor outside.

Twelve

Juliet kicked off her shoes and discarded her coat. She unbuckled her wristwatch, poured a glass of wine and sipped it, looking out of her bedroom window at the view of Manhattan twinkling in the night. She marvelled at the uncountable vastness of its steel and stone constructions and the windows dotting that vastness in shimmering pinpoints of silver and gold. She would have another bath, she decided. This time it would be for pure pleasure and she would luxuriate in the soap and bubbles of a deep and scented tub. It was exactly what she needed.

Juliet's muscles still ached slightly from the run of the previous night and the heat of the water bled away the tension. She lay immersed neck-deep, the bathroom illuminated by candlelight, her limbs floating, her eyes closed and the surface of the water perfectly still, glass-like in its unruffled smoothness. She felt drowsiness slip over her like gossamer. She could almost have descended into sleep.

The flames of the candles flickered. She opened her eyes and reached for her wine glass resting on the edge of the tub. As she did so she sensed low vibrations move across the floorboards and into the bath water. The tranquil surface shivered slightly and then began to ripple as the subsonic noise stirring it grew stronger beneath her.

Juliet did not flinch; it had become almost routine to her now, the travel of the heavy maintenance train as it trundled through the night on the subway line far below. Max had warned her about the effect. Then, in front of her mirror, she had witnessed it for the first time. Now, she pretty much expected it and felt the time would soon be upon her when she would not notice it at all. It was a tiny price to pay for the abundant charms of her gloriously sited new home.

She closed her eyes again. The aftertaste of the wine was sweet and complex on her tongue. Her thoughts were complex too, but immersed in the cleansing water and the hot haze of the steamy bathroom they did not threaten, as they sometimes did, to overwhelm her. Life was more good than bad and it was intriguing too. Possibilities were what distinguished life from mere existence, and she felt they were opening up to her.

She moved a bar of soap smoothly over her body, past a tiny, familiar mole on her upper back that she caressed lightly with her fingertips. Her hand slid down her legs, around her buttocks and she immersed her head in the water and then surfaced for air, moving an exploratory hand between her legs, touching herself, the touch of her soapy fingertips deliciously sensual, probing deeper with a caught gasp and shudder of arousal.

Something moved, jerking Juliet out of her erotic reverie with a jolt of surprise and fear. The wine in her glass had moved, the surface of it shifting, dimpling as though some phantom hand had gripped and shaken the stem of the glass. Suddenly she was scared, truly scared. This was not the melancholy feeling of intruding on an unquiet ghost she had felt at the apartment of the mobster suicide. It was more threatening than that, less subtle and more real. It was as though some tangible force was stealthily approaching her, malevolent, unseen.

She felt naked. She *was* naked. She could not have been more physically vulnerable, literally defenceless in her bath. She sat up, alert, straight-backed. She listened intently, slowly turning her head towards a faint and eerie noise coming from outside the bathroom door. Was it getting louder? Was it coming closer? She had to struggle against her own rising sense of panic to divorce what she was actually seeing and hearing from those sensations fear could make her imagine were real.

Juliet's hand brushed against her wine glass then and it toppled and crashed to the floor, a shimmering mess of purple liquid and shattered glass fragments spread across the tiles in the yellow candlelight.

'Shit.'

Cautiously, deliberately, she stepped out of the tub. She threw a thick bath towel over the broken glass and peered into the open doorway. She walked through it, the soles of her wet feet sucking at the wooden floor, leaving a trail of footprints in her wake. She entered her living room. Shadows played on the curtained window as headlight beams from traffic crossing the bridge skittered through its crisscross of iron girders. Her breathing, harsh, was her terror echoing in her ears, uncontrolled terror hammering at her chest, fast and hard and moistening her palms with it.

She hauled in a breath and strode decisively towards the window and gathering the fabric in both fists, flung the curtains wide, flushing the room with the night light from outside.

She turned around. The room lay exposed and innocent in pale moonlight. She could hear nothing but the faint traffic from below and the staccato drip of a bathroom faucet. When she held her breath and really listened, she could hear the hiss from the bathroom of one of her candles slightly guttering. There was no other sound, certainly nothing demonic or inexplicable or even slightly scary.

There was no old man standing staring at her from a corner, no wild-eyed ancient with a whisky and spittle-matted beard prowling gauntly through her private space, spying lasciviously on her. She really, really needed to get a grip on herself.

Her belongings lay where her own idleness and indifference had left them, still largely in the heap of boxes forming an uneven hill at the centre of the room. Nothing was out of kilter. Absolutely nothing was wrong.

She shuddered out a huge, ragged sigh of relief. 'Jesus Christ, Juliet. Calm the fuck down.'

Turning on the overhead light, she blew out the candles in the bathroom. She cleaned the mess of glass shards and spilled Merlot from the floor. Then, switching off the light, she let her eyes grow accustomed to the darkness before roughly towelling her hair and going into her bedroom. She sat on the bed and pushed a strand of wet hair the towel had missed from her face. It left a single water droplet on her index finger that rolled off her skin towards the floor as she swung up her feet and lay, relaxed now, on the bed. She closed her eyes.

Was it instinct or imagination, that feeling she had of being watched? She did not know, not for certain. But she felt safe now and so assumed it had been the latter. There had been nobody there, had there? She had looked and there had been no one to see. Old buildings creaked and moaned; their foundations and masonry, their very fabric, continued to move and settle for as long as they stood. They had a life of their own and it was sometimes audible, that was all. She relaxed and let fatigue and sleep claim her.

Thirteen

Juliet did not get a chance to talk to Sydney about the evening of the opening until they changed together after being on the same shift late in the afternoon a few days later. They were in the locker room. It was a location that lent itself to shared spoken intimacies and there was no real question that Sydney was, nowadays, easily her closest friend.

She had been since that concussed distress call Juliet had made on the day her marriage collapsed. Maybe she had been even before then, when Juliet had fooled herself Jack was her closest friend. But she did not really know what to say to Sydney about Max, because she was not at all sure what she felt about what had, or more precisely what had not, happened.

'I don't know what I expected.'

'You were expecting rebound sex, honey. Hot Landlord Rebound Sex.'

'I think the whole landlord thing is the basis of the attraction, actually. I see him less as someone who pockets the rent than as a sort of knight in shining armour.'

'You're not wet enough to play the damsel in distress, babe.'

Juliet smiled. She had been wet when she'd climbed out of the tub, later that same evening. She had been pretty damned distressed, too. Nothing odd had happened since, though. And she had seen nothing at all of Max either.

'I was desperate for a place to live and this guy hands me the dream apartment, on a plate. He's shy, unprepossessing, he's almost awkward, actually. But he's physically strong and capable. He's dependable and I get the sense he's just really solid inside.'

'And he's cute,' Sydney said. 'Don't forget that shallow but crucial detail.'

'He looked pretty good the other night,' Juliet said.

'He might be exactly what you need. I'm not saying he has to be for ever. I'm not saying it has to be for life or even for a month. But you need to move on, girl. Think of it as fate, doing you a favour for once. Maybe fate owes you a favour. You've sure as hell earned it.'

Juliet smiled again. Sydney hugged her hard and then left. She looked into her still-open locker, at the sticky residue left by the tape that used to hold in place the photos of her and Jack. They had symbolised the optimistic promise of a shared golden future. Juliet had ripped them out and torn them to pieces, treating their photos with the same brutality her errant husband had shown her heart. Maybe Sydney was right and fate owed her a favour, and she owed herself the reckless passion of no-strings sex.

Her phone rang. It was Jack, again, but this time she could not help herself. She answered it.

'Jack.'

'You picked up.'

'What do you want?'

'I just called to say hi.'

'Hi' would not do it. 'Hi' was wholly inadequate. He should be grovelling, pleading, shameful, shamed.

All at the same time she felt pleasure at hearing his voice, pain at the loss of him and disappointment at what he was communicating. Nothing would ever mend things between them but an apology would be better than nothing at all. The only word she thought it appropriate for Jack to say to her was a sincere, two-syllable expression of remorse. He needed to say sorry.

'Well, hi,' she said.

He was silent for so long, Juliet thought that the connection had been severed. Then he said, 'Can I see you?'

She didn't reply. She couldn't trust herself to, because she had missed him so much and wanted to see him so very badly she thought that if she spoke, she might weaken and accede to his request. In fact, she knew that she would. The only way at that moment to stay strong and resolute was to remain silent. She closed her eyes. She felt the phone shake in the grip of her hand with a tremor of trapped emotion.

Then he said it. 'I'm so sorry.'

It wasn't enough. Hearing it said just emphasised to her the enormity of the betrayal and the pain and humiliation he had caused her. She had been cheated on. The cheat was on the other end of the line, pleading for a second chance he did not deserve. 'Sorry' had just proven to be a pretty sorry word, in the face of what she had suffered. 'I've got to go,' Juliet said.

She had no sooner ended the call than her phone vibrated again and she picked up saying, 'It's not a good idea for us to talk yet.'

'Juliet?'

She recognised the voice. It was not her husband's. 'Max?'

There was a pause before he replied. He said, 'Listen, I'm sorry I've been out of touch for a few days. August died this afternoon.'

'Oh God,' she said. 'How awful for you, Max. How did it happen?'

Juliet felt sympathy for Max at hearing this news, but what she mostly felt was relief. She had vaguely thought her landlord might be deliberately avoiding her, out of embarrassment at their clumsy, fumbling conclusion to the night of the exhibition opening. And if she was honest with herself, she had thought there was something genuinely sinister about his grandfather, even though her suspicion had never been proven. It was a harsh thing to think, but Juliet thought it anyway. Life in her apartment building would be more comfort-able without that gaunt, staring sentinel who had occupied an address on the ninth floor that had looked like the junk shop from hell.

'He was in poor health. You must have seen that for yourself.'

'He seemed frail,' she said, 'but he didn't look like a dying man.'

'He'd had a number of small strokes, and they took

their toll. Nobody lives for ever.'

'So his death was not a shock to you?'

She heard Max clear his throat. 'I cared for him. I was the only person close to him. It is sad, of course. But his death did not come as a shock and I think of it really as a release. A release from the life of an invalid.'

'Of course.' This news was a jolting reminder to Juliet that she was not the centre of the universe. The discovery that the world did not actually revolve around her should have helped with her feelings about Jack, should have put the pain into some sort of perspective. But it did not. Emotion did not respond to objectivity; not in her case, anyway.

'Would you come to the funeral?' Max said.

'I hardly knew him,' Juliet said, surprised. 'We barely spoke.'

'He would have been a friend to you, had he lived,' Max said.

She thought about the old man's unsettling stare, the domestic squalor that had surrounded him, the sickening smell of whisky roused to warmth by tea. She remembered then the gift basket, each item it contained carefully chosen and individually wrapped. It was true, wasn't it? He had been kind in his clumsy way and she had reacted with disdain.

'All right,' she said, thinking that perhaps she had judged August too harshly.

'It would mean a lot to me.'

'Then of course I'll come.'

'Thank you.'

'I'm very sorry, Max, for your loss.'

'There are some things of his I need to dispense with. Actually, there is an enormous amount of stuff. There might be one or two pieces you could take. I couldn't help noticing how empty your apartment looks.'

She thought just for a second about making a joke about being minimalist by aesthetic choice. But it wasn't the time for wisecracks. Instead, she said, 'When is the funeral?'

'The day after tomorrow. In the afternoon.'

She nodded to herself. She could get someone to cover her shift. She was owed a few favours.

'I'll be there,' she said. She felt slightly hypocritical saying it because she had not really liked the little she had known of the old man and would not sincerely mourn him. But she had the strong sense that Max was on his own now and the sense of obligation she felt to him was pretty substantial. She knew what it felt like to be alone, how desolate and terrifying that could be. For his sake, she would go.

'When shall I come to your grandfather's apartment?'

'After the funeral, I suppose. I expect then would be most convenient for you.'

'Yes, that sounds best.'

'Thank you, Juliet. Sincerely, thank you.'

Fourteen

There were two funeral cars, the hearse and the black sedan that followed its sedate progress to the cemetery with Max and Juliet seated in their mourning attire in its rear.

Juliet had not attended a funeral since the death of her father. He had been cremated in a cardboard coffin after a humanist ceremony at a hippy commune in southern California. She remembered the smear of oily smoke from the incinerator against the bright blue of the sky. She had sweated then in her black wool suit in the West Coast summer sunshine.

She wouldn't be sweating today. The air conditioning of the sedan made its leather interior as chilly as a refrigerator. She was glad she had worn her best coat and her gloves. They were warm as well as possessing the necessary formality.

Max sat next to her in a black cashmere coat over a black three-piece suit that was so immaculately tailored it reminded her of Mike's comment about Max's probable worth. He wore a dark grey necktie and she had seen him check the time on a gold wristwatch with a black alligator strap.

She couldn't help looking at him as he sat next to her

in the back of the car, their bodies about eight inches apart. She didn't know him at all, but he was someone she would like to get to know: he was both physically attractive and somehow, innately mysterious.

Juliet wondered would it be frivolous to speak in the car; to make small talk with the grandson of the man whose funeral they were attending. She could not really gauge his emotional state from his appearance. He was dry-eyed and seemingly composed. Although he had told her that his grandfather's death had been a release, things were different, when a loved one was lying in a box in the car in front of yours. Things were different when that box was to be buried in a hole dug in the ground and covered by dark earth for ever.

In the event it was Max who spoke first. He said, 'Do you go to many funerals?'

'No,' she said. 'This is the first since my father's death almost a decade ago. Family doctors end up attending quite a few, especially in small communities. But my patients arrive and leave, alive or dead, as strangers.'

'Do you enjoy your work?'

'Very much.'

'Do you ever make mistakes?'

She thought about this question. 'You mean a misdiagnosis?'

'I mean have you ever killed someone who should have lived?'

Juliet did not much care for his turn of words. She actually thought it a rather extraordinary thing to ask. But she knew the honest answer to the question. 'No,' she said.

'People must be in awe of you,' he said.

'Hospitals are full of doctors, Max. Med school churns out more and more every year. We're pretty much two a penny.'

'When I met you, I got the impression you were proud of what you do. I was sure I could hear the pride unmistakably in your voice.'

'I am proud of what I do,' she said. 'It's just that what I do doesn't make me anything special.'

They were silent again for a while. Juliet was relieved that the conversation had stopped. It had been uncomfortably close to an interrogation, despite its brevity. Then Max turned to look at her and smiled and said, 'I think you're special.'

She smiled back. It was a nice compliment. 'Is that why you rented me the apartment?'

'I think it probably is, Juliet. I have never really had a job of my own.'

'You maintain your property.'

'I mean a proper job.'

'Your building must be worth a fortune.'

He shrugged. 'I've inherited that. The acumen that went into buying it was my great-grandfather's. I have never attended a job interview, or commuted to an office, or taken part in a training programme or a campaign or hit a target or earned a bonus. I've never had a colleague who wasn't a close relative. Work is an alien world to me.'

'Do you think you have missed out?'

'Of course I have.'

'Are you saying that you're lonely, Max?'

'If I am, then I will be lonelier with the absence of August from my life.'

Juliet nodded. She thought that this was true. But she remembered how socially at ease Max had seemed at the art opening. He had looked urbane and attractive and totally as though he belonged. He had appeared a damned sight more at ease there than she had felt.

She thought that if he wanted to, he could engage with the world much more fully than he did. Even if he didn't want to, with August dead, as the sole owner of the building he would be obliged to. And not playing nursemaid to a sick old man would also free up his time.

Juliet thought the dividing line between romantic loner and deliberate recluse was quite a fine one. There was something deliberate, wasn't there, about the isolation in which Max and his grandfather had chosen to live their lives. That was why she was in a single car and not leading a fleet of them to the cemetery. Where were August's friends? He must have made friends in a lifetime spanning eighty years. They could not all have pre-deceased him. But if he had friends, they had shunned his funeral.

Max took her arm when they reached the cemetery. They followed the coffin to the graveside accompanied only by an undertaker stretching up to hold a sheltering umbrella over their bowed heads to keep them from the strengthening downpour.

The pall-bearers were paid professionals, familiar with the ritual of burial and used to the weight of a dead man's casket. But August's coffin was a gargantuan thing hewn from oak and they slithered and struggled under their burden to the plot. It was as though Max had tried to restore to him the stature and substance in death that illness and increasing age had deprived him of in life.

The clergyman read the funeral liturgy. Juliet knew so little about formal religion that she was not even aware of his denomination, yet another gap in her social education that her hippie parents had failed to address.

The headstone was a large marble tablet, several thousand dollars' worth of engraved stone, she estimated, which Max must have had made well in advance of his grandfather's death. It was much too substantial and elaborate to have been carved in the time since the old man had died. She supposed it had only been waiting to have the date of his departure from life chiselled into its polished surface.

Max had certainly prepared scrupulously for this occasion. It was so neatly and grandly accomplished, it was almost as if the timing had been predetermined. If it had, she thought he might have hired professional mourners, though. The two of them were so solitary at the graveside it was actually quite pitiful. And he could have chosen a better day. The rain was close to torrential. It was turning the piled earth scooped from the grave to mud.

At the end of the service, Max was invited to drop soil onto the coffin before the excavators trundled forward to do their mechanical job of filling it. He walked gingerly across the flap of artificial grass neatening the graveside and dumped down a handful of black mud with an expression that said that he found the task distasteful. The mud hit the casket lid with a watery thud. He grimaced and one of the burial professionals handed him a wad of Wet Wipes.

Grief affected people in different ways, Juliet mused on the way back. Some people defer or delay it. She thought that probably was what Max was doing. He had shown no emotion at all from the moment the car had picked them up outside the building to the end of the funeral. August had surely been father, mother, uncle and brother all rolled into one cantankerous old man, hadn't he? Max had said he could be a pain in the ass, but he had also been the only living relative he possessed.

It had to be deferred grief. The alternative was too cold and disturbing for serious consideration.

He was so silent on the journey back, so lost to the possibility of conversation, that when he spoke she nearly jumped out of her skin.

'Do you believe in an afterlife?'

'I haven't given it serious thought,' she said. 'On balance, I probably do. I expect the question will gain greater urgency when I'm older.'

'Ghosts?'

She smiled. 'Sometimes. Depends on whether I've caught a really spooky movie. If I'm in the right frame of mind I can entertain the possibility, yes.' She thought about the man they had just seen buried, then roaming his familiar building, unaware that he was dead, a grim apparition defying physical laws. The image made her shudder. She said, 'You?'

'No. I saw my parents killed. They died in front of me.

I was six years old. If they could have come back, they would have done, to take care of me. At least, my mother would have. There are not many certainties in life, Juliet. But I'm pretty sure of that.'

Fifteen

Half an hour later, Juliet found herself in August's apartment for the second time in her life. It was hard to believe that she would never lay eyes on that strange old man again. She still had most of the toiletries he had put in his gift basket lying unwrapped in her living room.

She was used to mortality. But it was strange, thinking about a departed life when you were surrounded by the detritus of that life and August's apartment was just so full of *stuff*. When someone died, all their wisdom and erudition, all the skills and learning accrued over their lifetime went with them. Their virtues and vices, their failings and their personal triumphs just disappeared into the ether. In a sense, it was as though they had never been there at all. But with his belongings August had contrived to leave more of himself behind than most people did.

Max threw open the curtain over a huge window with a panoramic view of the Bridge and the river and the glittering island beyond. Light splashed across the arrayed objects, artefacts, furnishings and keepsakes piled and clustered and mounted and framed everywhere Juliet looked. The last time she had been here, age and whisky had suggested a sort of squalor. In the sunlight it had a different character; she was aware of lovely paintings and exquisite antiques, some of them seemed very valuable.

Max was looking at her. He looked like an art connoisseur in his three-piece suit now that he had removed his overcoat, or an auctioneer from one of those impossibly snooty art dealers like Christie's, maybe. He looked like a guy with a weekend house in the Hamptons and a serious yachting habit.

She could feel his eyes upon her, sense his observation, although she didn't find the scrutiny uncomfortable. He was watching her in the same appreciative way as she was looking at some of the beautiful objects in the room. There was nothing salacious or crude about it. Eventually, she returned his look. She said, 'Are you sure about this? Are you sure you want to do this?'

He nodded to her. 'I know you need a new bed, at least.'

She had let that slip, about her reluctance to sleep in her marital bed, when he'd helped her with her things. He had remembered.

'But some of this furniture is so beautiful. And it's yours now.'

'Pick what you want, Juliet. Take anything you want. The rest of it, I'm either going to sell, or throw away.'

'God, at least let me pay you.'

'No. Absolutely not. I don't want to profit from you in that way. I don't intend to take a penny from you for any of this. I merely thought I might be able to do you a favour.'

'You're doing me a lot of favours.'

'Accompanying me to the funeral meant a lot. It was beyond kind.'

'Then how about you let me buy you dinner? I've found a good place, terrific buzz, great young chef. You like jazz piano?'

Max grinned at her. He opened his arms. 'I can cook,' he said.

She smiled back at him. She didn't know him, not yet. She had reservations, but almost everything she'd seen and heard so far, she liked.

She took a few items: an antique silver candelabra and a flower vase Max told her had been made in Utrecht in the late eighteenth century. She also took an original and unsigned painting that to her unschooled eye looked like a Dufy. Over the next couple of evenings she unpacked her things and brought some kind of domestic order to her apartment.

She hung the Dufy on her sitting-room wall where the light from the window would bathe it in the morning. It was a view of a harbour, probably on the Côte d'Azur and it had about its smudged waves and sun-bleached canvas of its painted boatsails a suggestion of Scott Fitzgerald's *Tender is the Night*. She had read that one at Jack's insistence in his early, failed attempt to encourage her to share his taste for fiction. Most fiction bored her but that novel, she had loved.

She filled her Utrecht vase with lilies. She lit the candles she had bought for the candelabra which glittered in the light of the flames after the thorough polish she had given it to take the tarnish off.

All in all, her home looked fabulous, she thought. There was something slightly imperious, a suggestion of real splendour, about the proportions of the rooms and all the scrolled plaster ornate on the walls and the alcoves and pediments present throughout. But her thrown cushions and rugs gave it a human dimension and it smelled of her scent and soap and the beeswax on the wooden floors; it now had this snug warmth about it that was entirely personal to her.

She couldn't wait for Mike and Sydney to come over the following night and she was so excited about showing off her new apartment. Those items of his grandfather's Max had so thoughtfully offered her had made the place complete and she was anticipating the visit from her closest friends with something approaching pride. She had a home. Her new life had a proper setting and therefore a proper beginning. Her home would resound to the music of laughter once Mike began his dinner table patter.

She had to resist the temptation to think that there should be four of them. Mike and Syd were great company but she knew that their presence there would emphasise her own rudely inflicted predicament as a somewhat reluctant single woman.

She considered inviting Max to make a four but thought the dynamic would be wrong. She'd hate it if he felt left out. Sitting with other people's friends could be an isolating experience; he would not get the old jokes and fond references forged over years of friendship and confiding. And considering what he'd told her in the car she didn't want to make him feel uncomfortable. And then there was the fact that his presence could give the evening an unwelcome air of sexual tension. Because there was no doubt that her intentions towards him were not entirely honourable.

So, to make up for his absence tomorrow, she had accepted Max's invitation to cook her dinner. Socialising with him would wait and needed to anyway, until a respectable period of grief for his grandfather had been observed. It was too soon after the funeral for him to be thinking about her in the context of a relationship, however tentative those thoughts.

Sixteen

Her preparations for the arrival of her first ever guests went almost without a hitch. The only slightly irritating thing was that she did not get to wear what she wanted to. Juliet was not neurotic about fashion – a dress was a dress – but the clingy black number she particularly wanted to wear seemed to have disappeared. She spent half an hour looking for it without success before giving up and finding something else.

They arrived soon after, Syd wearing an elegant Empire maternity dress, and Mike for once looked really quite smart in a freshly pressed suit and crisp shirt and tie. He carried a house-warming present of a bread-making machine between his arms. It was an expensive affair of chrome and white ceramic and most homes would have struggled to accommodate its almost industrial dimensions. But hers did not. It fitted unobtrusively into the relative vastness of her kitchen as if it had always been there. It looked like it belonged.

'Bread,' Mike observed, 'the stuff of life.'

'Booze is the stuff of life, if your domestic habits are any indication,' Sydney said. She looked about her. 'Jesus, hon, this place is gorgeous.'

Mike too was looking around, flexing his arms, stiff from bearing the weight of their gift. 'When the baby is born, maybe we could come and stay here with you,' he said. 'We could use the extra space and you owe us a favour. Not that I want you to feel compromised into agreeing out of any sense of obligation.'

Juliet kissed them both and took their coats. She realised that she was very out of practice at this sort of thing and was suddenly relieved that she hadn't invited Max to make the four. With these two she didn't have to try, or make small talk, but with Max there, it would have been much more difficult.

'On the subject of the stuff of life,' Mike said. 'We did bring a couple of bottles with us.'

Juliet, holding their coats, looked at them both, a bit bemused. Mike had carried in the bread machine. Sydney, in her condition, was justifiably carrying nothing at all.

'Howard Hughes offered to bring it up,' Mike said.

Sydney giggled. 'Mike,' she said.

'Your shy millionaire,' Mike said. 'We met him in the vestibule. I was struggling to carry everything and he offered. Sydney told me who he was in the elevator.' He glanced back towards the door. 'He said he'd bring it up in a second. Hope he hasn't stolen it. You can never tell with these reclusive types.'

Sydney punched him on the arm.

To Juliet, Mike said, 'Even now, he could be squatting in the basement, guzzling wine straight from the neck of the bottle, singing to himself. Bob Dylan, I would imagine. Actually, more likely Leonard Cohen, going on the look of the guy. I'm assuming the building has a basement?'

But Juliet did not get the chance to reply. There was a knock at the door.

'Hallelujah,' Sydney said.

'I'm thinking more "Suzanne",' Mike said.

Syd turned to him and said, 'You are beyond hope.'

Juliet hung up her guests' coats on the way to get the door. Max was outside when she opened it. He was wearing jeans and a chambray shirt. Not quite his paint-spattered persona but nearer that than the gallery look or the way he had been turned out for his grandfather's funeral. He was carrying a box containing several bottles. Mike had been typically over-generous. He smiled and looked down at what he carried and said, 'House-warming party?'

'Not quite,' she said. 'Friends over for dinner. Sydney and her husband Mike. You remember Syd from the gallery opening?'

'I recognised her straight away when I saw her in the vestibule just now,' he said. 'I was down there replacing a light bulb. She introduced her husband. You have nice friends.' He held out the box he carried for her to take from him.

Juliet said, 'Won't you come in and have a quick drink?'

Max smiled and shook his head. 'I'm not dressed for the occasion,' which was true. 'I'll leave you to relax and enjoy yourselves in your new home with your old friends. But I'm holding you to our dinner date, Juliet. You haven't forgotten?'

'I haven't forgotten,' she smiled. 'You're cooking. I'm looking forward to it.' She took the box from him and he turned and walked away.

Juliet showed Mike and Syd around the apartment as they sipped their pre-dinner drinks. They were impressed by the décor and dimensions of the rooms, complimentary about what she had done with the place and incredulous about the rent she was paying for it. Mike tapped walls. Sydney raised her eyebrows. 'Some guys buying cars are tyre kickers. Some guys tap the walls when they're shown around a building. I'm lucky enough that Mike does both.'

'There's a lot of dead space here,' Mike pointed out. 'This place is pretty enormous. But it has the potential to be even bigger. Substantially larger, in fact. '

'I've heard that expression before,' Juliet said, 'about dead space.'

'There's a disparity between the interior shell and exterior wall,' Mike said. 'I suppose when the place was constructed, space wasn't at the premium it is now.'

'Larger rooms are fashionable now because heating is more efficient,' Sydney said. 'Back in the old days big rooms meant chilly New York winters.'

'You're probably right,' Mike said. 'But it wouldn't be built like this today, that's for sure. A discrepancy like that – the blueprints would certainly be interesting to look at.'

'Right now I'm interested in looking at a plate,' Sydney said. 'Lying laden on a table. From the perspective of a chair.' She winked at Juliet. Her hands were in the small of her back, pressing there. 'If we're done with the tour?'

The food she fed Mike and Sydney was pre-ordered from a restaurant and reheated in her stove. Juliet possessed a number of substantial attributes, but being a great cook was not one of them.

Dinner was fun, but inevitably the talk turned to Jack. 'You really need to embark on something new,' Sydney said, gently. She reached across the table and took Juliet's hand and gave it a squeeze. 'Have an affair, Jules. Keep it light and fun and reckless. See how you feel about Jack when you come out the other side. You need a different perspective on this from the one that you have. Jack is not the only guy in the world. He is not the only eligible guy. He hurt you pretty badly.'

'He devastated you,' Mike said, quietly.

Juliet looked sharply at him. Mike was not given to seriousness and was usually diplomatic. These two, though, had borne the brunt of it; they had taken care of her. 'Yes,' she confirmed. She remembered the prismatic shimmer of colour through the spray of their lawn sprinkler on that bright day of discovery. She remembered the sick feeling of dismay overwhelming her. 'He did devastate me.'

Mike was blushing. 'Sorry, hon,' he said. 'Tactless. Blame the alcohol.'

'You haven't had that much to drink,' Sydney said, 'yet. And all three of us know what you just said is true.'

'Excuse me,' Mike said. 'I need to use the bathroom.'

He seemed pale and preoccupied when he came back. Juliet put it down to embarrassment about his comment on what Jack had done to her. Mike was kind and essentially decent. But men like Mike generally spoke in a clubhouse code that did not allow for mention of subjects such as heartbreak and deceit.

Fifteen minutes later, when Mike was still pale and uneasy, Juliet began to wonder whether she might not have inadvertently poisoned him. The restaurant from which she had ordered the food was one their friend Corey had recommended. Corey spoke highly of the cuisine and the food Juliet had chosen from their menu did indeed taste delicious. But Mike looked distinctly queasy.

Suddenly, he put down his fork he had been eating with, and cleared his throat. He dabbed at his mouth with a napkin and then dabbed at his moist forehead and said, 'Sydney mentioned something to me, Juliet. When you were still searching for an apartment, you had a psychic experience?'

Sydney glanced at her. Juliet shrugged. She was not in the least offended. Syd told Mike everything. She enjoyed teasing him in public and making him the butt of her jokes, but she shared everything with him. Juliet supposed it was one of the reasons why their marriage had endured so happily.

'I thought I did, Mike,' she said. 'It was weird. I mean, you know what I'm like, pragmatic and scientific, but I sensed something really dismal in some rooms I saw. It compelled me to leave.'

'A presence?'

'More of a legacy, I think. It turned out a Mafia killer committed suicide there back in the bootlegging mob era. I don't think I sensed him, but I was somehow aware of his accomplishments, the fear and grief he'd been responsible for. There was a residue, almost an infection. Like it was contagious and still virulent. It was very unpleasant.'

'But no ghost?'

'No ghost as such, no. Why do you bring it up?'

'No reason.'

'Balls,' Sydney said. 'Tell her why you bring it up. Tell her why you bring it up now. I'm extremely curious myself.'

'It's silly.'

'Tell us,' Sydney said again.

Mike smiled. The smile was nervous and unsure, the expression on his face one Juliet had never seen him use before, completely uncharacteristic of his open, cheerful nature. He said, 'When I was in the bathroom just now, I felt as if I was not alone. It felt like someone was behind me, watching me. I have never felt so sure and strong an instinct in my life. I was absolutely certain of it. When I turned around, nobody was there.'

'So you were wrong,' Sydney said. 'Who would wish to watch you take a pee? You think people should pay? Like with a spectator sport?'

'No, Syd, I was right. I couldn't see anybody there. But someone was observing me. I know they were. I trust my instinct. I've made a pretty good living out of trusting it. I know what I know. I was not alone when I went to pee just now.'

The three people around the dinner table were silent for a long moment. Then Sydney pushed back her chair with her heels, levered herself to her feet with effort and stared at her husband.

'What?' he asked.

'What? What do you think? You think we're going to link hands and hold a séance? We're all going to the bathroom, Mike. The three of us are going to take a look.'

They trooped to the bathroom. Juliet switched on the overhead light. In their reflection, in the floor-length mirror, Sydney's bump looked enormous.

Their reflections were fractured in the mirror in the cabinet over the sink and the hand mirror on the bathroom shelf. They looked around, at the immaculately tiled walls and the high smooth plaster of the pale ceiling and the gleaming chrome of the faucets and the shower head. It was totally silent in the bathroom. Nothing gurgled or splashed or dripped. They looked and listened but there was nothing to see or hear.

'There's no one here. Except us,' Sydney said.

'No,' Mike said, 'there isn't.'

Not now, Juliet thought. That was how Mike wanted to end his sentence. He was too tactful to say the words and he probably did not want to risk a further browbeating from his indignant wife. But he was sane and sober and he was certain something had been there. *Someone.*

August, she thought to herself. The ghost of August with his unsettling eyes and spittle-flecked beard had stood watching Mike, staring at him so intently that Mike had become aware of the scrutiny he had been subjected to from beyond the grave.

Juliet shivered. It was ridiculous. She would dismiss the idea. She had not personally sensed the old man's whisky-soaked presence. She had not seen his spectre. She had seen him buried under six feet of ground in a casket from which David Blaine could not have escaped. There had been a ceremony, a solemn religious service. They had observed the custom of throwing dirt down onto the box. He was dead. He was gone for ever. *But you've felt it too*, a quiet voice whispered in her mind. *Before August died.*

The rest of the evening passed remarkably light-heartedly after that one peculiar episode. It was easy to forget the incident as they ate and laughed and drank too much, at least Mike and Juliet drank too much.

Her guests left after a tearful embrace at her apartment door at around one in the morning. Juliet saw that Mike had managed to get food on both his shirt-front and his necktie. It didn't matter. He could afford the laundry bills.

Syd took a last appraising look around and said, 'You've done very well for yourself, hon. This is exactly the start you need. Make the most of it. There's a lot that's right in your life and with your assets, a hell of a lot more that could be with just a little bit of effort. The world doesn't owe you anything. But you owe it to yourself to live a little more.'

After their departure, Juliet washed up and tidied the place, put the cutlery and dishes away before making herself a cup of lemon tea and pondering briefly on the evening before going to bed.

She did not feel spooked. She did not feel watched. She was sure she would have sensed any scrutiny, ghostly or otherwise. Poor August, she reflected, how could she think like that about an old and harmless man whose instincts had been gruffly kind and who his grandson insisted would have become her friend if he'd lived long enough?

Sydney had given her sensible advice. The Jack question would look different once she had enjoyed an affair, however brief or casual, with another man. It would seem neither so urgent nor as all-encompassing as it did. A carefree sexual fling would give her a fresh perspective. And she would enjoy it. There would certainly be no guilt involved. She was still legally married, but she was free to do as she pleased.

Seventeen

Max brought not only the food for their dinner, but the wine, readily decanted into a lead crystal vessel with the precisely elaborate facets of something crafted at least a century ago.

'You like old things,' she said, as he poured from the decanter into her glass. He didn't reply, just smiled slightly and got on with preparing the food.

'Wow, it looks like you know what you're doing.' Juliet was impressed with this new side of Max. 'You really are an excellent cook. I'm totally incompetent in the kitchen. Which is why I cheated and ordered in when Syd and Mike came round.'

'It's just practice. I had to learn to cook for August's sake. He needed good food when he was ill.'

'Lucky for him it wasn't me who was left to look after him. He'd have had cold beans straight from the can.'

Max laughed. 'He wouldn't have let you get away with that. He could be quite forceful when he wanted to be. But you should make more effort with your food. I mean, you are a doctor. I should add a clause to your contract banning canned food from this apartment. I just can't encourage that sort of behaviour,' he said. 'I couldn't live with myself if I did.'

Juliet looked at him. His face was animated and relaxed, and she was struck again by how good-looking he was. She felt a little flutter of excitement, as Sydney's advice rang in her ears. Maybe a fling with Max was exactly what she needed. If only he didn't live in the same block as her.

'Now pay attention. I feel it's my duty to teach you how to cook.' He took her through the preparation of the meal step by step. Instructed her on how vital it was to pre-heat the oven and regularly baste the meat. He showed her how to mix a salad dressing he had concocted himself.

'Pine nuts are the secret of a good salad,' he said.

'Sounds like something squirrels eat.'

'You heat them very gently over a flame in an iron pan. They cook in their own oils.'

She sipped the wine and its complexity on her tongue told her it was a prized vintage. Most men would have flourished the dusty bottle, made a show of uncorking it after making sure she saw the label. Max was not most men. That much was for sure.

'You like old things,' she said again.

He paused before replying. 'I'm not really one of the text-message-Twitter crowd. I'm not tempted to set up a Facebook page. I can see the usefulness of the Internet but am immune to whatever charms it's supposed to possess. Cyberspace is an ugly word, isn't it? Technology seems to be about telling everybody about your deep, dark secrets. And I believe secrets should be secrets.'

Juliet smiled playfully, her elbows on the table

between them, her chin resting on the knuckles of her linked fingers. 'So, what's your secret?' she asked.

Max did not reply. He just looked at her.

'Why aren't you married?'

'I never found anybody who . . .' he paused.

'Who what?'

'Got me, I guess. Understood me, or that I got. I just never found anybody right, I suppose. Compatibility can be a magical thing when you find it. It can seem a very elusive quality when you can't.'

Their gaze was shared, open. Juliet did not say anything. She thought that silence, at that moment, was the key to coaxing more out of this enigmatic man.

It worked. Max continued. 'And . . . I'm not very sociable. I guess because of the way I grew up, my whole life has been taking care of my family's building. I've already told you that I've never had a job. It's also true to say that I've never had a relationship that mattered.'

He expelled a sigh. Juliet sensed that what he had just said was a significant admission to himself, as well as for her.

'Going to that art opening the other night was a really big deal for me.'

Thinking of the failed kiss, colouring slightly, Juliet said, 'I'm sorry about that night.'

'No, no. Don't be. I was just surprised, that you—'

'That I what?'

'Wanted to kiss me.'

'Why wouldn't I?'

This time it was Max who blushed.

Juliet felt a stirring of sexual excitement, a thrill at the possibilities to come, at the potential the evening held for intimate acts with this likeable man. But events had their own momentum; passion its own choreography. What would happen would happen. Trying to rush it would just make things awkward. In the candlelight, the attraction of his green eyes was so absorbing that she had to drag her own gaze away from them.

She glanced around her apartment. It was inviting, gorgeous; it was hers. Something struck her, a feeling more profound than mere gratitude. She let out an audible sigh of contentment.

'What?'

'It feels like what I used to look at, always from the outside. Other people's houses. Warm, safe, home. And you did it for me.' There were tears in her eyes. She breathed out a slightly ragged breath. Emotion was costing her composure, but she didn't much care. Composure was for the Emergency Room, for colleagues and the patients in her care. Max was a friend and very soon might become her lover. It could happen at any moment.

'You've made me secure,' she said. 'I'm happy here.'

'Good,' he said.

He did not add to that, he didn't need to. She could hear the satisfaction, almost the relief in his voice, at what he had done for her. It mattered to him. She sensed with certainty that his emotions ran far deeper than his willingness to express them.

The moment came when all the food was eaten, the decanter drained, the coffee drunk. The candles were guttering as Max finally rose to go. Juliet opened the door for him and they paused and lingered in a moment of shared sexual tension.

'Landlord,' Juliet said.

'Tenant.'

'Messy . . .'

She closed the door on him. She stood for a moment leaning her weight against it. She turned and looked through the peephole but there was nobody there. She bit down on her lip and then opened the door and looked down the hall at her retreating guest. He had heard the door open and now he turned and paused, a questioning look on his face. Quietly, Juliet said, 'Come back in.'

He was still for a beat of time. The physical pause was so long that she didn't think he was going to do it. And then he walked back along the hallway, through the door, into her arms and her devouring kiss.

Eventually the kiss broke. They stared at one another, their eyes burning with desire. She began to unbutton her blouse. She had dexterous surgeon's hands, but her fingers felt clumsy in the passion and nervousness of the moment.

Max strode across the room and he lowered the blind. Juliet slipped her blouse from her shoulders letting it fall, then unhooked her bra and shrugged out of it. She stood semi-naked in the candlelight, her breathing heavy, almost coarse, her skin tingling, exposed.

Max had been rooted to the spot by the window for a moment, before he walked over to her, unable to keep his hands from reaching out and touching her. He examined her with his fingertips and his eyes, seeking and discovering her with a rapt look of wonder on his features. 'You're so beautiful,' he said.

She took off his shirt, running her hand up his arms, along a latticework of tiny scars etched on to his forearms. His expression changed when she did this and she could not tell whether her doing it pleased or angered him. The latter she thought; it was turning him on, as he pushed her down and continued to stroke her. She could feel his heat and the tensile strength of him and hear his breathing grow more rapid and shallow.

She started to feel uncomfortable. There was something frenzied about the way Max was touching her. His absorption was too intense to allow her to relax with him.

'Max.'

But he did not respond.

'I can't do this,' Juliet said.

The expression on his face did not alter. Max did not appear to understand what she was saying. It was as though she had not said anything at all and her body stiffened with alarm.

'I can't do this,' she said again. 'I can't get him out of my mind.'

Max stopped touching her. She was aware of his harsh breathing, his heat and intimate proximity. His voice, when it came, was guttural. 'What are you talking about?'

'Jack.'

Max got to his knees. He got to his feet. 'I was going too fast,' he said.

'I still only know his smell,' Juliet said. 'The way he touches me.' *His sound and rhythm*, she thought, *his tender, intuitive confidence. His gentle strength.* In the presence of this stranger, she missed the intimate attentions of the man she loved. 'I don't want it to be this way,' she said.

Max swallowed hard, bringing himself under control. 'I understand.'

'You get it, right?' Relief made her voice eager. She did not want to hurt someone who had been so kind to her, someone whose vulnerability she had sensed was really quite raw.

'I'll call you tomorrow,' Max said. Calmly he walked out of the front door and closed it quietly but firmly behind him. She gathered her clothes and put them back on.

Juliet sat on the floor, hugging her knees up against her chest, shaken and suddenly insecure. The home that had felt so comforting earlier suddenly felt like a stranger's domain, an alien place crammed with odd trinkets and props and mysterious keepsakes, and items of furniture from a history more frightening and more unsettling than she could ever imagine.

Eighteen

Max believed that perspective was a very important influence in determining events and their outcome. He had studied people. He had watched them intently and learned from his observations. He knew their weaknesses and fallibilities, their appetites, their vanity and their greed. He knew that people were often governed by fear. He considered himself something of an authority on the subject of fear.

By and large, people believed what they wanted to believe. But if you could dictate their perspective, you could make them believe what you wanted them to. It was quite an easy trick to pull off. And anyway, he had practised it to the point where it was second nature to him.

He had taken great pains to eliminate chance from his life. He was risk-averse, cautious, the opposite in temperament of a gambler. He did not enjoy spontaneity or feel comfortable with the notion of surprise. He had been surprised in his childhood by an event so awful it had made him dread anything he could not predict or manipulate. He was deliberate and methodical. It was important to him to be in control. His intelligence and his meticulous preparation generally overcame any variables and put him several steps ahead of what was happening at any given moment.

It was chance he had to thank, though, for his first encounter with the woman who would later become his tenant. Had his grandfather not taken ill at that particular moment, had he not been obliged to take him to the hospital on that specific night, he might never have laid eyes on Juliet Devereau.

He had caught her at the time of her greatest vulnerability, when desperation drowned out any suspicion she might otherwise have had. He was therefore doubly grateful to chance. And his gratitude was deep and sincere because that brief and wordless study of Juliet had been more than just the snapshot of a glamorous professional absorbed by her work; it had been love at first sight.

He had never felt the emotion before. But he knew it was not simple lust he felt. He had never felt the need for love, never, to his knowledge, suffered from its absence in his life. For Max, romantic love was more than slightly hazardous. Love of this sort was often prefaced by such adjectives as 'hopeless', 'endless' and 'bottomless'. It was an impossible emotion to control.

But if you could manipulate a person, cleverly and completely and without them knowing you were doing it, you could make them reciprocate the feelings you had for them. And then love wasn't hazardous at all. You were not its victim; you were its beneficiary.

The night that he first laid eyes on Juliet a door separated the two of them. He was in the waiting room, patiently waiting for word on his grandfather's condition from the physician who had wheeled him away to examine him. He had been there almost an hour. Waiting was what you did in waiting rooms.

She was in a room beyond it and all, to his untrained eye, was chaos in there. The door kept opening and closing on medics rushing in and out, their scrubs heavily smeared with the deep crimson of arterial blood. There was the glimpse of the patient, a boy chained to a bed, bleeding profusely from what Max gathered were gun shot wounds. There was the boy's mother, hysterically weeping for her son, restrained by a capable nurse.

Juliet was calm and lovely and Max did not yet know her name. He saw her look down at the wounded boy with an expression of compassion on her beautiful face. He distinctly heard her say, 'I'm going to take care of you.'

Not 'we', the hedged bet of collective responsibility, but 'I'. This woman was going to take it upon herself to save the patient's life. Her skill would determine the outcome and if he died, she and she alone, would shoulder the responsibility and face the recrimination of his grief-stricken relatives. She was slightly built for so heavy a burden, but strong-willed, Max could tell. He was impressed. More than that, he was beguiled.

She introduced herself to the hysterical mother who was praying in Spanish, a language Max recognised, but didn't understand. 'I am Dr Devereau,' she explained. Her calm, her tranquillity, seemed contagious. She took the woman by the arm and said, 'We need to operate immediately. I need you to hold back so that I can do my best with him. You must try to remain in control of yourself for as long as there is hope.'

The woman nodded. She was open mouthed, staring at the splashes of her son's blood on Dr Devereau's white coat.

To the nurse, the doctor said, 'Let's go.' The medical team, grim-faced, Dr Devereau unquestionably at the head of them, wheeled the boy swiftly out towards the Operating Room. There were bottles of plasma and blood attached to brackets above the gurney he was on, and an oxygen mask over his face. He was unconscious and his complexion had a bluish tinge. To Max his prospects did not look good. The patient was evidently far closer to death than he was to life.

Max was left alone. There were other people waiting there, but they did not count. After the dramatics of what he had just witnessed, after an encounter with Dr Devereau to which she had been oblivious, he felt flat and empty. He was indifferent to the fate of the wounded boy. He had enjoyed the drama though, and relished the performance of its star.

Max endured a vigil that lasted most of the night. He had brought his grandfather to the hospital unconscious. He knew they would not bring him around abruptly. If they did so, the shock might stop his heart. They would wait until he revived to assess his condition. Communication was a part of the procedure. He had learned that through previous visits. They would ask his grandfather questions. Max wondered would August be capable of coherent speech after this latest episode. The decline in him was rapid and seemingly relentless.

A few minutes before dawn, he looked up to see August being brought towards him in a wheel chair. The old man looked pale and very elderly and frail and there was sweat beading his forehead. He seemed alert, but also pained. Max took a handkerchief from his pocket and gently dabbed at his grandfather's brow.

The doctor pulled Max to one side, out of his grandfather's hearing.

'It's another stroke, isn't it?' Max asked.

'No. It was a panic attack. He lost consciousness because he fainted.'

'But he thought he was dying.'

'Yes,' the doctor said, 'but he also thought he was going crazy.'

'I don't understand,' Max said.

'These are normal signs of panic disorder. I've called in a script for Klonopin. He should probably see a psychiatrist. Does he get much mental stimulation? Does he interact with people his own age?'

'He values his privacy. He interacts with me.'

The doctor looked unhappy with this reply. 'I know it can be difficult, dealing with a semi-invalid.'

'Do you? Have you done it? Do you do it every day?'

'There are agencies. There is a support network. Without stimuli, people suffer mental atrophy. I can give you some contact numbers.'

Max was suddenly distracted. Through the swing doors towards the OR, Dr Devereau had reappeared. She was in her swabs, a surgical mask loose around her neck, just out of surgery and talking to the shot boy's mother. The doctor looked tired and drained and gorgeous. She was a creature with the power to restore life to someone from whom, but for her skills, it would certainly have slipped away.

He could not hear the conversation, but Max watched attentively until he saw the mother raise her hands to her face and begin to cry and he knew the tears were her expression of joy and relief. He could not help but smile in admiration at what the beautiful doctor had accomplished.

He heard the doctor attending his grandfather say something to him. He repeated it, 'Are you OK?'

Max snapped out of his reverie. 'Yes, thank you. I'm absolutely fine.'

'Should I get you those contact numbers?'

'Don't bother. When he is well, my grandfather has all the stimulation he can handle. But he is not what you would call a garrulous individual. He has no gift for friendship. He prefers his own company. I'm grateful for your efforts and I am sure the medication will help, but your advice is misguided.'

Max turned and wheeled August away and out the door. In the corridor beyond, he saw a bulletin board full of notes and ads. The name Devereau was printed prominently among the cards and papers pinned there and of course, it caught his eye. It was not all that common a name after all. If it was her, she was seeking an apartment and if the size of the hand-printed letters on the card was an indication, she was doing so quite desperately. At the bottom of the ad there were several hanging tabs with her surname and the same phone number written on each.

What happened next happened in slow motion for Max. He made a decision that would take him into territory he had never attempted to explore before in his life. He would plan every step of his expedition with meticulous care. He was a meticulous man; attention to detail was one of his distinguishing characteristics.

With calm and excitement competing in him for ascendancy, he unpinned one of several identical cards advertising a cab company from the board, took a biro from his shirt pocket, flipped the card over and, in neat and precise capitals, wrote, 'APARTMENT FOR RENT'.

Nineteen

The first part of Max's plan worked perfectly. There was a moment, just after she had moved in, when he thought that his grandfather might expose him and ruin everything, but in the end the moment had worked, to his advantage.

It had been the afternoon after the one on which she questioned him about the gift basket left outside her door. August had been ill and shaky and the shakiness had made him truculent and difficult, and there had been the possibility that he might have become, in his truculence, disastrously indiscreet.

Max prepared a syringe of medication for him. Sweating, jittery and angry, August waited for the needle to be plunged into his arm. He said, 'Is this how you get your women now? What is wrong with you?'

Max just looked at his grandfather. He hoped the look was vulnerable. Vulnerable, at that moment, was exactly how he felt. So much depended upon the old man's cooperation. He had already invested a great deal emotionally in successfully luring Juliet to live there. He did not want anything to arouse her suspicions. He wanted her to remain in blissful ignorance.

She had to think that it was her idea. The possibility

of romance had to occur to her without his obvious influence. His was a passive role in the proceedings. He knew that she had been too badly hurt to welcome a sexually aggressive approach. She was ripe for the method of seduction that perfectly suited his character and inclinations.

'I know what goes on in this building,' August said. 'Just like I know what goes on in your head. You think I don't understand how your brain works? You're just like your father.'

On the August scale of insults, and Max was wearily familiar with the entire list, this was a severe one. August had despised his son-in-law.

'I'm your daughter's son,' Max said. 'Your blood runs through my veins.'

'More the pity,' August said.

Max dug his nails into the flesh of his arm. Crescents of blood oozed where the skin broke with the savagery of his grip on himself. It was an unconscious gesture, a nervous reflex. He was oblivious to the pain it caused, but the habit had scarred his forearms with tiny curves of pale skin raised in hardened bumps.

August said, 'Why don't you stand up for yourself, present yourself to people like a normal human being?'

Max didn't respond. He could not even begin to know the answer to the question, which he thought unfair and pointless. Things were what they were. He had been shaped by circumstance. He was, for better or for worse, what his world had made him.

'You're jealous and perverted like your father,' August muttered.

Something snapped in Max. 'That's enough!' he said. 'I take care of you. You depend upon me. I do not ask for gratitude. I do what I do for you out of loyalty. I don't deserve your abuse.'

'My contempt is what you have,' August said. 'And you have earned all of the contempt I possess.'

Max did not reply. He had gathered control of himself again. His grandfather's slights could do him no real harm, so long as they were confined to this private dialogue.

'She was beautiful,' August said. 'Your mother was gentle and generous. She was my only daughter and she married a weak man. She married a weak man and then she compounded her sin when she gave birth to another.' He clenched a shaking fist and hit Max with it feebly against the chest.

It was almost touching, the way in which the old man persisted with violence when his blows no longer carried weight. The pain he had inflicted when Max had been very young had been savage and severe. He could no longer do it, yet he still tried. It spoke for his strong will and enduring instinct for cruelty. You had to admire a trait so stubborn, Max thought, smiling to himself.

A knock sounded sudden and loud against the door. Both men glanced towards the sound. Then Max grabbed the hand that had hit him and pierced it with the syringe point deep between two of the knuckles, in the soft flesh there. He depressed the plunger.

August gasped.

Max whispered, 'Do exactly as I have asked you to.

Say you gave her the gift basket. It will help her get accustomed to the new apartment, to the neighbourhood. It will make her feel comfortable and at home. Do this, Grandfather. Do it for your grandson. Do it out of the love you know you have deep down for me. And do it for her.'

The drug was already working. August looked more relaxed, almost blissful. Gently, he grazed Max's face with the back of his hand.

'I'm all you've got.'

'God help me, you are.'

Another knock rapped loudly at the door.

Very quietly, August said, 'This building is mine. Everything inside of it is mine. *Everything*, Max. You understand that, don't you?'

Where his grandfather was concerned there was a time to stand up for yourself and a time to back down and Max knew the difference between those moments very well. He smiled sweetly and murmured, 'Yes, of course I do.'

Apparently satisfied by this admission, August opened the door to Juliet as Max shrank back into the shadows of the cluttered room. He stood very still and listened.

August said, 'There you are.'

Juliet said, 'It's overwhelmingly thoughtful, the gift . . .'

Max crept further back, confident that his grandfather was simply smoothing out things with Juliet according to the agreed script. He did not think he would be heard or his presence in the room sensed and he knew that he would not be seen. He had a talent for concealment and observation and knew how to exploit them.

Max had ensured that he would be at the gallery opening that night simply by following Juliet. Showered and groomed, he changed into clothing that he calculated would give him the right quality of urbane acceptability and stylishness. He wanted to delight her with how aptly he could fit in to a situation where his very presence would surprise her.

He wanted the surprise to be a pleasant one, of course. So he spent some time studying the party, learning the lexicon and choreography of this glittering social ritual before committing himself to a confrontation with his prey.

He watched her talking to the friend he had learned was called Sydney. Sydney was a doctor too, and heavily pregnant, which made her conspicuous amongst the crowd the event had drawn. Max was somewhat mystified by the appeal of the event itself. Abstract and performance art left him cold. Most of the artefacts assembled there were crude and childish, but he wasn't that bothered. The crowd was a useful tool in enabling him to time his moment with Juliet perfectly.

Right next to him, a guy cuddled up with his girlfriend and said, 'Sometimes I think all I ever do is work. Twenty-four-seven. So, I decided. I wanted to stop, come out, feel Brooklyn. You know?'

To Max's ears and mind, the words sounded authentic, the sentiment spontaneous and true. It was something he could borrow and use. Juliet would be convinced. She might even be charmed.

She looked a bit lost to him. She toyed with some tit-bit on a cocktail stick and then dumped it uneaten in a trash can. Some guy approached her, feeding her an obvious line and she laughed it off and retreated away from him, shirking eye contact. She held out her hand when a waiter came by with a tray of champagne flutes, but she hesitated and withdrew the hand without taking one. It was clear she wasn't enjoying herself.

She still hadn't seen him. She did not become aware of him until the moment he approached out of her line of sight and then deliberately bumped into her in a manner contrived to seem wholly accidental.

'Watch it,' she said. Then she looked up at him. She seemed genuinely surprised and happy to see him. She asked him what he was doing there.

Smiling easily Max looked around and gestured expansively and said, 'Sometimes I feel like all I ever do is work. Twenty-four-seven. I decided I wanted to stop, come out, feel Brooklyn, you know . . .'

She did know. He could tell by the look on her face. It was what people called empathetic. It was not pitying or guarded; she understood him. They were the same; he was normal. He felt that this was going very well.

It continued to go well on the walk home. Max found that he could speak to Juliet very naturally if he just followed her conversational leads. So long as he paid attention to what she said and particularly to her tone of voice, he could reply in kind. The tone of voice was important because some of what she said was meant ironically. This was particularly true when she talked about her job and domestic situation. The tone told you that she was making fun of herself and the way to react was with a knowing smile and a nod, rather than to take her words at face value. He quickly discovered that with Juliet you could comment by not commenting at all, which suited him.

Things continued to go better than Max could have hoped right up to the moment of their failed kiss outside her apartment door. He recoiled when she tried to kiss him on the mouth.

It was not that he did not want to kiss her. Quite the opposite. But he had never kissed or been touched by a woman in his life and he had succumbed to nerves when the moment arrived. He had not expected it, had not had time to prepare for it. The spontaneity of the moment took him completely by surprise.

She said, 'I'm sorry. God, I'm an idiot.'

He said, 'No. Don't be sorry.'

'Of course,' she said, 'it's a bad idea.'

'I didn't mean it that way,' Max said. He felt that he was digging a hole for himself with his words and that everything he uttered made it deeper. The confidence he had felt walking her back from the exhibition opening had disappeared into the hole.

'I'm confused,' Juliet said, 'out of practice. I'm reading the wrong signals.' She laughed, opened her door and vanished inside her apartment.

Twenty

He had blown it. Max stood in the gloom of the hallway outside her apartment door and closed his eyes in anger and frustration. His nails dug through his jacket sleeves into the flesh of his forearms in savage self-reproach. He could play at being normal but he had felt a million miles from normal in his crass failure to cope with a kiss. He wanted that kiss so badly. He craved her affection, her body, her tender soul. He had to have all of her, but to get her, he would have to do better than this.

He opened the door to his own apartment and then entered the passages. He wanted to have her, but in the meantime, in the passages, he could observe her. He had designed them himself, a secret catacomb empire running between the spaces in which people lived their lives and the supporting walls of the building. He had constructed and concealed them, with their myriad hidden entrances and discreet galleries of strategically placed and disguised peepholes with painstaking care.

Here he could observe Juliet. He could scrutinise her as she went about her private life with complete unself-consciousness. He would study her and enjoy the sensation of simply watching.

Soon there would be better and more satisfying things between him and Juliet Devereau, but for now he wanted to watch. It was what he'd always done, crouched in the dark passageways to observe people's most intimate rituals. It was how he'd grown up.

Some of the passages were no more than crawlspaces. But that was a technical detail. It was a secret window on a forbidden world; it was his refuge and his domain and the precious secret he kept to himself. It was also the key, Max thought, to his power over other people. It gave him an edge of which the people he chose to watch were completely unaware.

Max knew every stray cable, every cord and section of electrical wiring, every inch of plaster and lattice and the nature and destination of every pipe that thrummed as he scurried, sure-footed, to where he wanted to go. He could navigate his way by feel and by the sound of the domestic lives being enacted beyond the walls behind which he silently encroached.

It would be fair to say he had enjoyed his happiest and most complete moments watching from behind the apparent blindness of the walls between which he roamed.

Now, as he headed in the direction of Juliet's apartment, August's earlier admonishment was still ringing like a dull ache in his skull. He was not strange or a coward or in any way perverse. He was what his unfortunate childhood had made him. He was incomplete, but he was certain he'd found the person who could change all that. With Juliet beside him, he could emerge finally out of this strange solitary world.

He reached the place he was looking for. He groped in the narrow confinement of the passage, pulling out a wooden chair he placed carefully on the floor and sat on. He was facing a pillowed section of wall insulation. He reached out and removed a plug of it, revealing a large peephole that looked on to Juliet's living room. He peered through it, carefully, watchfully, his breathing shallow and a thrill coursing through him that he could barely suppress.

There was no movement, no occupant. The lights were on, but there was no one there. He stood and moved along the passage and pulled the stuffing from another peephole. This one gave him a view of the kitchen. And this time there was something for him to see as Juliet passed by the kitchen door, turning out the light as she went. He looked back and saw that the living-room light had also gone out.

Further up the passage, a warm glow of illumination suffused a small area against the wall. It was the bathroom peephole and Max assumed the glow was provided by candlelight; it had that waxy suggestion of yellow heat. He approached it feeling breathless by what he was likely to see, water churning through the thrumming pipes filling the tub with her chosen balance of hot and cold.

Max imagined that she would take her bath as hot as her skin could endure it. She ran very hard when she ran and the way to ease the aching muscles in those long and luscious calves and thighs of hers was to immerse herself in heat. Sweat would break out in tiny droplets on her unblemished skin. He stood still in the silent dark, his body taut with expectation, his breathing fast, hissing through his nose in rapid puffs. In just a moment, he would see it.

The view he had of her bathroom from the passage was from behind the two-way mirror on her bathroom wall. To Max, it was like a cinema screen. Except that this showing was exclusive, private and the movie enacted for his entertainment and gratification alone. No one but him would ever enjoy this particular show. Juliet was the star. Her performance would be unselfconscious, because she would never know she was giving it. On balance, Max thought the scenario just about perfect.

A film of condensation covered the mirror. He was right; the water in the tub would be very hot. He put his fingers silently against the cool glass and stroked its smooth surface contemplatively. He moved his face closer to it, inches from it, as though doing so could broach the opaque secrecy of the steam on the other side.

Suddenly the view was swept clear. Juliet was standing there, in front of him, inches from him, still clothed, oblivious to his presence, carrying a glass of wine that she put down carefully on the edge of the tub.

She walked out of the bathroom. Streaks of water slid down the mirror. They left small vertical trails on the glass. His breathing got faster. He could barely control it. It would not be audible to her, but he could hear his own heart hammering in his chest and he felt light-headed with excitement.

She came back into the bathroom naked and slid into the tub, the water lapping deliciously around her, sighing with heat and relaxation and unseen by him now, cloaked by night and shadow.

The frustration of that moment nearly made him groan out loud. He couldn't stand it. He wanted to share the moment. He wanted to be with this naked woman, to share the intimacy of her company. She would not see or even sense him. He could steal into her presence without her ever knowing.

Max moved swiftly through the passages until he came to a small door disguised in the panelling of an old, unused wine closet in Juliet's kitchen. He sighed in satisfaction. Just being close to her, hearing her movements, letting the scent of her waft over him made his body hum with arousal. Silently he stole down the corridor. He was in her bedroom when he heard her wine glass smash. He was shocked. He hadn't made any noise at all, but something had spooked her. She must have sensed she was not alone and had got out of the bathtub; he could hear water dripping from her naked body as it splashed softly onto the wooden floor.

He was behind her bedroom door when she entered, went to the window and flung wide the curtains, exposing the room to the night light outside. He was frozen, immobile and silent.

She said out loud, 'Jesus Christ, Juliet. Calm the fuck down.'

She walked out, back to the bathroom to deal with the mess of spilled wine and broken glass he supposed; back to dry her dripping body and her wet hair. It was his moment to slip away, enough time to retreat unseen to the kitchen and his secret exit.

But he didn't take it. He felt unsatisfied. There was more that could be enjoyed without compromising himself and being discovered. Although he was risk averse by nature, he was too excited to retreat, so instead he came from behind the door, and swiftly moved towards Juliet's bed, and slid silently under it.

She was still dripping from the bath when she came back in. Her feet and lower legs came into view. He lay still, feeling the weight of her settle above him on her mattress, seeing a single drop of water explode in front of his face as it dripped from a frond of her hair, hearing her exhale as she relaxed and prepared to let sleep claim her.

Under the bed, Max aligned himself with Juliet's recumbent body and waited until her breathing became deep and regular. Then he reached up with his hand, feeling the solid weight of her against his fingertips. Her mattress moved slightly as she breathed, the springs sighing subtly with each expansion and contraction of her chest. Pulsating with excitement he forced himself to lie still, breathing with her, until he was certain she was asleep. And then his free hand reached for his erection, rubbing in time with her breathing, biting his lip to stop himself groaning aloud, until his pace increased and became frantic as he sought relief from his almost painful arousal.

Eventually, Max slithered out from under Juliet's bed. He could smell the scented soap on her skin, the apple blossom fragrance of the shampoo she had used on her hair. Under those distractions her own odour lay; warm and subtle and deliciously feminine. He looked at her from above where she slept and he breathed in the breath she exhaled, studying her face for a long moment before departing her room. She did not waken.

He could smell too his semen, puddled in a damp patch, drying on the belly of his T-shirt, the taint of it, a stinking reminder of what he had done. It followed him like a sour reproach when he entered the passages through the secret doorway beyond her kitchen wine store and made his way back through the labyrinth to his own apartment.

There, he passed through a door fitted to the back of his closet. He emerged with practised nimbleness; no one to see his re-entry into the world of normality. He stripped and threw his dirty clothing into his laundry bin. He showered, scrubbing hard with a bristle brush, feeling soiled within, stained indelibly by what he had done, the temptations he had surrendered to.

He made himself a cup of coffee. She drank wine, but Max thought intoxication might unleash urges worse than the ones that drove and alarmed him in equal part even when sober. He should sleep, but his emotions were in turmoil; an image of Juliet, water dripping down her naked breasts, tormented him. August was right, he was an abomination, what he had done could never be construed as conventional behaviour. Nothing, not even the fact that she had led him on, teased him with her nakedness, could justify or excuse his later actions. But, surely, as long as Juliet never discovered it, he could carry on as normal, and he would never take such a risk, or treat her with such disrespect again. She deserved more from him.

He stood up decisively. It was time to take action, to make sure that he stopped himself behaving like that again. He fetched his toolbox from the utility room, went to his closet and nailed shut the secret door that gave on to his warren-world of hidden voyeuristic opportunity.

When this was done, he lay on his bed – single, in narrow contrast to hers – and looked at the shadows on the ceiling turned to capering demons by the shifting light of the night city through the window. *They are my demons*, he thought, before sleep finally claimed him.

They were his demons and he had no control over them at all.

Twenty-one

Max really had seen his parents die. He had told Juliet the truth about that.

For his sixth birthday, Max's parents bought him a toy theatre. It was made of wood and colourfully painted, and the players on the stage were puppets manipulated from above. He loved staging their performances, creating little lives, personalities and dramas for them. His puppets had become his friends. But it had not been enough.

It did not compete with the fascination he had for the secret study of real people. You could not, of course, manipulate those that you observed. But you could predict their actions and when your prediction was proven to be correct, there was a thrill of accomplishment to be had. It wasn't so bad, when they surprised you. When they confounded your expectations, it taught you something more about them. And it helped to eliminate the possibility of their surprising you again.

It did not come as a surprise when his father shot his mother, but it was a shock. In his bedroom, he had heard the arguments between them at night, but had not known what was wrong between the two of them. He would not discover that until the eve of his thirteenth birthday when August, maudlin and drunk on whisky and grief for his murdered daughter, told him about his mother's infidelity.

There was a terse quality to the hushed dialogues he heard that told the young Max two things. The first was that their quarrels were too serious simply to allow them to shout at one another. The second was that they did not want their only child knowing what had driven the wedge between them.

He was in the pantry on the evening of their deaths. He was not hiding or deliberately observing them. He was actually stealing cookies when his mother came into the kitchen to season something she had slow-cooking on the stove and he saw her ivory blouse and black skirt through the slats in the pantry door. He heard her humming something, 'Lara's Theme', from the film *Doctor Zhivago*, one of her favourites.

He munched on a chocolate chip cookie, smiling at his mother, thrilled, if he was honest, to be observing her secretly, to have this view of her that she would remain for ever unaware of. He felt his unseen study of his mother gave him an importance greater than that ordinarily accorded a child.

At the age of six, Max would not have used those words to describe his feelings. He would not have possessed this vocabulary. But he remembered the occasion very accurately and the words reflected his six-year-old feelings with absolute truth.

His father came in and stood behind his mother and said something very quietly to her. She was bent down from the waist with the oven door open before her and her body stiffened when he said what he said but even with his alert ears, in the cool, slatted quiet of the pantry, even though he had stopped chewing and stood watching with the cookie a congealing mess in his mouth, Max could not make out his father's words.

Later in his life, Max saw old newsreels of Nazi death squads. The executions took place in a forest, not in a kitchen. But the mechanics of it, the basic choreography, was the same.

The victim would kneel before the executioner who would shoot them once in the back of the skull with a bullet from a 9mm pistol. Max did not know then the specifics of the gun his father took from out of his suit pocket. It would take August to inform him of that on that whisky- and grief-soaked night a few years into the future. But that, essentially, was what his father did. He took out the pistol and placed it against the back of his wife's skull and pressed the trigger and there was a sharp report, and a sharp odour filled the kitchen that Max later learned was called cordite.

That first bullet skimmed his mother's head.

In the Nazi newsreels, the victims always slumped, like puppets with their strings abruptly cut, to the forest floor. In their kitchen, his mother did not slump over the open oven. She stiffened and then rose and turned and faced his father.

'No,' she said. 'Daniel, for the love of God—'

And he shot her in the forehead, leaving a hole in her head that was the size of a quarter, bright crimson in colour, and there was the smell of more cordite and she did slump to the floor, the life leaving her in a surprised rush. And his father let out a scream higher and more startling in pitch than Max would have thought him capable, with his deep speaking voice.

Then his father opened his mouth wide, put the barrel of the pistol into his mouth, closed his eyes and pressed the trigger. There was another explosion of sound. The top of his head erupted, blood and bits of bone fragment spattered on the ceiling and Max's father fell to the floor beside his dead wife.

It was very still in the kitchen after that. Max swallowed the rest of his cookie. Neighbours were alerted by the noise. By the time they arrived, Max was out of the pantry and lying like spoons with his mother weeping. The tears were genuine. He mourned his mother bitterly for years.

He tried to re-enact the death. He did it with his puppet theatre. He painted the gory death wounds onto the puppets and created dialogue to add colour to the scene. Sometimes he would contrive a happier outcome, where his mother talked his father out of it. Sometimes his father did not kill his mother at all, just killing himself in front of her as she seasoned her stew at the stove.

On a couple of occasions, he had his mother wrestle or trick the gun from his father and turn it on him in self-defence. This scenario did not really work, though. His mother had been too gentle a woman to use physical force. His father had a weak character but it was from his father that Max had inherited his formidable physical strength.

The re-enactments stopped when August caught

him. His grandfather beat him with his belt so severely across the buttocks that Max was unable to sit comfortably afterwards for a full week. August burned the theatre and the puppets in an incinerator in the basement of the building. It was after that, when Max was eight, that the nature of his games became of necessity more secretive.

He had realised eventually that his grandfather would never love him. August looked at him and saw his father. He had been no way culpable in the death of either of his parents. He had nothing to do with his mother's infidelity or his father's disastrous reaction to it. But his grandfather looked for the traits in him that had led to his mother's dissatisfaction with his father. He searched for weakness. And because he wanted to so ardently, of course he found evidence to suggest that it existed, as if present in some crippled, mutant gene that disfigured his personality.

His parents had loved him, Max was certain of that. And he had loved them, although he had stopped loving his father when he saw him shoot his mother dead. And Max could not love August. He loved his mother's memory and that was all. He had had a brief, adolescent crush on the child of one of the apartment's tenant families. August put an end to that too, as painful as it was humiliating. And then Juliet had come into his life.

He had made up the story about the six-hour operation to try to save his shot mother's life because he wanted Juliet's sympathy. He thought he'd succeeded. But Juliet had dashed the hopes he had for them in the cruellest manner imaginable. He couldn't understand what had gone wrong. The dinner he had cooked had been a triumph, everything had been going exactly as he'd hoped, and then, after kissing him, taking off her clothes, leading him on, she'd rejected him. And it was not his fault. He had performed flawlessly; she had been the one to blame. She'd led him to believe she wanted him, and then she'd said no. Obviously the influence of her ex-husband was still poisoning her mind and there was nothing he could do about it.

Twenty-two

The morning after the disastrous dinner and its shameful aftermath, Max felt as if the whole terrible episode had happened years ago. In fact, he wondered whether it had happened at all. Maybe the next time they met, she'd look at him with the same friendliness and he'd wonder what he'd been worrying about.

Then he saw her. He was walking, a few hundred yards from their building, and he saw her race through the rain, huddled in her coat and head down, across the sidewalk and into the doorway of a deli. And the memory of her deliberately bared breasts and the warmth of her breath and the taste of her lips as she willingly kissed him came back so vividly, he could not hide the truth of it from himself any more.

Max wondered what to do. Whatever he said, it was going to be embarrassing for both of them. They would be obliged to revisit the awkwardness of the previous night and the prospect of further humiliation and rejection filled him with dread. But what could he do? He had to know one way or another what she thought. So he followed her into the deli.

She was paying for her sandwich when he went through the door. She turned to leave and saw him and she smiled and the smile was awkward, as he had known it would be.

'Hey,' she said.

'Hey,' he mirrored back. He moved to kiss her then, on the mouth, starting again where they had left off, except this time determined to get the choreography of romance absolutely right.

She averted her lips so that the kiss was delivered to her cheek. Did she wince slightly, when she turned her head? No, he decided, he had imagined it. But she had deliberately avoided his lips and he was stung by that.

He needed to deal with it. The only way to do that was head-on. There was too much at stake for prevarication. Max said, 'I wanted to talk to you.'

'Yeah,' she said, 'I'm sorry. I suddenly felt weird. It had nothing to do with you. I just need time.'

'It's OK,' Max said. 'That just tells me you take being with someone seriously. I like that.'

She didn't say anything. The way she didn't comment on what he had just said inflicted a slight feeling of panic on him. He thought that he might be able to provoke her into responding how he wanted her to with a bluff. She'd made the first move after all. She had taken off her shirt last night willingly. He had seen the desire burning in her eyes by candlelight. He had seen the dark, delicious contrast of her nipples against her pale skin. He had not been imagining that. She liked and desired him, didn't she? She had to. 'But . . . I was thinking about it,' he said, 'and maybe we shouldn't have done that, living in the same building.'

'Really?'

'There's a saying, isn't there, about mixing business and pleasure? We're not exactly in business together, but you know what I mean. We have a tenant–landlord relationship.'

'We do,' Juliet said, nodding. 'We certainly have that.'

'I suppose there's two ways of looking at it,' he said. 'You can be sensible and cautious and correct. Or you can just act on instinct, doing what your feelings tell you to do, guided by your emotions in the moment.'

'I'm not quite clear on what you're driving at, Max; at where you're coming from here.'

'I honestly didn't mean for anything to happen,' he said. 'I'm just so used to having August around. I just wanted company. I wouldn't want it weird between us.'

Her posture changed as she relaxed and a slight frown lifted from her brow. She said, 'I'm so glad you feel the same way.'

He could hear the relief in her voice as she clearly thought they both felt the same way: that it had been a mistake, a miscalculation they had been able to escape without either of them incurring damage or indignity.

It was a disaster. Max could feel the fury and frustration building in him: she'd kissed him first. How could she dismiss him from her life as if he was just some stranger? It wasn't fair. It wasn't how it was meant to be. But he couldn't show any of this to her; all he could do was stand there with a stupid smile glued to his features, being who she wanted him to be, just a sweet and stolid acquaintance; someone to call upon if a fuse needed fixing or if her central heating failed. He had been bumped in a sickening moment from romantic lead to also-ran, and he had done absolutely nothing to deserve it.

'It's meant a lot to me,' Juliet was saying.

And Max knew that she meant the snug comfort blanket of his unthreatening, asexual presence; the shelter he had provided and his vigilance in keeping his new tenant comfortable and secure. Twelve hours earlier, she had been on the verge of making love to him, abandoning herself to their shared passion. Now he was little more than a fondly thought of employee. His status was nearer the hired help than the man who shared her body and bed.

He nodded, numbly. Around him, the deli bustled with conversation, wisecracks, complaints about the weather, shouted orders for food, off-menu requests, speculation about the ball game and the next big title fight. He ignored it. It was life, of a sort, but held no appeal for him and he had always ignored it. But he had never in his life felt quite so numb, quite so isolated from things. *It feels like a sort of exile,* he thought, as Juliet treated him to a cute wave and walked out of the deli, having dismissed him entirely as a significant part of the new life she was embarking upon.

He left the deli without even completing the pretence of ordering anything to eat or drink. What was the point? She had gone. In her absence he no longer needed a pretext for being there. One of the staff shouted something at his retreating back but Max ignored him.

He climbed the stairs to his apartment; nine floors, eighteen flights. He was fit and strong and reached his destination barely breathing more heavily than he had at the outset, at the bottom of the first set of steps, but he barely noticed. His mind was otherwise engaged.

He had tried and failed to orchestrate matters the conventional way. Somewhere he had missed a step in the tricky choreography of the dating ritual or stumbled over a line of dialogue. The mimicry only took him so far. After a while he was dependent upon his own instincts and personality and he had neither the experience nor the confidence to carry things off successfully.

There was only one avenue left to him. He would have to revert. He stood in his apartment with the closet doors flung wide and looked at the hidden aperture he had so recently nailed shut, believing it to be for the very last time. He'd meant it the night before when he'd decided to try to do the right thing. But it wasn't as simple as he'd thought. The passages gave him power and it was clear that he would have to use that power if he was going to get what he wanted. Because without Juliet, there was no longer any point to his life.

He would have to extract the nails. Resolutions were all very well but he needed to study his subject further. He needed to learn everything he could about her if he was to overcome the setback he had endured that morning.

Faint heart never won a fair maiden, the saying ran. He had heard his grandfather say it. And he was the possessor of a strong heart. He would not give up. He would restrain himself and restrict himself to what was respectable in his behaviour once beyond this wall. He would act with dignity and good taste. But he would have to go back to his hidden domain or he would never learn how to go forward in his life.

Twenty-three

Max did not remember the very first occasion on which he had ventured into the passages. He knew that he must have been very young. He thought he had probably been about four or five years old when his fascination with other people first began to intrude upon and then influence his own behaviour.

The O'Donnells had lived in Juliet's apartment back then. Phil O'Donnell was a high-ranking member of the New York Fire Department, having climbed the promotion ladder to a level where he only wore a uniform for ceremonial gatherings. His wife, Patricia, was a part-time teacher of music and drama, and it was the music that first drew Max into the passages. It was the repeated playing of scales and the plangent chords of classical exercises that first attracted him to the honeycomb of secret spaces that haphazard building and conversion work had endowed the building with.

The O'Donnells had a daughter called Kate. He remembered that she was very beautiful. In fact, she had looked almost uncannily like Juliet Devereau.

She had not looked like that when he had first seen her; when he had been five and she about eleven and he was restricted to glimpses in the elevator, or on the sidewalk outside the building. She had looked like that when she reached the age of about fourteen and achieved what Max now knew was termed puberty. He had not known that word then. He had sensed the change, though. Even as an eight-year-old, he had been aware of Kate O'Donnell's budding sexuality; the way in which she was ripely blossoming into womanhood.

He had bored his first peepholes by then. They gave him intimate views of every room in what was now Juliet Devereau's apartment. He could watch the O'Donnells go about their family business for hours, fascinated, his attention span belying his years as he watched Phil O'Donnell carelessly caress his wife's breasts through her blouse after returning from work, removing his suit coat and tie and pouring himself an inch of whisky.

Everything about the way that people behaved together surprised little Max. He could not predict what people were going to do, how they would act or react to what other people close to them did.

The notion of closeness was strange. There was physical closeness, of course. That was just proximity, the way a family chose to confine themselves, living together in a single space, apparently preferring one another's company to solitude.

Max didn't understand this. He liked solitude; he revelled in it. He knew that his fascination for others would be considered odd and his spying upon them met with disapproval. This made him careful of being caught, almost preternaturally alert. And of course, it isolated him. He could not share his secret and his secret made him unique.

The other closeness slightly baffled him. This was the closeness that encouraged Kate to sit on her father's lap when she was close to being a full-grown woman. He would hug her and stroke her head and croon to her in a sweet tenor voice.

'Tell me about the difference between a man and a woman, Daddy.'

'I'd say it's fairly plain.'

'I mean the real difference. What's the reason the men on the construction sites whistle at us when Ma and me walk by?'

'It's because they know no better.'

'We don't whistle back.'

'Do you want to?'

'Of course not.'

'I'm glad to hear it, Katy my love.'

And later, after Kate had long gone to bed, her parents would lie in theirs and Max would watch through the wall, listening.

'Have you seen the way she's developing, Phil?'

'I'm not blind.'

'She will need to be told about intercourse. She will need to be told about male urges and the mechanics of it.'

'I'd rather you told her about the mechanics of it.'

'Shy about the theory, Phil? I've never known you shirk the practical side of things.'

Laughter then, shared and deliberately muffled, which Max did not really understand the reason for and hoped was a prelude to their coupling. He liked to watch that. He liked to hear Phil snort like a pig and his wife whimper like someone in pain. He liked the way Patricia O'Donnell's brassiere straps dug into the soft flesh on her pale shoulders.

But Kate was the star. Sometimes she would sit between her mother's knees as her mother sat and brushed her hair. They would murmur things Max could not catch and laugh together and it mystified him. Kate was old enough to brush her own hair. She was not a helpless baby.

Max liked mornings in the music room. That had been turned into a study by the time Juliet Devereau rented the apartment. But back then, in the O'Donnell era, it was a music room where Patricia O'Donnell taught her students.

Kate was a gifted musician, at least to Max's inexpert eyes and ears. She would come into the music room in the mornings before school, still in her nightgown with her hair blowsy and sleep smudging the corners of her eyes. And she would play songs for her secret audience of one, lurking silent and still, watching her from behind the interior wall.

She would play tunes by Elton John and Fleetwood Mac that Max would recognise on radios left on windowsills or fire escapes throughout the neighbourhood on summer nights.

She would sing with the gift of her father's perfect pitch and Max would listen, knowing in his heart that the performance was just for him and naturally thrilled at the fact, as any eight-year-old boy thus privileged would be. Best of all, though, he had liked her bath times, until that pleasure had been ruined by August.

Max could not forget his grandfather's brutal grip on his neck, or the stink of shit that had followed them as August had hauled him through the passages, trailing dust and humiliation, to a punishment that had left him bruised and aching for a week.

Now, he looked at the nailed panel that accessed his secret world. August had grown feeble in the thirty years since the event Max so vividly and shamefully recalled. And then he had died.

Max would require his claw hammer to grip the nail heads and pry them from the wood. He needed to reopen his access to Juliet's world so he could approach her afresh.

It was ironic, just how strongly she resembled the fourteen-year-old girl he had loved all those years ago. Maybe he was destined to have someone who looked exactly like that in his life. Working with his hammer, using the strength he had acquired since his far-off, puny childhood, he thought that was it; it was fate that had led him to Juliet. He did not really believe in coincidence.

It had not been a coincidence that they had encountered one another at the hospital. There had been nothing coincidental about the timing of the failure of her marriage and her need for an apartment. The fact that she looked the mirror-image of his first infatuation was either a doubly implausible lightning strike or it was destiny. Ripping out the last of the nails, re-opening the route to his future, Max was pretty confident it was the latter.

Twenty-four

Juliet was just finishing her shift when one of the nurses stuck her head round the door.

'Hey, Juliet, Holstrom wants to see you in his office before you go.'

Juliet glanced round in surprise. 'Really? Why?'

'I don't know, but it's not usually good news.' The nurse grinned. 'Just joking, I'm sure it's fine. No one's died on you recently, have they?'

'OK, thanks. I guess.'

Despite the reassurance, Juliet was nervous when she knocked on Holstrom's door. She wasn't due a promotion or a pay rise so this summons could only mean bad news. It confirmed, she thought with a sinking heart, her feeling that she was being watched, had undergone some sort of probationary spell to see if her disrupted home life was affecting the quality and consistency of her work.

But since she'd found the apartment and had Max as her custodian-cum-sentinel watching over and taking care of her, she was sure she'd been back to her best. Her decision making had been confident, her energy levels were restored, and her concentration was back on song. She missed Jack as she imagined an amputee might miss a severed limb, but she was over the shock of his departure from her life. Physically, she was finally getting some quality rest. She entered Holstrom's office tentatively.

'Sit down,' Holstrom said.

Holstrom had placed his visitor's chair to one side of his desk. He deliberately avoided the formality of a face-to-face with a desk between him and the person to whom he was speaking. She looked at the pictures on his desk that proudly showed off his family and felt a familiar stab of envy at the stability of Holstrom's contented home life.

He opened a desk drawer and took a letter from it and pushed it across the desk towards her. It had some kind of official stamp on the face of the envelope, which was slit open, so obviously the letter had already been read.

'I apologise for having opened what it transpired was personal mail intended for your eyes only,' Holstrom said. 'But I will say two things in mitigation. The first is that it was not addressed to you by name. The second is that I have a duty of care to all of my staff and you are no exception.'

Juliet opened the letter. It had been handwritten across two pages of flimsy paper. The writing was laboured, but it was clear that whoever had written it had put a lot of effort into the task. She smoothed and steadied the pages and read what they had to say.

Dear Pretty Doctor,
I suppose I should really thank you for saving my life. That's your job and all, and you must be awful

178

good at it because everyone on the ward tells me either of the bullets you took out of me could have done for me if it hadn't been for what you did back there on the operating table.

I'll take that as Gospel, doc, but forgive me if I don't fall down before you and weep like my mother tells me she did with gratitude. It's all a question of perspective, you see. There's yours, there's hers and there's mine. And then there's the law's perspective on a cop killer. For reasons you will no doubt understand, the view taken by the New York State Prosecutor on this particular matter is a very dim one.

There's no point denying I did what I did. I would if I could, but I can't. There were witnesses. The forensic evidence would have nailed me even if there weren't. It wasn't exactly self-defence and it wasn't exactly cold-blooded execution. It was somewhere between the two. But I loaded the gun, took it into the store, held the place up and shot back when those two cops gave chase and shot at me. And one of them is dead.

Would you have struggled so hard to save me if you'd known I just offed a cop? A guy with a wife and two young kids? A guy with ten years on the force and two bravery citations to his name? Maybe you would. I think in all fairness that you probably would have done your best because saving lives is your reason for doing what you do.

But I have to tell you that you should have

failed, lady. It would have been an outcome better for all concerned. Lockdown in solitary will be my sentence and it will end when I eventually die in a cell. I've got a girlfriend who has already consigned me to history and a kid with her I will likely never see again. I got a mother too old to travel the distance to where they will probably put me for prison visits.

If that doesn't sound like much of a future, that's because however you stack it, it doesn't add up as much of one. Even a moron could see that I would be better off dead.

It would have given the dead cop's widow some consolation as I'm sure you can appreciate. It would probably have helped his kids accept the loss of their father more easily when they get older and start to give what they've been deprived of some serious thought.

Everything's perspective, pretty doctor, like I said. Everyone's is different. It's your job to save lives and nobody, including me, could hold that against you. They tell me you performed a kind of miracle in saving me in surgery that night. Maybe you did. But the miracle wasn't welcome and it turns out, didn't do nobody any good.

Sincerely,
Carlos Leon

When Juliet had finished reading Holstrom said, 'Written from the hospital bed where he's recovering under armed guard.'

'I read his notes before I operated,' Juliet said. 'He's eighteen. He's a child. He can't buy a drink in a bar.'

'He can pull a trigger and because he chose to do so, a cop is dead.'

'I wouldn't have done anything differently.'

'I would sincerely hope not.'

'He has a point about perspective.'

'He does,' Holstrom said. 'He seems to have an instinct for philosophy. It's unschooled, but he will have plenty of time, where he's going, to catch up on his reading.'

Juliet nodded.

'How are matters looking from your point of view?' Holstrom said.

'My situation is much improved. It's more secure than it's been over recent weeks.'

'That's good. I'm very happy to hear it. You are well thought of, Juliet. The work you do here is invaluable.'

'Thank you.'

There was a slightly awkward silence before he said, 'Do you have any plans for tonight?'

For an insane moment, Juliet thought he might be coming on to her. No, it was too ridiculous. 'Why do you ask?'

'Because a letter like the one you have just been obliged to read could cast a cloud on your evening. That's all.'

My evening, she thought. *Carlos Leon's life.* She said, 'I'm planning to relax by myself. I'll listen to some music or read a magazine in the peace and quiet of my new apartment. Believe it or not, being able to do that is a luxury for me.'

'It sounds about perfect,' Holstrom said. 'It also sounds therapeutic.'

She laughed. 'Do you ever switch off, Dr Holstrom?'

'Like I said, I have a duty of care to my staff,' he said. 'I can't switch off. I can, however, reduce the glare of the light, a little.'

'I don't understand that remark.'

'I think you do.'

And then she did. They *had* been keeping an eye on her. Her hunch had been right. And he thought it was no longer necessary for them to do so. That was the meaning of his oblique little metaphor.

She got up and walked out of her boss's office and strode the familiar corridors on her route out of the hospital. She was glad he'd waited until the end of her shift before calling her in to show her the letter. If she'd had this on her mind while she worked, she could have started doubting herself. Carlos's words had shaken her. She had been moved and saddened by what he had said. He painted a bleak future for himself and for the family of the dead cop, but she had told Holstrom the truth. She wouldn't have done anything differently. She still believed absolutely in her healing vocation. The moral case for choosing one life over another could be persuasively made, but it was not her job to make it. That was one of the two reasons her powers were not godlike. She did not sit in judgement. She tried her best to save the life of every patient confronted by the threat of death.

The other reason she was not godlike, was that whatever skill she possessed, and despite what people like the young cop killer's mother chose to believe, she was not capable of miracles. She relied on what she had learned and the knowledge she had accrued and her nerve. Carlos had survived because she was good and he had been young and strong.

She got off the subway two stops short of her destination, needing time to think about things, and stopped for coffee at the first café she came to. The letter had made her think about Jack, and that word perspective was bothering her. She wondered about how events might have looked from his perspective in the period of the disintegration of their marriage. If she had thought to ask at the time, their marriage might not have disintegrated at all.

She knew that she had been very absorbed by her work, pretty much from the day she secured her job at the hospital. But she couldn't blame the break-up of her marriage on her job. Most doctors showed the same dedication that she did, so how did they manage to keep their relationships going? What did Sydney or Holstrom do that she hadn't?

If she was really honest with herself, she had taken Jack for granted a little. At the outset, it had been that old cliché, the attraction of opposites. But she had never taken the interest she might have in his ambitions and aspirations. He had been passionate about his writing and she had been: what?

She had tolerated it. She had treated it the way someone might their partner's hobby. Except that it had not been model ship-making or stamp collecting, had it? Over the course of their marriage his writing had proven to be a lucrative career and he had a growing reputation and readership. He had gained the respect of his peers and been shortlisted for a couple of literary prizes and because she had been disengaged from it, she had inevitably become disengaged from him.

But the other night it had been Jack's arms she had wanted around her not Max's, however sweet and handsome her landlord was. She was not over Jack, she could admit that to herself now.

Her libido wasn't over Jack either. Which was disappointing, she mused, draining her cup and watching people idle by in the autumnal sunshine outside. She wanted to hold on to Jack and have him hold on to her as they walked through the park kicking their way through the piles of leaves. She wanted the familiar scent and weight of him and the delicious way his breath hitched in his chest when he made love to her.

Were those experiences gone for ever? Could she ever forgive him for what he'd done? Shouldn't she take her share of the blame for their failure to make a real go of things together? And if he really was remorseful and she still refused to forgive him, did she actually spite herself by stubbornly allowing her wounded pride to take precedence over her deeper feelings for Jack?

She rose to go. 'Retail therapy, Juliet,' she said to herself on the way out of the café door. It was her little joke. She intended to buy groceries. She needed bleach and detergent and kitchen towels. And something to eat. She looked up at the sky. Her walk home had begun in sunshine, but it had grown overcast now and rain was starting to fall in the large, sporadic drops that suggested a mighty downpour to come.

Twenty-five

Max stood and watched her sleeping. He was content, for the time being, simply to watch and listen to the noises she made as she slept. It was an intimacy he enjoyed because he was the only person who could see and hear her at that particular moment. And he could smell her smell of perfumed slumber, which was a deliciously private sensation.

But the urge to touch her was growing in him. He did not think he would be able to resist it for very much longer. Her skin was so luminous and smooth in the moonlight and would be silky and warm against his fingertips.

His right hand descended. It had a weight and will of its own. It hovered an inch above the succulent swell of her breast. He could feel himself salivating and had to resist the instinct to swallow. He would likely gulp and was scared the sound might wake her. The blood was pounding in his brain and he was only able to control his respiration, keeping it silent, because he had trained himself through long practice.

His reaching hand was the thickness of a cigarette paper from her flesh when Juliet stirred in sleep and mumbled something. 'Jack,' she said. She stretched her limbs and turned onto her side and her head rose blindly from her pillow.

Max quickly retreated on noiseless feet, out of the bedroom and down the hall, into the kitchen where escape awaited in the dark maw beyond the wine closet. But in his haste, he hit a metal serving bowl sitting on the counter with his hip and sent it clattering to the floor where it landed with a loud and resounding clank.

He caught it on the bounce, then froze on his haunches and waited. He listened, straining his ears for the sound of springs shifting within the mattress and the thump of drowsy feet across the wooden floor.

In the bedroom, Juliet's eyes opened. Again, she had the feeling that she was not entirely alone. It was a curious, disorientating sensation, unlike the ghostly presentiment she had felt in the haunted apartment. It was nothing to do with the supernatural. It was more a wary instinct that something was slightly and deliberately out of kilter in her home.

She sat up. All was silent. But something had woken her, hadn't it? Something or, more likely, someone. Rodents and roaches did not make the sort of noise that would wake a sleeping person. Anyway, Max was far too solicitous a landlord, she knew, to allow vermin to encroach on her living space. He was the thorough sort who would deal with pests decisively.

Max heard the telltale sigh of bedsprings as Juliet sat up. He slid through the door that accessed the wine closet. Then he opened the passage door, skilfully concealed as a piece of panelling. He groped for and found the light that would illuminate the section of passage he was in. Then, secure once more and concealed, he went to one of his peepholes to discover what Juliet was doing, awake and apparently suspicious.

Juliet turned her head and saw a weird seepage of light in the hallway and when she climbed off the bed and went into the hall, she saw that the light was coming from the kitchen. Had she left the refrigerator door open? She couldn't have. It would be making more noise. And anyway the shade of the light was wrong for the fridge. The fridge light was yellow. This was a sort of electric blue.

Driven as much by curiosity as fear, she entered the kitchen. She wanted this problem solved. She was sick of feeling weird in her apartment, she wanted to get the thought of intruders or spectres or any of that sort of shit out of her mind, and the only way to do that was to find a logical explanation.

The light was coming from a doorway she had barely noticed; a doorway that she had thought led to nowhere because it had been painted over and lacked a doorknob to open it with. It lay opposite the fridge and from its top edge, against the wall above the fridge in the kitchen darkness, it now projected a thin strip of electric blue light.

Max watched her walk into the kitchen. Then he caught his breath in terror as he saw what she saw. He had left open the doorway to the passage! He had left it open only a chink, but the passage light had leaked through the wine closet door and she was seeing it!

Juliet extended a trembling hand towards the door. She was very nervous about what she might find beyond it. But she needed this mystery solved, and she had to be brave.

'Fuck it,' she said to herself.

She fingered the outer edge of the door, then gave it a firm push, stumbling slightly as it opened inward on a large space within her kitchen wall. There was no blue light beyond her kitchen, in the space. What light she saw by came from the kitchen to her rear, as she stepped into the closet and took in its dusty and neglected detail.

Against the rear wall, there were piled wine racks with one or two bottles still in them. She groped for and found a light switch, the unfinished floorboards of the space she had accessed creaking under her feet. A naked overhead bulb flared into yellowy life.

It was just a wine closet. Space was at such a premium in any rental apartment and yet this once had space to spare – secret space – space she could colonise and utilise for herself.

'Wow!' The sound of her own voice reassured Juliet, so she carried on talking to herself. 'If I cleaned it up, got Max to fix the door, this would be cool.'

Max stood only inches away from her. He was aroused, taut with excitement and fear. At any moment, he could be discovered, and you didn't have to know precisely which of them you were, to enjoy the thrill of the cat-and-mouse game.

It came to him then, that the solitary thrill was no longer enough for him. He craved a shared experience, now. With her beauty and sensuality Juliet had done that for him and among the mingling of emotions he felt for her, he felt a degree of gratitude. Many of his feelings for his tenant were selfless and even noble but the overriding one, at that moment deep in the night in his secret hideaway, was naked desire. It was time to take things further.

No longer afraid, Juliet stood in the wine closet, wondering about its history, and thinking about how she could use this space. She yawned. Now the adrenalin had seeped away, she was exhausted. If she listened quietly and hard, beyond the familiar tick of the refrigerator, she could hear night traffic outside coursing through the city that never slept. But she needed to sleep, and in the morning she'd show Max the wine closet before she went for a run.

In bed, Juliet thought about Max and how lucky she was to have him around to help her. The guy really was a godsend, she thought. It could have turned so awkward between them after the disastrous dinner the other night, but he'd cleared the air with her. Thank goodness for that, she thought as she drifted off to sleep. She would hate to have any unpleasantness between them.

Twenty-six

Max was waiting for Juliet's call the next morning. He maintained the building, after all. He had risen early, as he habitually did, and had rehearsed his surprised expression as he prepared his tools after putting on his mundane, familiar, paint-spattered attire.

Juliet met him at the door. 'Hi, Max, thanks for coming. It's strange that I never noticed this little place before. I had kind of a weird experience last night when I thought I heard something, and the door to it was just sort of standing open.'

'Sounds interesting. So what scared you last night?'

'Oh, nothing. I just thought I heard a noise in the kitchen and then I saw this light. But it was probably something outside. So, here it is. What do you think?'

Max put his well-rehearsed expression of surprise on his face. 'Wow! Look at this!' Under the guise of examining the walls, Max surreptitiously made sure that the door from the wine closet to the passages was properly secured. It was. He noted with a grunt of satisfaction that it was so well concealed he would never have known it was there himself, had he not painstakingly crafted it.

Juliet stood behind him as he looked. He could smell

sleep and last night's perfume on her. She planned to pound the streets in her Nikes and she would not shower until afterwards. After she showered, she would smell of that apple-scented shampoo she used. He fancied she was close enough behind him that he could feel her breath, warm as a caress on his neck. But he knew that was just a treat provided him by his imagination.

'I never realised your kitchen had a wine closet,' he said. 'There's one in August's old place, but they must have covered yours up years ago.' He turned to her. She was nodding, buying it. 'Old buildings have secrets.'

'And you like secrets.'

'Do I?'

'You told me yourself that you do. You told me over dinner.'

'Yes, I did. I remember now.' *About a million years ago when I was something more in your mind and that moist place in your underwear than a handyman.*

'I think it's kind of cool,' Juliet said. 'Can I use it?'

'Sure,' Max said. 'It could do with a little neatening up, though. I'll do it while you're out today.' He swung the closet door back and forth. 'This needs to be fixed. I don't want it coming off the hinge.'

Juliet smiled. 'Thanks for being such a friend,' she said.

Max felt so crestfallen at her expression and tone as she said this that the return smile he felt obliged to offer froze like a rictus on his face. He did not want to be her friend. He did not have any interest in being sweet, dependable Max, the caring and capable guy who cosseted her building. There was nothing in the role for him but disappointment and frustration.

'Sure,' he said. Pulling himself together he treated her to his most sincere smile, the one he had spent much time perfecting. 'A friend in need,' he said.

He remembered the night gleam in her eye when she shrugged off her blouse and her breasts were revealed before him and it now seemed like a beautiful dream. He wanted to get back to that mood between them, charged with passion and possibility and sexual danger. But he didn't know how to. He did not know whether it was possible to conjure it up again.

He was furious after she left, venting his anger by using his cordless nail gun, triggering each nail with a percussive whump as he secured fallen shelves and strengthened the wine closet door-frame and made a rattling beam on the ceiling rigid and stiff. When he had completed this work, he put the nail gun high up on one of the newly fixed shelves and stepped back to examine the racks, making sure that they were correctly aligned and concealed the hidden door. They were. A curious cop would never find his hidden portal; a master carpenter wouldn't spot it now.

Max switched off the wine closet light and closed its newly hung door and got a flowered mug from one of Juliet's kitchen cabinets. He filled it with coffee. He toured the rest of the apartment, leisurely, sipping the strong black brew in the chintzy mug. He had a plan for the place. It was formulating neatly in his mind and he was not a man to squander opportunity.

Twenty-seven

Juliet was on a break on her own in the small ER staff room when she surrendered to the impulse to contact Jack.

There was a dead guy on a gurney under a taut sheet on the other side of the wall, about two feet from where she stood. Blood had leaked in big crimson blossoms through the sheet. He had been stabbed in a bungled street robbery for the fifty dollars he had just taken from a cash machine.

Juliet had tried to save him but the blade of the knife had nicked an artery; the bleeding had been catastrophic. She had held his hand as he died, his grip on hers growing weaker as life leaked away. He had been aware that he was dying until the moment that the light dimmed in his eyes and they closed and he was gone.

Being surrounded by death made you aware that life was short; too short for prevarication or for wasting time not doing what you really wanted to. And the dead guy on the gurney had reminded her of Jack. They had the same colouring and hairstyle and had been roughly the same age.

There was nothing to link the two of them except a chance resemblance. There was no real rationale to calling Jack because she had lost a patient only moments earlier. It just felt overwhelmingly to be the right thing to do. An orderly came by and nodded deferentially to her then went next door and rolled the gurney and its stiffening human cargo away.

She dialled. Then she snapped shut her cell phone before the call registered. She rolled her eyes in exasperation at her own lack of courage. She hit redial and then almost instantly disconnected again.

'Oh, my God,' she said to herself. She felt nervous and stupid, embarrassed and girlish, excited and somehow determined. She typed a text into the phone: *I miss you.* Then she sent it and suddenly vulnerability was added to the stew of all the other things she was feeling. She glanced at the door, glad at least that she was alone.

She poured coffee from the machine into a Styrofoam cup, aware of a slight tremor in her hand she would have to bring under control before returning to her shift. She sipped at the lip of the cup. The coffee was tepid. Her cell phone, in the pocket of her white coat, signalled an incoming text. She drained her drink and threw the cup into a trashcan and took the cell from her pocket and looked at the caller ID. The message was from Jack: *I miss you too.*

An image came to her then, an involuntary recollection that was as vivid as it was totally unexpected, of her and her mother in their family trailer. Wan sunshine from some piece of southern California scrubland spread through the net curtain covering the scooped-out oval of metal framed window and glazed the old Formica of their breakfast table with its million tiny scratches. Her mother was seated opposite Juliet, sipping from a glass of lemon tea, her smile as pale and insipid as the morning sunlight. It had been winter, Juliet remembered. The sky was an unsullied blue, but the weather had been chilly that morning.

Her father was not there. It had been in the time of their free-love period, when her parents swapped partners with a hippie insouciance. Except that her mother, that morning, had not looked insouciant. Her mother had looked wistful and even sad. The dark patches age and a rackety lifestyle were putting prematurely under her eyes had looked like tender bruises. A song had been playing on their tinny little transistor radio, Stevie Nicks singing something by Fleetwood Mac, a yearning, melancholy ballad.

Her mother had sat and sipped her lemon tea, wearing an unbleached cotton smock and twists of ribbon and coloured string in her artfully plaited hair. And she had looked totally bereft, and Juliet, who had been ten or eleven at the time, had resolved to herself: *I will never let this happen to me. When I grow up, I will never allow myself to become as lonely as this.*

And now, with the blood of a stab victim freshly scrubbed from her hands, and the awareness of Jack's absence from her life like a hole at the centre of her world, she finally understood exactly how her mother must have felt that day. And she did not want to go on feeling this way. She could not let pride get in the way of her happiness, and with her new insight into her own behaviour, she finally made a decision. If Jack was truly sorry, she would forgive him and take him back. They would make a real go of things. She missed him because she loved him and the text he had just sent, in its truthful brevity, told her that he felt exactly the same way she did.

Max opened Juliet's closet to reveal her clothing, the individual items hung neatly on their rails. She favoured a simple wardrobe; at least where the palette was concerned. She did not wear vibrant shades. Her clothes were monochromatic; black, grey, ivory, cream. He ran a finger along the line of garments. It stopped when it stroked something silky to the touch, a blouse. It was the same blouse she had shrugged from her pale shoulders when he had almost made love to her.

He gathered a bunch of the slippery fabric in his fist. It was hard to get a good grip on, as she was herself. He brought it up to his nose and sniffed its scent, its residue of Juliet. He breathed in, burying his face in it, allowing it to unfold and envelop his features, his face wearing an expression close to bliss.

He examined the contents of her underwear drawer. There was not much of the exotica in there. She was a practical sort of woman, wasn't she? The queen of the emergency room.

There was a pair of sheer silk stockings and the suspender belt to hold them up. The stockings were black. He supposed she had worn them on special, romantic occasions but it hurt him to speculate about exactly what those occasions had entailed because he had not been involved in them. There were two lacy slips it thrilled him to touch because she wore them under her clothing, where no one could see them. He pressed his lips into the cups of her bras. She was shapelier than Kate O'Donnell had been, but Kate had only been fourteen years old the last time he had been privileged to study her in her nakedness.

He used Juliet's hairbrush to brush his own hair, carefully removing the two or three strands plucked from his scalp from its pad of bristles when he had finished.

He spent quite a long time in her bathroom, just staring at the empty tub. There were some strands of hair caught in the circular metal grid of the plughole and he teased these out between his fingers and put them in his pocket to keep. It was early days for souvenirs of her and where she was concerned his ambitions were much greater than the hoarding of a few intimate keepsakes. But he considered it only human nature to take of her what he could, when the opportunity arose.

It was exciting being in her bathroom. It was much better than spying on it from a passage peephole, separated from it by the obstruction of a wall. That was OK, but this was infinitely better. Spontaneously, without really knowing he was going to do it until it was done, he climbed fully clothed into her tub, lay down and stretched luxuriantly there. The sheer thrill of lying where her naked form had been was overwhelming, and he closed his eyes for a while, savouring the memory of his first view of Juliet in the bath, soaping herself, her hands wandering down between her thighs.

He shuddered and opened his eyes, now was not the

time to give in to his arousal; he still had too much to explore. Turning his attention to Juliet's bathroom sink and the items on the shelves below the mirror, his gaze alighted on Juliet's toothbrush. It was an electric tooth-brush and the urge to use it, to have the shuddering bristles that cleaned her mouth in his, was over-whelming.

He was using the brush when he saw her through her apartment window, returning along the sidewalk from her hospital shift with a large bag of groceries between her hands. He had been using the brush for so long that his gums were sore and when he plopped it out of his mouth he saw that the head was pink with blood. He rinsed it quickly in her sink and shook and then blew the bristles as dry as he could in the time he had before he needed to make good his escape.

Twenty-eight

When Juliet exited the lift, Max was standing at the entrance to his apartment across the hall. As she juggled with the grocery bag and the keys to open her door he said, 'Hey.'

'Hey.'

'Let me help you with that.'

'No,' she said, 'I've got it, really.'

But he was determined to help her, and more than that, he seemed agitated and nervous. His breath smelled of spearmint, as though he had recently brushed his teeth.

He took her groceries. She unlocked the door and led the way into her apartment. He followed her into the kitchen. She knew that if he looked into the bag, he would see that she had bought the same ingredients for dinner that he had cooked for her the other night.

He did look. And then he smiled that sweet smile of his. 'Cooking?'

'Yeah.'

She walked out of the kitchen, discarding her coat as she went.

He put the bag onto the counter and began to unpack

the items it contained.

'You don't have to do that,' she said from behind him. The words sounded funny to her own ears, her pronunciation weird.

He turned to look at her. She was brushing her teeth. She had her toothbrush in her mouth. Max started and then staggered, his arm hitting the bag on the counter, tipping its contents on to the kitchen floor, bags of vegetables bursting, a roast chicken breaking free of its packaging in a richly aromatic cloud of onion gravy.

Max stared at the mess, he looked mortified. 'I thought I smelled chicken.'

Juliet quickly spat toothpaste into the kitchen sink. She switched off the brush and looked at the mess. 'Shit.'

'I'm sorry,' Max said. 'Let me make it up to you. I can help make dinner.'

'No,' Juliet said, 'it's really OK.'

She picked the chicken up off the floor and tried to wash it off. She needed to busy herself or she thought she might lose her temper with Max. She did not want to do that after he'd been so helpful that morning, but she didn't want him there now, inarticulate and clumsy and crowding her just when she needed the space to prepare and organise what he had just inadvertently sabotaged.

She heard him gulp in a big breath and noticed drops of sweat gathering at his hairline. *What's eating at him anyway?* she wondered. *Surely it couldn't still be the events of the other night?*

Then he spoke, and her heart sank. 'I wanted to try

and speak with you about something. It's been a little confusing for me, because you kissed me first.'

Fuck. She had thought them both reconciled to the fact that any chance they had of ever having a physical relationship was dead and buried. And there was something else; there was something stubbornly childlike about his logic. It sounded resentful. 'What do you mean?' She tried to keep the impatience out of her voice.

'You made the first move,' Max persisted. 'And now you act like nothing happened.'

'I'm sorry,' she said. 'We were just getting to know each other.'

Max was silent. It was a charged, petulant silence.

Juliet said, 'It's seeing whether things work or not. That's what people do.'

'That's not what I do,' he said.

'You need to be mature about this.'

'Where is there a rule written that I need to be anything about this other than disappointed and upset?'

'You're blowing events out of proportion.'

'I don't believe that I am. You can manipulate my feelings, Juliet. You've proven to be very skilled at that. What you cannot do is dictate them to me.'

'I have not tried to do either.'

'Haven't you? Forgive me if I beg to differ. Actually, forget I said that. Beg is the wrong word in this context.'

'In what context?'

'You know very well.'

'I genuinely don't.'

'I genuinely think you do.'

She bit down on her lip. She shook the chicken dry and dabbed at it with a paper towel. She really didn't need this now. The inference was that she had led him on and then slammed the door in his face. She could see how he might think that, but it was an immature conclusion, unreasonable considering the matter had been discussed and agreed amicably between them. Hadn't it?

Max levered his way off the counter he was leaning on and walked out of her apartment without saying another word.

Minutes later, he was watching her. She was still in the kitchen. She was preparing a meal in exactly the way he had taught her to do when they had enjoyed their romantic dinner together about a million years ago.

He moved silently along the passage to the peephole that gave him a view of the living room. He saw that the table was set for two. It was the table that had belonged to his grandfather; she had chosen it and he had carried it into her apartment for her, to her warm show of, what had seemed at the time, sincere gratitude.

Max was beginning to understand. He was first incredulous and then furious but there was no mistaking what she was doing. She was preparing to wine and dine another man.

In the refuge of the wall, hurt and angry, Max stole through the gloom to look upon Juliet again in the kitchen. Her cell phone was on the counter, ringing, shifting slightly with the vibration. She picked it up and when she saw who was calling, smiled broadly and shook her hair the way women did when they were pleased and playful.

'Hi,' she said. In the one word, her voice already sounded flirtatious. It was a new tone to Max's ears. It was one she had never used with him.

'Ten minutes sounds good,' she said. She walked out of the kitchen and out of sight.

Max scampered through the passageways, trying to keep her in view as he passed the hidden peepholes peppering her walls.

He found her in the bathroom. She was brushing her teeth again. Knowing that the brush had shared the interior of both their mouths sent a visceral thrill jolting through him, just as it had earlier when the sensation had been so strong he'd knocked the groceries off the counter. But the feeling was nothing like so strong or pleasurable now. She had brushed her teeth on returning from her shift out of habit, just to remove the canteen food and machine coffee staleness inflicted by a shift at the hospital.

This was different. She was brushing her teeth now to freshen her breath in anticipation of a kiss. She had put wine and candles on the table. Her dinner guest was clearly not her pregnant friend and her sloppy mess of a husband. Max had never romanced anyone, prior to Juliet, in his life. But he had seen the movies that had taught him how to behave on his one dinner date with Juliet and he was sure he could read the signs very clearly.

He had to decide what to do. He felt the hopeless devastation of rejection and the pain was too great for him to endure without doing something that might deliver him relief from it. These walls were his womb as well as his kingdom; he had always felt safe here. But the time might have come for him to do something he had never really considered doing before. His pain compelled him to do it. He had to act, or he thought the agony consuming him might drive him mad.

He entered her apartment through the panel from the passages to the wine closet and walked into her kitchen; he knew she wasn't there because he could hear the whine of the electric toothbrush still in use in the bathroom. He stole into her living room and looked around quickly for her bag.

He spotted it. He still had time. He was cool and unafraid, impressed by his own nerve and initiative. No one had called her since that man, a few minutes ago. If he were punctual, he would be here in a little over five. He took Juliet's cell and looked for the most recently dialled call. There was no name next to the number when Max brought it up on the display, but it was definitely him.

Max was writing down the number quickly on his palm with the biro from his pocket when the door buzzer sounded, loud and abrupt from the hallway.

He had no time to escape. He still had Juliet's cell phone in his hand. He stood as rigid as stone and watched her walk right past him to the front door.

Twenty-nine

Juliet took a quick look through her spyhole before opening the door. Max, in his new mood of gloomy, awkward persistence, had made her slightly wary. But all she saw through the lens was Jack, familiar and gorgeous, reassuring in all his glorious, joyful contradictions.

'Hey,' he said, into the spyhole. 'I brought a friend.'

She flung open the door and immediately heard a yap and a bark. She looked down as Amelie, their pet terrier, jumped in excitement around her knees. She bent and picked the dog up and it lapped her face. 'Amelie!' Juliet said. 'I missed you so much.'

She glanced from the dog to Jack. He was beautifully dressed, and was bearing a bottle of tequila and a bag of limes. 'Wow,' she said. 'Look at you.' She bent and put Amelie back down on the floor.

Jack smiled at her uncertainly. There was a formality to him, as though he did not know quite how to behave or quite what to expect. 'Didn't really know what to wear to a dinner like this. I'm nervous,' he said, confirming the impression. 'Here.' He handed Juliet the bottle.

She said, 'Let's sit in the living room.' They walked there, Jack sat down and Juliet sank to her haunches and removed Amelie's lead, allowing the little terrier to scamper happily, exploring the apartment. She knew that Jack had brought the dog to break the ice. He really was nervous and there was something endearing about that. And the thought of ice made her remember the tequila bottle she had just put down on the table with the bag of limes.

'I'll fix us both a drink,' she said. In the kitchen, she reached for two glasses from a shelf and started to prepare two margaritas; coaxing ice cubes from a tray, slicing the limes, rimming the glasses with salt, trying in the unthinkingly familiar ritual to steady her own nerves. Things were looking good. The fact that Jack was nervous reassured her, but a lot depended upon the outcome of this evening and yet there was so much over which she had no control. For a start she had no idea what Jack was going to say, so she could not even predict her own reaction to his words.

They sat on the sofa and sipped their drinks. They were together and still a chasm apart and the silence grew more uncomfortable between them the longer it stretched out. Juliet did not think it her responsibility in the circumstances to fill the space between them with congenial chat. In the end though, because she could hear the little dog skittering unsettled from room to room, she said, 'What's up with Amelie?'

Jack said, 'She picked a fight with a German shepherd at Doggie Day Care.'

'Why are you taking her there?'

'I've been out of town a lot the last few weeks,' he said.

Juliet nodded. *With a woman*, she thought, gloomily. Out of town romancing someone appreciative of his writing as well as his looks; someone literate and cultured and beautiful and probably very rich.

'No,' Jack said, reading her mind. 'It was professional rather than personal. It's promotional stuff; publicity. It's fulfilling a contractual obligation. I wasn't doing what you might think.'

'I wasn't thinking that at all,' Juliet said. She said the words emphatically but to her own ears, they sounded hollow. There was another awkward silence and she wondered how long they would be able to delay confronting the subject of Jack's affair. They would have to address it at some point that evening. He must have come there prepared to be honest, even if he wasn't really contrite.

'This place is huge,' Jack said, changing the subject.

'And cheap,' Juliet said.

'How much?'

'Thirty-eight hundred.' She could not disguise the pride in her voice. She did not even try.

'Are there other apartments available?'

'For who?'

'For me.'

'You? I don't think we're quite ready for that.'

Jack said, 'We could be like Mia and Woody.'

'He cheated on her too,' Juliet pointed out.

'Right,' Jack said. 'Right . . .'

'I don't want to talk about it,' Juliet said. She got up. She looked at the now empty glass in her hand. She reached for the glass Jack was cradling but it was still almost full and he shook his head. She sighed and turned and walked into the kitchen.

'I can tell you everything that happened,' Jack called after her.

'I don't want to know,' Juliet said.

'You were never home. I almost literally never saw you.'

'That isn't true.'

'Even when you were there, you were preoccupied by your work to the point where you might as well not have been.'

Juliet tossed fresh ice into her margarita glass. She added tequila. She sliced another lime. She said, 'Please don't tell me you slept with someone else because I was working too hard.' At her feet, agitated, Amelie had appeared and started to bark. When Jack replied, she could hardly hear what he was saying for the barking. She picked the terrier up. She turned back for the living room with her drink in one hand and Amelie cradled in the other arm.

'I'm not saying that at all,' Jack said. 'I was sick of being alone every night. I honestly thought you didn't care any more. We weren't connecting. I wanted—'

'A housewife.'

'I wanted you and you weren't there,' Jack said. 'You were all I ever wanted. Just you.'

There was a hesitation between them. Juliet would not let it become a silence. There had been enough of those. She said, 'I've been with someone else.'

Jack took a deep breath. He closed his eyes and then opened them again and she saw that his fists were clenched and he had grown suddenly pale. It was obvious to her that he did not want to hear this and equally obvious that he needed to. She could embellish the story and thought that maybe he would deserve it if she did.

She remembered the words Mike had used in this very room to describe what Jack had done to her. *He devastated you.* She remembered the rainbow shimmer on their lawn and the empty dismay in her belly as she fought the concussion and shame on that August afternoon.

It was a lot to forgive, wasn't it? She probably deserved her pound of flesh in revenge. More than a pound she thought. She could give Jack the graphic blow by blow of a fictional passion and he would believe every syllable and squirm accordingly. And part of her was tempted to. But she decided she would not do that. She was not playing games. She had not invited him here merely to score points off him.

'It was a flirtation. For a moment, it felt amazing. He was attractive, intriguing. He was nice.'

Jack did not say anything. His head was bowed, listening to her. He was looking at the floor.

Juliet cleared her throat. She said, 'I want to be clear about something. I want you to be clear about it too. He was nice, my flirtation. But he was never you.'

'Was he the guy with the glasses?'

Juliet said, 'How would you know that?'

'I followed you one night. I was going to ring your bell, but . . .'

'. . . you followed me?'

'I know, I'm sorry, it sounds wrong, even a little creepy. But I had to do it. I was beginning to understand what I stood to lose, what I'd maybe lost, for ever. I had to do it, just like I had to call you when you refused to take the calls. It wasn't good any more.'

'What wasn't?'

'Anything, Juliet. Life.'

She looked at him. He was looking back at her now. He shrugged. 'Life without you,' he said.

He looked away again, down at the floor, thinking, she supposed, that he had said too much, like a gambler who displays too early a hand that isn't strong enough to win the game. And now he had no more cards to play.

It did not matter to her. It was neither game nor competition and either they both won, or neither of them did. She reached for his hand and held and then kissed it. He touched her face, stroking and caressing the skin around her eyes and mouth, touching her the way a potter might, shaping his most precious clay. They kissed, then. And to Juliet the kiss was perfect. Their mouths melded. The kiss eventually broke and when it did, Juliet took Jack by the hand and led him into her bedroom.

Thirty

Crouched on a shelf in the kitchen, Max watched almost all of this drama unfold. The little he did not see of it, he clearly heard. He had not left the apartment after taking Jack's phone number. His urge to stay had been too strong. He had hidden in the kitchen, where the dog had almost alerted Juliet to his presence as he crouched in the shadows above a cupboard beside the cooking range.

They had been oblivious, too wrapped up in the charged moment of their reconciliation to sense him. Desperate to get closer, Max had managed to creep into the living room where he hid behind the sofa. He was so close that he could feel the body heat emanating off them as they embraced. He could smell their mingled scents, and his indignation and fury almost choked him. It wasn't fair. This man had betrayed her; when Max had met her, she'd been at her lowest point. He had sensed the despair and desperation coming off her; she exuded it. And he had been the one to rescue her.

She'd still be trudging the streets of New York trying to get her life back together if it wasn't for him. And how did she repay him? Was this gratitude? Was this justice? Was this how he was going to be rewarded for his kindness and chivalry, with a coquettish shrug of rejection in favour of someone who had broken her heart?

The little terrier was barking again. They barked at intruders and he wasn't one. He had been crouching atop a kitchen shelf when the dog had cocked its head and sniffed his presence in the shadows there and taken exception to him. Maybe it was just loyal to the interloper who'd brought it here on the leash. Maybe it thought three was a crowd.

He would have to leave before the animal alerted them to him. The barking would raise their suspicions eventually.

They were in the bedroom. Their voices low. He could hear them, but it was a strain to do so because their shared tone was confidential and intimate.

The guy said, 'You ever get the feeling you are being watched here?'

'Jesus. Not you too.'

'What do you mean?'

'I invited Mike and Syd for dinner. Mike thought someone was in the bathroom, watching him pee.'

The guy laughed. There was not much humour in the laugh.

'An old man owned the building when I first moved in. He was probably very nice but he was creepy too in that way old men can become when they don't see enough daylight or have many friends. He died.'

'You think he's haunting the place?'

'The idea occurred to me. But the odd noises, the feeling of being awoken sometimes and then seeing nobody there. Those sensations preceded his death.'

'Maybe that's why the rent is so reasonable. You share the apartment with ghosts.'

It was Juliet's turn to laugh. She did not sound terribly amused either.

'I'm going to see what's bugging Amelie,' Jack said.

'And then?'

'And then, my darling, we are going to get properly reacquainted.'

Life had always been unfair, Max thought, creeping off towards the kitchen and his access to the passages. He had been dealt a terrible hand in the parents who had deserted him and the grandfather who had bullied and beaten him mercilessly after their deaths. Even when his physical strength had left him, August had still taunted his grandson cruelly, humiliating him at every opportunity, always reminding him that he and not Max owned the building.

Before Juliet, Max had merely existed, but with her came the promise of a real, vibrant life. That's why he'd manipulated her into moving here, that's why he had planned to own the building. And now he did own it; every brick and inch of plaster and floorboard and ceiling joist and frame of window glass. It had all been going so well. Until he realised that he owned no part of her. His plan for her had gone awry and he deserved better.

August had disconcerted Juliet. Max had picked up on that. He had wanted her to be comfortable. He had wanted the apartment she had just rented to be her dream home. So he had injected August with an increased dose of the sedative he had been prescribed.

The dosage had only been fractionally greater than

what he was ordinarily administered with. But practice had made Max an expert in the potency of his grand-father's medication and he knew it was enough to stop his faltering heart from beating altogether.

August had known. He must have felt the extra volume of the liquid pumping into his vein or noticed that the chamber of the syringe took fractionally longer to empty as the lethal dose was discharged from it.

'You've killed me,' he whimpered.

'You were cruel in life, Grandfather. Try not to be pitiful in death,' Max replied coldly.

'Why have you done this to me?'

'For everything you have done to me. If I thought I could have done it without raising suspicion, the moment would have come much sooner.'

'So now you are a murderer.'

'I am what you made me.'

August shuddered and closed his eyes. They opened again. The pupils were pinpricks and he was sweating and his skin had grown translucent. 'Hold me, Max,' he said.

'Hold you? Why?'

'So I don't die alone.' With the last effort of which his body was capable, he held out his arms for a dying embrace.

Max rose from beside him, shaking his head. 'Go to hell,' he said, before leaving the room, closing and locking the door behind him.

And he'd gone through all that for Juliet. He had extinguished the life of his only living relative in a warm and selfless gesture of welcome to the woman whose life he dreamed of sharing. And it had gained him precisely nothing.

He made for the bedroom peepholes. There they were, kissing on the bed. She was stroking her husband's hair as the passion grew between them. A part of Max felt a strong compulsion to watch what they did together. But he was torn, conflicted, consumed by so much righteous jealousy that in the end he could not bear to witness it.

He pounded through the dark passageways like some prowling minotaur, his domain feeling less like his animal kingdom than the tunnels of some dungeon in which he'd been unwillingly confined.

He did not know what to do. He was struggling to retain control of emotions that had never been so provoked in his life. He knew he still had the will and the cunning to change things, to influence the outcome of events. There was really no point in his existence if he did not have that, was there?

Thirty-one

Juliet lay on the bed in the aftermath of their love-making. Jack was dressing, looking to her like he knew he had to go but was reluctant to leave. His body language was as she remembered, before she stopped noticing him and he looked beyond her for attention and whatever else he'd sought.

He hadn't found it. Not in sexual gymnastics with the trophy blonde. He said that he had slept with her perhaps half a dozen times and never again once Juliet had left. She believed him. He was not a good enough actor to fake the level of remorse that had shown on his face.

He told her he had feared he would never again share a bed with Juliet, and that her absence had told him he was losing the woman he loved completely. Juliet believed that, too. You had to take some things on trust.

He sat, shirtless, on the bed beside her. He pecked her shoulder and she said, 'I'm sorry dinner burned.'

He said, 'I'm not.'

They kissed.

'I want you to stay.'

'I have a live radio interview scheduled for first thing tomorrow morning. I haven't prepped for it at all and I do need to. It's the last commitment on a national book publicity tour. I'll be free, after I've completed it. We have the rest of our lives in which to enjoy one another's company and this time, we are going to get it right.'

'I didn't take you seriously,' she said. 'I mean, what you did, what you do. I guess I knew how much it meant to you, but not what it could mean for you.'

'For us,' he said.

'I remember one occasion. You showed me a book cover, the design for the second hardback. I was on autopilot, thinking about some new operational procedure that hinders excessive bleeding. I barely looked up. Do you remember what I said?'

'You said, "now we're cooking with gas".'

'I think that was the moment in which I lost you, Jack.'

'And now you've found me again. And thank God you have.' He sounded like he meant it. 'Could you meet me for lunch tomorrow?'

She nodded.

He got up and put on his shirt and began to button it. He said, 'You want to keep Amelie tonight? Watch dog?'

Juliet shook her head. 'No pets allowed,' she said. 'Why the offer?'

'I'd almost rather not say. I could hear the pride in your voice when you told me what you're renting this place for.' He glanced around, wrestling with a cuff. 'And there's what you've done with it. Great location, stunning views, endless space, stylish décor – I could go on. At first sight, it's the dream apartment.'

'But . . .?'

'I don't know. I don't want to rain on your parade, Jules.'

'Writers shouldn't talk in clichés.'

'I don't want to spook you,' he said.

'You won't,' she said. 'I've toughened up without you. The reason why I left you meant that I had to.'

Jack ignored the barbed comment. He probably thought that he deserved it. 'I've sensed something of what Mike did, I think. I don't really believe in ghosts. Or at least, I didn't. But there's something about this place that would make me happy if you left it.'

'And move back in with you?'

'Why not?'

'Because it's too soon?'

He shrugged. He was fully clothed, on the point of departure. He had Amelie's leash looped over one fist. 'I wouldn't stoop so low as to try to deliberately scare you back into my bed, Jules. You wouldn't go for it.'

'This place is not haunted, Jack. I've been somewhere that was and let me tell you, it was fucking terrifying. The hair wouldn't sit down on the back of my neck for two hours after I left. It was like the walls were screaming. I've had a couple of frights here caused by elderly plumbing and a maintenance train that runs at night. And my own imagination. Fiction writers don't have a patent on imagination, you know.'

He smiled at her. She thought the smile apologetic. He would say no more on what was actually a touchier subject than she was allowing herself to believe. He said, 'Lunch tomorrow?'

She blew him a conciliatory kiss. And he left.

Thirty-two

As the front door shut behind Jack, Max stole on silent feet into her kitchen from the door in the closet. He saw the glass from which she had been drinking. She had moved from the margarita to wine. The smudge of lipstick on its rim told him that the glass was definitely hers. He took a small syringe from his pocket and plunged its clear contents into the glass, before disappearing back into concealment.

Juliet walked into the kitchen about ten minutes later not yet ready for sleep, after the excitement and magnitude of the events of the evening. She picked up her wine glass and took a long swallow. For the first time in what seemed like a very long time, Juliet was looking forward to her future.

She switched on the kitchen radio. The station she had it tuned to was playing a song by Fleetwood Mac. Stevie Nicks was singing it in that strong, declarative, histrionic style of hers. Juliet was reminded of her mother, faded and lovelorn in their mobile home in the scrub of California.

She would read Jack's books, she resolved, as she sipped her wine. She would read them because they mattered so profoundly to him and he was such an important part of her life again.

Juliet's cell phone rang. It occurred to her that the coverage here really was as intermittent as Max had warned her it was. It was an inconvenience, but he'd been truthful enough in warning her.

She expected Jack and a mumbled, romantic goodnight, maybe with the newly cantankerous Amelie growling in the background.

It was Sydney. She said, 'You OK, baby?'

'You have a real baby arriving imminently, Syd. You should be asleep. You should maybe have been asleep a couple hours ago.'

'Just checking on you.'

'Mike's ghoul has vacated the bathroom. I'm absolutely fine.'

'Not afraid of the dark?'

'The dark suddenly doesn't seem as dark as it did.'

'Oh? That sounds like a significant development. You'll have to explain that one to me.'

'I will. You know I will.'

'Night, hon.'

'Night, Syd.'

Juliet yawned, surprising herself. She was more tired than the hour would normally have made her. Sex hadn't used to make her feel sleepy, quite the opposite. Maybe she was emotionally drained, but she shouldn't be, because emotionally she felt stronger and happier that evening than she had for months. She was tired, though, she conceded to herself, yawning again. She swallowed the last of her wine. She rinsed the glass. She brushed her teeth with darkness almost impinging at the edges of her vision. She barely made it to the bed before descending into deep slumber.

Max stood above Juliet in her bedroom, watching her. Lozenges of bright colour in hues of amber and red cast by the lights of the night traffic on the bridge outside slipped across the walls and ceiling of her bedroom. They inked what he could see of her skin above the bed sheet partially wrapping her. He could smell the odour of recent sex rising in the warmth of the bed from her recumbent body. There was something tartly insistent about it, he thought. It was a new smell to him; a strong but still subtle secretion, part of her secrecy he would get to know well.

Her cell phone began to ring again, a sudden sound that startled him. The display was backed by a green pulsing light as the device vibrated with life on her night stand. He retreated into the dark corner of the room where the light from the traffic did not impinge and the glow of her cellular was too feeble to illuminate. He was entirely still there, patient and implacable, unafraid, curious as to whether this summons from outside would wake her.

It did not. The drug was too potent. He emerged from his dark place and crept over to the bed. He studied her some more. She lay on her back, peacefully. He had delivered her this calm period of rest. He did not expect she would be grateful for it. But then she'd never know, would she? He was too careful, too clever.

He sank to his knees and rolled onto his back on the floor. As he had before, he slipped under her bed, where he was just a mattress thickness away from Juliet's sleeping shape. He twisted and edged in careful fractions of movement until the excitement in his groin insisted to him that he was perfectly positioned.

He moved his hands up and pressed them against the mattress feeling her weight. He began to breathe in rhythm with Juliet. He lifted her. He lifted her even higher, aware of her density and warmth and his own strength and growing sexual urge.

Juliet's hand flopped from off the bed and hung limply a few inches from his face. He looked at it for a long moment. Very slowly, he lowered his hands from the mattress. He slid towards the hand. He did not dare to touch it; did he? *This time it might be safe*, he thought. She was so deep in her narcotic sleep that she would not feel his caress.

He moved his lips to her palm, smelling the skin of her hand, inhaling her. He kissed her softly and felt her move in response sensually in her sleep, and moan with an unconscious pleasure.

Max slipped out from under Juliet's bed. He knew he was about to cross a line, but the reward was so sweet that it vastly outweighed the risk. First, though, he had to take extra precautions. He would have to ensure that Juliet remained oblivious to what he intended for them to do together.

He ran back through his secret passages, emerging from the labyrinthine route in the now vacant apartment his grandfather had occupied until his death. The old man's medication was still in August's bathroom cabinet. That was where he had earlier acquired the sedative he had slipped into Juliet's drink.

August's denuded library roused no feeling in him as he passed the vacant shelves, making for the bathroom and an ampoule of something that would befuddle Juliet's senses and rob her of consciousness should his careful attentions rouse her. A drug imbibed orally was nowhere near so strong or swift in its effect as one injected.

He was sure he wouldn't wake her. He would be gentle. He wanted to make love to her, not violate her. He would be tender and grateful because she would satisfy his desire and bring an end to the loneliness that he had endured for what seemed like the whole of his life.

When he returned to Juliet's bedroom, he brushed off the dust of his travels before cleaning his teeth with her toothbrush once again and tidying his dishevelled hair with her brush. He thought briefly about attiring her in something sexy from her underwear draw but decided against that. Instead, he arranged her on the bed in the attitude he remembered seeing her in when she had been with her husband a few hours earlier.

With a wry smile, he sat on the bed next to her, remembering how he had kissed and then licked out the cups of her bra on his first proper inspection of her clothes. No need for that now. He had her, the woman of his dreams. He had no need for keepsakes and mementoes.

Max was pleased with himself. He was not just clever and imaginative. He was courageous, doing this. He was excited too, as he touched her bare neck, the tresses of her hair and the warm, satiny smoothness of her cheek. The pad of his thumb paused against the resistance of her lower lip. He used it to part her lips, slightly opening her mouth, seeing the tip of her tongue like a ripening red bud succulent between her teeth, before moving in to kiss her properly for the first time.

Juliet's eyes opened wide. She groaned, blinking, trying to see straight. She was drugged and bleary, but coming around, so much stronger than August, of course, so much younger and more vital. He had misjudged the dose and hadn't given her enough sedative to keep her tranquil and him safe.

Max fumbled in his pocket for the syringe. His erection got in the way and panic made him clumsy. Finally he was able to take the syringe out of his pocket and remove the cap from the needle. He reached for one of Juliet's feet.

On the bed, Juliet was trying to look at him. She was trying to raise her head but she could not control her muscles. He could see them spasm in her neck as she tried to raise the weight of her head.

He pushed the point of the needle under her toenail. He knew enough to know that there the injection would not leave a mark. He depressed the plunger. She whimpered in pain as the shock of the needle coursed through her body. He watched her through a film of tears as the drug did its work and her body swiftly returned to a supine state of relaxation and rest.

Having to do this to her had made him cry. It was a tribute to his love for her. He didn't remember crying since he had curled up beside his mother's dead body. The salt tears coursed down his face as the conflicting emotions mingled and churned inside him.

Thirty-three

It took the persistent buzzing of her alarm clock to wake Juliet the following morning. It was a sound somewhere between an angry bee and the blade of a band saw shrieking its way through vibrating layers of ply. She had never heard her alarm clock go off before, she realised dully, fumbling for the button that would make the noise stop. It was a precaution only; she always woke up a few minutes before the alarm was set to sound.

Her head hurt. She tried to inventory what she had drunk the night before, but her mind was not co-operating with its usual clarity. That was a symptom of a hangover in itself.

She knew what caused hangovers. The principal culprit was dehydration. Then there were congeners. They were the chemicals that fixed the colour in alcoholic drinks and they were toxic so they made you feel bad if you ingested too many of them. They were not added to tequila. She had drunk two margaritas the previous evening. Congeners were at their most concentrated as an ingredient in rum and port. But they were also present in red wine and she had drunk red wine the previous evening too.

It was true that she had gone to sleep without drinking her habitual night glass of water. She remembered barely staying conscious long enough to brush her teeth. But she had drunk nowhere near enough alcohol to feel as bad as she felt. Her head hurt. It really thumped. And there had been that strange erotic dream she had experienced and now only vaguely remembered.

Slowly, she examined herself. She could see or feel nothing out of the ordinary.

She was late. Or she was going to be late, if she did not hurry to get ready for work. She quickly showered and dressed and then walked into the living room, feeling nervous and exposed, not at all sure why she was feeling those things instead of the elation she should have felt after her evening of reconciliation with Jack.

She did not feel rested. She felt raw and numb at the same time, contradictory sensations, true, but that summed up how she felt. The numbness was the hangover bit. The rawness came from that sense of exposure, a suspicion she realised had been too vague in her before now to find a name. But Juliet did feel exposed that morning, as she got ready for work in her apartment. She felt watched, almost nakedly on show. Something was not right about her situation. An insistent and growing intuition told her so. And she trusted her intuition. In her profession, it had more than once saved patients' lives.

The ghost of August did not roam, dribbling into his beard with lust for her, in the night. She did not believe that. But Mike: beneath the ramshackle persona was a sensible man who had made a fortune out of his alertness. The apartment bathroom had spooked him.

Jack had been spooked too, hadn't he? He had been most reluctant, in that old phrase, to rain on her parade. But he had felt the need to warn her urgently enough to do it anyway.

She caught a flash of movement from the monitor in her sitting room that was linked to a security camera rigged in the vestibule. It showed a construction worker entering the building. That gave her an idea that solidified in her mind during her swift walk to the subway station. By the time she reached the main entrance of the hospital and pushed her way through the doors, her idea had become a plan.

At seven o'clock that evening, Max was at the grocery store. He really thought that by now, he should be shopping for two. The meal he had cooked her had made for a wonderful dinner and up until the end, a wonderful evening too. The chicken had been moist and tender and the roast potatoes, basted in goose fat, were perfect. The parsnips had been sweet and succulent, burnished by a light brushing of virgin olive oil. The Lynch-Bages he had taken from his grandfather's wine store had been a bottle of the coveted '62 vintage. He had decanted it perfectly.

All that meal had done in the end he thought as he drifted between the aisles, had been to inspire the one she cooked for that superciliously smooth husband of hers, that glib adulterer she had demeaned herself by allowing back into her life. The ingredients had been identical.

Apart from the wine. The wine had been something indifferent, a budget bottle of generic Californian Merlot. He had experienced no qualms adulterating it. She had deserved that, for her tasteless copying of the meal he had cooked her and for inviting back into her life the man who had betrayed her. Her treatment of him, of Max, had been unscrupulous and cruel.

But he was a forgiving man, he thought, selecting half a dozen choice yellow plums. And he was an optimist. And he believed the adventure of Juliet had a long way to evolve before it was all played out.

At two minutes past seven, a security technician called Tom Fanning was helping Juliet place the second of two miniature video webcams. They were tiny, inconspicuous by design and then deliberately concealed. The first of them had already been placed on a bookcase in her bedroom. Tom was attaching the second on a bookshelf in the hallway.

'It's like a Dictaphone with a voice activator,' he said. 'The record feature is triggered by movement.' He moved his hand in front of the camera, then added, 'It's wireless and feeds directly into its own hard drive that can be played through your TV or computer.

'These positions will cover as much of the apartment as possible with just two units. But it still leaves the kitchen and bathroom uncovered.'

'That's OK,' Juliet replied. 'As long as I've got the

bedroom and the front door covered, I think I'll be pretty secure.'

'It has automatic night vision,' Tom said. 'So no need to leave a light burning. It'll catch whatever moves.'

Juliet nodded.

'You gonna sublet?'

'What?'

'Most people put these in for parties or if they're gonna sublet, or for babysitters. Make sure no one misbehaves or messes up the place or steals anything.'

'Oh, yeah,' Juliet said. 'I'm gonna sublet.'

She still didn't feel right. It was like there was a layer of insulation muffling her senses from the world. She was thirsty, had felt parched all day and had noticed Holstrom frowning at her from behind the glass of his office when she fumbled with a stethoscope monitoring a patient's heart rate.

She had measured her own pulse and it had felt sluggish and a bit thready. Her resting pulse rate was normally in the mid-fifties, low she supposed because of her fairly extreme exercise habit. But that morning it had been around forty-eight, which was lower than it ever was normally. She had felt worse than sluggish, she had felt almost sedated and she knew these were not the symptoms of a hangover.

She stood at her door and watched Tom take the elevator down, after thanking him for his handiwork. She was still leaning on her doorframe five minutes later when the elevator doors opened and Max walked out onto their floor, a bag of groceries in his arms. Juliet gave him what she hoped was a friendly smile. She still had a lot to feel grateful to the guy for, even if she found herself liking him less since his petulant verbal outburst of the previous evening.

He did not smile back. He looked if anything a little bit startled to see her there. He was not shocked enough to repeat his trick of the night before and spill the contents of his own grocery bag all over the floor, but she certainly seemed to have given him a fright.

It didn't matter, not really. What mattered were her plans for the night, a reciprocal dinner with Jack, who she felt sure would find a way to sharpen her dulled senses. She would pack a bag and stay over. There may be balance to strike between not rushing things and making up for lost time but really, all she wanted to do was be with Jack.

She watched Max self-consciously juggle his burden of provisions and his keys as he unlocked his apartment door. It did not really matter if they were no longer friends. Their moment had come and gone without amounting to anything. He was a solitary sort of individual when all was said and done, even if he seemed to have expected more from her than she could give. But there was only room in Juliet's heart for one man and fuzzy as her thinking might be, she was certain it wasn't Max.

Juliet went back inside. She packed a duffle bag, drank yet another glass of water and went to the toilet. She was starting to feel normal again, at last. She paused by her front door, sure for a moment that she had forgotten something. Then she remembered that she did not need to switch on her spiffy little surveillance cameras. They were motion-activated. They did all the switching on they needed to do, all by themselves.

Thirty-four

Max came to at 4 a.m., looking at his wristwatch to confirm the time, seated in the chair he used when he studied her from his array of bedroom peepholes. Juliet was not there. She had not returned from wherever it was she had gone. Where was she? This was not part of his plan. He had not predicted this random behaviour from her. The apartment he had leased her was her refuge from heartbreak and insecurity. It was her bastion against a cruel and sometimes hostile world and he could not imagine where she would go and be happier and more contented than there.

And then he could.

She had to be with *him*. She had returned to the arms of her creep of a husband. It was his embrace in which she would now be cradled, asleep and apparently safe from any further emotional harm.

Max did not think that he could bear it, but he had to have confirmation before he could think about how to act, how to respond to this changed set of circumstances. His strategy, such as it was, had been predicated on her staying put in the apartment. She had a lease agreement to honour, for Christ's sake! They had entered into a contract and he expected her to be principled enough to keep her side of their bargain. The place was a steal at the rent and she knew it. Even the husband had more or less intimated as much, the previous night.

Max decided that he would have to follow her. He would wait until she left the hospital at the end of her shift that evening and see where it was she went. He could not simply wait for her to come home from work. That would be torture for him, unendurable because she might not do so. She might stay away for a second night.

Facts had to be established. Suspicions needed to be confirmed. Threats, if they really existed, needed to be eliminated. He had to act decisively. He thought that August, his baleful and disapproving grandfather, would actually have been proud of this bold and decisive new Max. He had tapped into a vast reserve of resourcefulness and courage. He met challenges head on and with ingenuity too. He was a different person really, a more complete and able human being than he had ever been before, now that he had Juliet in his life.

It was clear that Juliet needed him as much as he needed her. He was obviously the best thing for her, the person who, in the long run, could make her happiest and most content. He just had to convince her of the fact.

Thirty-five

Jack met her from the hospital and they went together to a Brooklyn deli where they sheltered from the rain and drank coffee at a table by the window.

Condensation clouded the window; the past clouded their conversation. They should have talked about this last night, but going to bed seemed so much easier. Making love required no dialogue and told her the most important thing: they still loved each other. They both wanted a new beginning, but it would not be achieved without some discussion of how things had ended between them. And that was difficult.

'I take responsibility,' Jack said, 'for everything.'

'You don't want to plead mitigation?'

'I don't.'

Juliet sipped her coffee. The street outside through the steamed glass had a phantom quality, like a dream. She said, 'You're very magnanimous. Does the pleasure you got from your affair contribute to this generous frame of mind?'

'Please, Juliet.'

She sipped coffee. She did not feel the way she knew she sounded. She felt anything but lofty and detached. And the truth was that she found the moral high ground a lonely spot to occupy. It was short on home comforts. 'Just trying to establish the facts,' she said.

'The fact is that I ended the affair.'

'Because you grew bored with her?'

'I was never really interested in her.'

'You fucked her, Jack. You were making a pretty enthusiastic job of it when I caught you.'

He did not say anything. He just offered a slight shrug.

'So you didn't like her sparkling personality or her book-group intellect or her drop-dead looks. So it was what? Friction?'

'I'm not proud of having done it.'

'What went through your mind when I caught you? What did you think when your injured wife poked her disfigured head through our bedroom door and witnessed the pair of you in action?'

'I was shocked. Then I was ashamed and sorry.'

'Not sorry enough, Jack.'

'I called the hospital, to find out what had happened to you. They put me on to that martinet Holstrom. He wouldn't tell me.'

'He has a duty of care. So did you, to your wife. He happens to take his seriously. He has lofty ideals. He has a sense of honour and integrity. He's loyal. If these are concepts new to you, you can find them in any dictionary.'

'I called Sydney. She called me something unrepeatable and hung up. I called Mike at his office. He wouldn't even come to the phone.'

'Tell me truthfully why you ended the affair.'

'Because she wasn't you.'

'She wasn't me when you began it, Jack.'

He was silent for a while, playing with his cup, twisting it between two fingers on its saucer. 'You weren't you either,' he said eventually. 'You'd become a stranger to me.'

'We'd become strangers to one another,' Juliet said. It felt like a concession, saying it. It also felt like the truth. She said, 'And now?'

'Now I want to make it up to you. I want you back,' he said. He smiled. The smile was small, tentative, far more hopeful than confident. 'I don't really care if your friends continue to ostracise me; I don't particularly need their approval. I'd like to win yours, though, however long that might take to achieve. It took the loss of you to teach me just how much I love you. What I'd like is the chance of a fresh start with you. I know I don't deserve it, but I'd like that more than anything in the world.'

A few minutes later Jack paid the check and they left the restaurant, kissing under the awning out of the rain and then hugging each other tightly before parting from one another on the sidewalk.

Jack walked with his head down and his hands in his raincoat pockets. To Max, watching him from a doorway across the street, he looked oblivious to the downpour soaking his hair and seeping through the shoulders of his clothing. It was as though the weather could not depress his mood. He walked with the light tread of a man given a reprieve by a woman he had deceived and simply did not deserve to get a second chance with.

Max raised the hood of his track top and followed. He heard Jack start to whistle. The tune was not one he recognised, but it certainly sounded jaunty, given the awful weather and the dismal vista of wet streets and gridlocked road traffic. Max closed the distance between them to a few feet. His own tread, in his rubber-soled boots, was silent. He was careful to avoid splashing in any of the sidewalk puddles on the route.

Jack paused in front of him. He had reached the steps of his subway station. He was about to descend them when Max threw himself forward and collided directly with him.

'You want to watch where you're going,' Jack said, sounding surprised and indignant, as though the impact had taken the gloss off his mood.

'Fuck you,' Max growled, from under his hood. He took an abrupt step forward and shoved Jack violently, catapulting him down the stairs.

Thirty-six

Back in her apartment, as she sat and read a magazine on her sofa, for the first time in a long while Juliet felt both happy about her future and more relaxed about the present. There was a glass of wine at her elbow and music playing softly on her hi-fi over the faint hum of traffic from the bridge below. It was now forty-eight hours since she had had her surveillance cameras installed and in that time, they had recorded nothing she had not triggered herself.

Obviously, paranoia had been getting the better of her. It wasn't really all that surprising, was it? She had been emotionally bruised. The letter from the cop killer had jolted her into the realisation that sometimes there were violent and desperate perspectives totally in contrast to her own. Her assumptions had been undermined by that letter. It had proven to her that the world was not always the place it seemed to be.

But at least she had her apartment. There was no intruder. The sense of being watched she had experienced had been a fraught combination of nerves and insecurity. She had thought she had got through the ordeal of separation and homelessness relatively unscathed, but the experience had obviously exhausted her and she was only now really recovering.

She turned the page, absorbed in the article she was reading in her magazine, enjoying the luxury of her leisure time, making a mental note to start the novel written by Jack she had picked up earlier in the bookstore.

In the kitchen, though, where the cameras did not see, an uninvited visitor lurked beside the open wine bottle on her counter there.

Five minutes later, when she entered the kitchen to pour herself another glass, Juliet had her apartment entirely to herself. No sign remained of her intruder, no clue that anyone but her had visited her kitchen that night. Nevertheless, when drowsiness overcame her, she felt glad she had the surveillance cameras installed and ready to record any movement that might take place during the night.

She was startled awake the following morning. Something was moving softly behind her curtains, shuffling against the window pane. She sat up and grabbed a handful of curtain fabric and pulled it aside. Movement exploded in the pale triangle of light and space and revealed the grey and white whirr of feathers. Juliet realised that pigeons on the sill had been responsible for the peculiar noise she had heard. There was something odd about the light; it was bright, the sun higher in the sky than it should have been, the shadows less oblique than she was used to seeing them first thing in the morning.

She glanced at her wristwatch. It was almost ten o'clock! She leaped out of bed and grabbed the land line.

Despite her urgency and a bewilderment not far short of actual panic, she felt fuzzy again, her senses dulled. Where was her adrenalin when she needed it? Once again she almost felt sedated, insulated somehow from the sights and sounds and feel of the physical world.

Once was an occurrence she was prepared to shrug off. But this was the second time it had happened to her. Twice was more than just coincidence; twice amounted to a set of symptoms.

Someone answered her call. 'Hey, it's Juliet Devereau.' Her mouth felt cottony and dry. She had a full water glass on her bedside table. As parched as she was, she did not understand why thirst alone hadn't woken her before now.

Something caught her eye. An object that should not have been there lay on the floor under the night table. She bent down and picked it up. It was a syringe cap. It was a familiar enough object to her but totally alien in that environment. How the fuck had it got there? She looked around the room, trying to figure it out, her dulled brain attempting deductive reasoning; as effective, the way she felt, as trying to sprint through fog over ice. Her gaze fell to the empty wine glass on the bedside table.

From the phone receiver, a voice said, 'Hello?'

Juliet said, 'I'm sorry I'm late, but somehow I've seriously overslept. I'll be there as soon as I can.'

She dropped the phone and started to dress. Her mind limped dully from what it was that was making her behave like this, to what would happen as a consequence of being late. ER doctors were not expected to be perfect, despite the popular perception. But they were expected to be totally reliable. If they were not reliable, they could not be counted upon and that meant they could not be trusted.

This was an easy conclusion to reach, even in her dulled state, because she knew it already. On the rushed journey to the hospital, she put her slowly clarifying mind to the problem of how to find out the things that she didn't know.

It was her subway ride that gave her the idea. She was seated opposite a sleeping construction worker she assumed had just come off a graveyard shift. He was dust-covered with grime-rimmed eye sockets and hair matted from wearing a hard hat.

He was cradling a lunch pail and with the eyes closed in his thrown-back head and a slackly open mouth, he looked about as alert as she felt. Then they rounded a bend and the carriage lurched. He slumped forward and the pail slipped from his grip onto the floor where it opened up with a clatter that woke him.

He leant forward, clearly embarrassed, scooping up the spilled contents of the pail, gathering an empty yoghurt pot, a half-full bottle of Pepsi Max, the remains of a sandwich wrapped in foil, an apple core and a bottle of pills with an upside-down label spelling the familiar word Demerol.

Poor guy, Juliet thought, through her own slowly clearing stupor, *having to take painkillers of that strength to get through the working day. Hope he isn't working high up. Hope he isn't working where he needs his agility and wits about him halfway sedated on that stuff.*

And all at once it occurred to her that that was how she felt; she felt like she had when she had just had her wisdom teeth removed and the dentist had written her a script for Co-Dydramol and she had taken two of them, dry-swallowed on an empty stomach before a glazed evening in front of a TV schedule she could not afterwards remember.

She would take a toxicology test when she got to the hospital. The idea that she might have been drugged was outlandish. But the symptoms made it the obvious cause of how she was feeling, didn't they? She needed to get to the bottom of this mystery and she was schooled in diagnostic discipline. Taking a toxicology test was as logical as it was crazy.

It was only as she entered the main doors of the hospital, that Juliet remembered her surveillance cameras and, in her rush to get out of her apartment and into work, the fact that she had not checked to see if they had recorded anything new. She could not check her cameras, but she could check herself.

She took the blood sample herself, extracting a vialful from her arm with a hypodermic. She took a urine sample too. She filled out a full toxicology screen panel, put everything into a Ziploc bag and handed the bag to an ER technician with a fully completed work order for a TR to be carried out urgently.

On her break, Juliet ran into Sydney in the doctors' lounge. She was far more alert now than she had been earlier in the day. Her head had cleared and she thought she was probably functioning at a level so close to 100 per cent that no one would notice the difference. No one except Holstrom, anyway.

Quietly, Sydney said, 'I saw you were late again today.'

Juliet lowered her own voice in reply. She did not want the other staff members in the lounge to overhear what she had to say. She said, 'I slept through my alarm. I never oversleep and you're right, it's happened twice in two days.'

Sydney smiled. She cocked her head, amused and said, 'So what's going on? You been out late?'

'I've been seeing Jack.'

'Oh, no. Jules . . .'

'We're taking it slowly. It's going really well.'

'What about the cute guy at the exhibition? The guy from your building?'

'Max. Yeah. Didn't work out. Was never going to.'

'I hope he's a good loser,' Sydney said.

Juliet shrugged. 'Everything is going really well,' she said. 'Or everything would be, if it wasn't for this weird sleep disorder thing.'

'Disorder, babe, is when you don't sleep.'

'I do,' Juliet said. 'Like a log.'

'So buy a louder alarm,' Sydney replied. She gave Juliet's arm a consolatory squeeze and stood and walked away.

Juliet considered it all. Her mind had cleared, but there were no answers coming into focus. The clarity only brought the questions into greater and more urgent relief. The only thing she was certain of was that for Sydney to comment on her erratic time-keeping made it a general talking point among the entire department. She really would have to find a way to put a stop to it just as soon as she possibly could.

Juliet had little appetite for lunch. The sun was shining after the heavy rain of the previous day and the air had a crisp cleanliness to it she thought might help clear the remaining clouds from her head. So instead of eating in the canteen, she bought a sandwich and sat outside, in the ivy-clad quadrangle that offered a bit of quiet and seclusion behind the hospital's X-ray department.

She unwrapped and ate her sandwich very deliberately. She knew it was tuna and mayo because that was what the label said. She knew it contained slices of cucumber because they were freshly cut and crunched audibly between her teeth. She could not really taste anything yet, she realised. But for the texture of what she chewed, she could have been eating cardboard.

When her cell phone started to vibrate in her pocket, she assumed it was Jack. But it was Holstrom. She frowned. Her last conversation with her boss had been a bleak one. She did not want to hear that the boy she had used all her powers to save had strung himself up or opened his wrists in his cell. The tone of his letter had told her Carlos might well be a strong candidate for a suicide attempt. It would not be an attention-seeking cry for help; it would be the real deal with him.

But Holstrom wasn't calling about Carlos at all.

'I am looking at the admissions list for last night,' Holstrom said. 'Am I right in thinking your estranged husband is Jack Devereau, the author?'

Fear clutched at Juliet. Suddenly she did not feel quite so wrapped in cotton wool. She could taste the residue of fish and sunflower oil in a slick coating over her teeth. She was aware of the strength of the autumn sun, warming her scalp under her hair. She must have moved on hearing Jack's name, because a pigeon stabbing at the sandwich crumbs between her feet was startled by the reflex and took flight.

'He is. Why do you ask?'

'He was admitted to the hospital last night. Apparently he was pushed down a flight of subway steps. He suffered heavy bruising to his coccyx and his sternum and his head was cut. His right knee was badly jarred, exacerbating an old high-school football injury. He walked out of here, apparently. Though I suspect it was more of a limp. He will live, Juliet, but he was pretty badly bashed up. He did not recognise his attacker. The police are treating it as a random incident of unprovoked violence.'

'It must have been random,' Juliet said. 'Jack hasn't an enemy in the world. Well, aside from the odd book critic.'

'Critics don't push authors down flights of steps.'

'No,' Juliet conceded. 'They don't.'

But she ended the call uneasily. There was a chill creeping through her, making the hairs on the back of her neck stand on end and the gooseflesh rise on her arms. She had never been a great believer in coincidence. Things were stacking up. There was no defining pattern yet, but things were definitely out of whack.

Thirty-seven

Jack walked gingerly towards Juliet's apartment building. Max watched his progress from nine floors above. He felt fairly satisfied at the damage he had inflicted on the man. Even from the angle and distance from which he watched, Jack's gait was laboured, handicapped by a brown grocery bag that looked full and heavy. He must have shopped locally, Max thought, or he would have taken a cab in his condition, hampered by his injuries and burdened by the weight of a bag. He was too far away for Max to be able to make out details but he expected that pain, and possibly the drugs prescribed to ease it, would make the man dazed-looking and pale.

Jack was now at the door of the apartment building. Max watched him grimace and juggle with his cell phone. He did not put it to his ear. He was sending someone a text message and Max didn't need to be a genius to guess who that someone was. Max watched Jack slip the phone back into his coat pocket. Then the acuteness of the angle put him out of sight as he approached the building's door.

Max was standing in Juliet's darkened bathroom, holding one of her dresses, stroking the silky smooth fabric, speculating on what kind of occasion she would wear it, how she would accessorise it, whether she would ever wear it out with him, when he heard Jack come in.

Max's immediate thought was one of incredulity. He could not believe that Juliet had taken the insolent liberty of giving this stranger a key. Max was the one who determined who should come and go freely in his building. It was not something Juliet should have taken it upon herself to do without consulting him. The guy was strolling along the hallway towards the kitchen as though he was here by right; as though he owned the place. Despite his limp he was almost swaggering. To the crackle and staccato thumps of groceries being unpacked, Max hid behind the bathroom door and waited. The dress he had been stroking hung forgotten from one tightly clenched fist.

Jack stood right next to the newly refurbished wine alcove. Its door was wide open. He had brought with him two bottles of wine. One was a nice Chilean Merlot, a decent wine, but nothing special. The other bottle, however, was a very special wine indeed. It was a '64 Château Margaux he had bought in the hope of opening in celebration. Maybe not this evening, but soon, when he put the vital question and Juliet agreed that they should move back in together.

He opened the Merlot and left it on the counter to let it breathe. The Margaux, he decided, he would store in the appropriate place. So he entered the wine closet looking for a rack, hoping his prized bottle would not lie there for long enough to gather a patina of dust. He switched on the light. And that was when he noticed that the back wall of the wine closet was cracked.

The crack was not natural. Panelling fissured along the grain of the wood from which it was made. This crack was a straight vertical line, like something deliberately and very neatly contrived. He walked towards the closet's rear wall and looked at it more closely. Then he pushed at the crack experimentally, and it swung back on concealed hinges, revealing a labyrinthine space. He could see plaster rough over brickwork and rodent droppings on a stone floor.

'What the fuck is this?' Jack said out loud, momentarily stunned. He had never seen anything like this in his life. There was something profoundly clandestine and also unmistakably menacing about what he was looking at. He could think of no purpose for it that was not sinister. He was damn sure about one thing: Juliet knew nothing about it.

He pushed the door back fully and put his head into the space and peered around. It was a secret passage. It extended into the gloom to left and right of where he stood and at intervals was suffused by feeble patches of light. He walked fully into the passage. It was high enough for him to stand in.

'Shit,' he said to himself.

His instinct was to get out of the apartment. He knew that the mind responsible for this perverse secret architecture could only be as dark and foreboding as the passages it had fashioned. He wanted to escape because he thought that his discovery was very dangerous. But he also wanted to warn Juliet. She must never return. His instincts told him that she wasn't safe here. No one was safe here. Anyone who entered this apartment was merely prey to whatever creature lurked in these corridors.

Several details that had failed to trouble him individually now began to stack up for Jack and form a disturbing pattern.

The rent charged for this place wasn't just competitive. For the location and dimensions of the apartment, the rent was absurdly low. No realtor had been involved in brokering the tenancy. Juliet had told him that the owner of the building had recently died. Just as she had told him that the references she had supplied had never been checked.

There was Amelie's skittish behaviour on the evening of his dinner here. The dog had been nervous when she should have been overjoyed at being reunited with Juliet. And Jack had felt himself a strange sense of being observed; it had seemed to him as though the two of them were somehow on display.

He had wondered if the creepy old guy Juliet had told him about, the dead guy whose table they ate from, was haunting the place and watching them. He'd mentioned what he'd sensed to her only very reluctantly and because he thought she might be somehow threatened by it.

He turned from the kitchen into the hallway and stopped dead in his tracks. Looming before him with a grinning, fixed stare was the guy with the glasses.

Jack saw him tense and recognised the spasmodic swiftness of the movement and the hatred and fear that prompted it and he knew with cold certainty that this was the man who had pushed him down the subway steps. The hooded top had obscured his features when he'd done that. But there was something singular and unmistakable about the way the fellow moved: quick and somehow furtive at the same time.

Max took a step towards him. Jack knew that he was going to have to fight to get out of Juliet's apartment. He knew about the fight or flight response to the impending threat of physical confrontation and flight was not an option here; not unless he found a way of descending nine flights safely from out of one of the apartment windows.

A fight with Max was not an enticing prospect. He looked strong and though he did not look sane, he looked focused and determined. Jack wasn't afraid of him though. He was furious on his own behalf at the unprovoked subway assault, and utterly disgusted at what that skulking labyrinth he had chanced upon had done to breach Juliet's privacy.

'You have no right to be here,' Max said.

'You've no business talking about rights,' Jack said. 'What are you, some kind of Peeping Tom? Some kind of fucking pervert?'

Max winced slightly at that. There was truculence in his tone when he said, 'You never deserved her.'

'What?' Jack said. 'Get out of my fucking way, you creep. Back off, or I'll hurt you with a smile on my face.'

But Max was the only one of the two of them who smiled.

Thirty-eight

Juliet's cell phone rang and she saw that someone had sent her a text message she had not yet read. She answered the call and recognised the lab technician's voice as the woman said, 'Doctor Devereau?'

'Yes?'

'I faxed the toxicology report you ordered.'

Juliet stepped into her ER station and grabbed the fax from the machine. She read it with a dawning sense of horror. The list of medications that had been identified from her blood and urine read like a lexicon of sedatives and sleeping draughts. The words Vicodin, Valium and Demarol were irrefutable in black capitals on the one-page report.

She opened her unread text. It was from Jack. It had been sent half an hour earlier and said, *Dinner at your place, 7pm, don't be late! x*

Five minutes later she was in the street making for home, still in her scrubs, her cell phone at her ear, silently imploring Jack to pick up. He didn't. She left a message. 'Jack,' she warned, 'don't go into my apartment. I don't know how the fuck it happened, but somehow . . .'

The call dropped with a series of beeps.

'Fuck.' She did not bother to call back. She just ran down the street at greater speed. She wasn't dressed for running but she'd never run faster or more urgently in her entire life.

I don't know how the fuck it happened but I've been taking a cocktail of drugs in the evening. It's madness. But there's method in the madness because the drugs all have complementary and overlapping effects. They all do the same basic job on the human body and mind. Their aim is temporary oblivion and they make me wonder just how much they've made me oblivious to.

I've been the victim of a violation. I've been the victim of a planned crime, carefully carried out. Every premeditated crime shares two characteristics: opportunity and motive.

Opportunity was an easy one, but motive? *Oh, Jesus,* she thought. She would have closed her eyes, had she not been running down the street at full speed. It hardly bore thinking about. Neither did the jeopardy Jack might have placed himself in with his chivalrous gesture of cooking her dinner.

She rode the elevator to the ninth floor and fumbled in her pocket for her keys. She paused for just a half-beat as she passed Max's door. When she reached her own, ominously it was already open. She had to gather her courage before she found the will to enter her own home.

'Jack?' she called.

Nothing.

She moved through the living room, towards the kitchen where she saw the bag of groceries that Jack had brought. It was only half emptied, there were still items on the counter. It was entirely out of character for him to have left things like that. He would not have left vegetables that needed chilling to wilt. He was, by habit, punctiliously neat.

With an effort that was almost palpable, she went through the rest of the apartment, looking for something unusual or anomalous, but there was nothing she could identify as out of place or strange.

Except when she returned to the living room. There, she noticed a red blinking light on the screen of the surveillance system. It was the signal to indicate that something had been recorded. It meant that there had been movement in her apartment while she had been absent from it.

She hit the playback button. She saw Jack enter the apartment with his grocery bag, his gait slightly stiffer than usual, as though he was nursing sore muscles after a really strenuous workout. He disappeared into the kitchen, but that was the last thing recorded.

There was no record of him leaving the kitchen. And the kitchen wasn't covered by the cameras. But there was no record of him leaving the apartment, which, since he wasn't there, there should have been.

Juliet was dwelling on this mystery when she saw that the surveillance system's screen listed another recorded incident. The time of the recording was 2.31 a.m. the previous night. It meant that someone or something had been moving around her apartment as she slept.

Her finger paused over the playback button. She felt almost sick with foreboding at what it might reveal. For a moment, she was too afraid of what had been filmed to press the button and view it. She knew, though, that she had to. She took a deep breath and pressed the button and the screen flickered revealing the security camera view from the living-room feed.

The screen showed the living room and in the upper left-hand corner, the entrance to the bedroom. Playback jumped ahead of time to find a moment of movement in the room. In jerking, time-cut style editing, Juliet watched the image of herself from the night before as she walked back to the bedroom. She saw that the time at which she did so, was 23.05 p.m.

The recording stopped. Then it jumped forward in time again. It showed 1.05 in the morning. Almost two hours after she had turned in, something shifted in her apartment. She thought she sensed movement, on the edge of the frame, near the front door? Maybe it was actually near the kitchen.

A figure abruptly stepped into the frame. Juliet gasped in fear and physically recoiled, forced back by the sheer shock of what she was witnessing. Deducing something from an item of technology was not the same as seeing an intruder, looming on the screen in the early hours of the night in her private space.

The figure was facing away from the camera. Who was it? Would she recognise him? *Motive*, she thought. *Opportunity*. In excruciating slow motion, as if somehow sensing the hidden scrutiny of the lens focused on him, or at least wary and suspicious, the figure turned. And Juliet felt dread shudder through her as she recognised Max. She expelled a pained whimper. The figure on the screen paused. And then he passed into her bedroom and out of the reach and sight of the camera lens.

The screen went to static and then to black. And then the time code showed 1.55 a.m. and Max slipped like a burly phantom out of her room and across the screen before disappearing once more from view. The screen went black again. And then it came on, showing daylight, a frantic Juliet rushing, late for work at the edge of the frame and the time code spelled out 10.03.

He had been in her room for forty-five minutes while she had been oblivious to his presence. He had contrived that, hadn't he? To what end had he drugged her so comprehensively? She thought that she probably knew the answer to the question, grotesque as the answer would be. She wondered did she have the strength to find out, conclusively. She was shaking, on the verge of hyperventilating, and only her medical training and a supreme self-discipline was preventing that from happening now. At the edge of hysteria, with hands made clumsy and disobedient by dread and panic, Juliet grasped the remote and changed the feed on the monitor to the bedroom camera.

The screen displayed a close, high-angle view of the bed. Juliet entered the room and put her water glass on her night table, then picked it up and took a sip, put it down again, pulled back the duvet and settled into bed. She saw that her eyes radiated a red glow on the screen, as though caught in the flash of a cheap, disposable camera.

The film jumped forward in short, staccato cuts, revealing her own toss-and-turn movements during a restless slumber. Then there was a long moment. Juliet just lay in it, at its centre, when suddenly, Max entered the room.

At first, he just stood at the foot of the bed. He seemed to be staring at her. Then he sank to his knees beside the bed and sort of slid and shuffled under it. He had vanished from sight, the movement in the room had ceased and the screen went black. Juliet, watching the monitor, had to fight to prevent herself from breathing a sigh of relief. But worse was to come, the strong part of her mind insisted to her. Much worse. He had not sedated her merely to do this.

The picture clarified with a start. The time code had shifted forward by ten minutes. Max was rising from under the bed. Ambient light from the street and bridge traffic below, painted him purple and his eyes were scarlet so that he looked like some grim and determined demon.

He took off his shirt. He methodically stripped off the rest of his clothes, the deliberation in his movements a demonstration of his sureness that his victim would not wake, then he peeled back the duvet and poised over her. There was some slithery item in his fist, a piece of clothing Juliet could not properly make out. He draped this across her naked groin in a movement so formal it seemed almost ceremonial. Then he climbed onto the bed and straddled her. He squirmed and thrust spasmodically, huge in the camera's eye, until finally he shuddered to a stop.

He extricated himself from her and, as Juliet watched, aware of the loudness of her own breathing in her ears and the cold sweat that had broken out all over her body, he crouched over her, moving in pecking stabs of motion for a while, kissing her, she supposed, but from the angle at which she watched in horror, less like a demon now than a large arachnid eating leisurely at something stunned but still living at the centre of its web.

Somehow she managed to squeeze the remote's stop button. The image on the screen disappeared, as though retreating back into nightmare, its rightful domain. It was an abomination. But she knew it had happened. The toxicology report had shown how he had prepared her for her ordeal and his sick gratification. The surveillance camera had recorded what he had done. The remaining mystery in the churn of Juliet's nauseated mind was how on earth he had got in.

And where on earth was Jack?

Thirty-nine

There was a knock just then at the door. Someone banged their knuckles against it three times. In the charged silence that followed, Juliet crept to the door and looked through the peephole. Max stood outside in the hallway. She caught her breath and moved away from the door on silent feet. But then, behind her, as she reached the living room, she heard the doorknob start to turn and remembered that the door was not locked.

A moment later Max peeked his head into the living room. He was neatly attired. In one hand he carried a bottle of wine. Juliet could see enough of the label to see that it was Château Margaux. Seeing her he smiled, easily. He looked very relaxed, as though everything was totally normal and he hadn't a care in the world. 'You just get home?'

'Yeah.' Standing where he was, at the entrance to the living room from the hallway, he was blocking her escape route.

He handed her the bottle. She took it. 'I found this great old vintage in August's wine closet,' he said.

'I'll open it,' Juliet said. She did not honestly know how she had taken it from him without fumbling the bottle to the floor. She was controlling the urge to tremble only by brute force of will. She felt a mingling of disgust, anger and fear. But the fear was the dominant emotion. Where the hell was Jack?

She stepped into the kitchen. Max followed her, which was only natural, she thought, while thinking him the most unnatural man in the world. He was a creature dragged from dark subconscious dreams, a beast made flesh, standing behind her, watching her in black, secret amusement. She started to pick at the foil of the bottle neck with a paring knife but could not control her mutinous hands. They were shaking too much to achieve the task.

'Here,' Max said, 'I can do that for you.'

He took it from her, opened the bottle and poured two glasses, spilling a little of the wine as he poured. He gestured for her to sit at the kitchen table and she did so. She did not feel in thrall to him but she was more terrified than she had ever been of anyone in her life. She was alone in the presence of a madman.

Max was clearly insane. He was sexually obsessed with her. Risk and retribution did not inhibit him. He did not fear being caught and punished. It made her wonder bleakly what steps he might have taken to make sure he wouldn't be; it made her wonder what his insanity and carnal appetite would drive him to do now.

For the moment she had to live in the moment, she did not feel she had a choice. She must not provoke or confront him or otherwise inadvertently pull the hair trigger of his rage. She had to bide her time and recognise her opportunity to escape him when it came.

He slid a glass of wine towards her. He gestured over

her right shoulder and said, 'Could I have that towel?'

Juliet turned to reach for the towel and when she turned back to hand it to him she saw his hand move across the top of her wine glass. Had he put a sedative into her drink? Had he spiked it again?

'Thanks,' he said, taking the towel. He mopped up the spillage and then stood to put the towel back and she swapped their glasses in the brief second while his attention was elsewhere. She did it deftly. She did not think that he could have noticed. She took a sip. He did the same. He seemed to be watching her, she thought, every bit as carefully as she was watching him.

Max said, 'You OK?'

'Exhausted,' she said, 'not sleeping well.'

She took out and checked her cell phone for a signal. She saw him watch her do it. There wasn't one. He had said that at the outset, hadn't he? He had said that cell phone reception was poor and sporadic in the building. It might have been the only unequivocally honest thing he had said to her. Where was Jack?

'I like this wine,' Max said.

Juliet had started to feel dizzy.

'Here.' He offered her a napkin. She had started to sweat. She did not bother to thank him. She checked her phone again and saw that she now had a signal.

'I'll be right back,' she said, feeling light-headed as she rose from her chair, starting to punch a number into the phone, hearing her own voice as a stranger's, thick and slurry.

Max took her free hand and held it. 'Why are you calling him?'

'Where is he?' She felt barely able to speak. She could not properly fill her lungs with air and her mouth would not shape the words in the way she intended.

'Why would you give him a key to my building?'

'Oh, God. You know where he is, don't you?'

'All you do is betray me.'

'What have you done to him?'

He squeezed the hand he had grabbed, hard and suddenly, and Juliet screamed as she felt her tendons crack and knuckles bunch with the crunching force of his grip. She yanked away from him and staggered, her balance badly impaired.

'You put something in my drink,' she said. But the drug did nothing to take the edge off her terror. She felt that growing inside her, uncontrolled.

'This time you will be awake,' he said. 'You will enjoy the experience fully conscious.'

She still had the paring knife in her pocket. She only had a fraction of time in which to act, perhaps only seconds. She took the knife from her pocket and lunged, slamming it blade-deep into his shoulder twice before Max could fend her off, pushing her to the ground. She heard the knife land on the kitchen floor with a clatter where she could not reach it.

He stood over her, breathing heavily. There was no pain on his face and no surprise. Just a dark fury that she realised now, too late, his facial features had been made for. This was the real him. He had no need to mask his nature or intentions any more. He said, 'Stop. Making. Me. Hurt. You.'

It was the tone you might adopt with a truculent

child. It was a tone that told her in five words that this man had never really related normally to another human being. People were there only to obey him. Anything but slavish obedience would be interpreted as an unacceptable slight. He lived in a world in which he made the rules and nobody was his equal. He would find a way to justify everything he did, however terrible. He always had, hadn't he?

Forty

The awful certainty came to her as she lay on the kitchen floor, with the contorted face of Max above her, staring into hers, that Jack was dead. She was on her own. Instinct for survival jolted through the drugs and she lashed out at him with a foot, scrambled to her feet and grabbed a carving knife from the knife block on the counter. He came up behind her and she spun and lunged at him, snagging the long, sharp blade of the knife on his shirt. He stepped back. She ran at him again with the knife raised high. He retreated into the wine closet, closing the closet door on his own hand in a bid to escape the frenzy of her attack, Juliet slashing at and slicing open his forearm in a deep wound as he did so.

She had the gratification of hearing him gasp once in agony as he pulled his hand through the gap and closed the closet door behind him. And she had the satisfaction of knowing that she had trapped him in there. At least, she had when she had pushed the refrigerator on its side to block the door from being opened again.

She stumbled. Whatever drug he had slipped into her wine glass was taking effect in her system, numbing her, making her slow and clumsy, deadening her nerves, overcoming her ability to think and act. It was as though she had blundered into a narcotic swamp and she did not know how long she had before it engulfed her completely.

She staggered into her living room and tried the landline, but it was dead. She had no time to think about how that had happened. She took out her cell phone but there was no signal. She reeled towards her front door. But it would not open. It was as though it had been locked from the outside. She had an insane vision then of Max outside her door, clutching his injured arm, bleeding on to the hallway floor with a leer of triumph on his face having locked her in and secured her in his prison. She shook the thought from her head; it was impossible. The door did not lock from the outside, did it? And Max was safely secured in the wine closet. He was her prisoner, not the other way around.

But the drug was forcing her further into that swamp. She lurched around her apartment, trying to get a signal on her cell phone. It was no use. There was nothing.

She tried to assess her situation, but it was becoming more difficult by the second for her to concentrate. She slammed a fist into a wall in sheer frustration and the bright flare of pain cleared her mind for a couple of minutes.

She was stuck, trapped in her own apartment with no way to get out, no way to raise the alarm and there was a wounded madman confined – for now – in her kitchen wine cellar. And she was drugged. That was her predicament and it was grim and dangerous and getting worse as the drug further enfeebled her. The question was what could she do?

She checked the Internet, because she should have done that before, she thought, chiding herself. Her computer booted up but there was no broadband signal. She tried to connect three times before giving up on that. She went and piled what weighty items she could against the refrigerator to securely wedge shut the door of the makeshift prison occupied by Max.

She tried to break the glass of her living-room window by throwing a hardwood chair against it. Plate glass hitting the sidewalk in a shower from the ninth floor of a Brooklyn building would have alerted curious eyes to what was going on up there, wouldn't it? But the glass was tough, the chair heavy and her throw a puny effort in her drug-weakened state. The chair bounced harmlessly back into the room.

She went into her bathroom. She rifled through her medical cabinet, grabbing headache pills. She knew of course how they worked, which chemical ingredients they comprised. They contained caffeine and the stimulant pseudoephedrine. She slammed down four pills, gulping water after them.

Juliet went and sat on her bed. The temptation to bury herself in her duvet and seek what refuge she could in sleep was almost overwhelming. But that was the effect on her mind of the cocktail of drugs Max had slipped her, she knew. Sleep here had been anything but a safe refuge. This had been the scene of her violation. The apparent safety of her bedroom was a thin and probably fatal illusion.

She looked out of the window, over the gables and gantries of the great riveted iron bridge; over the twinkling waste of the East River to Manhattan and its million twinkling lights and stone canyoned enormity. And the reality hit her of how alone she was in the looming, indifferent vastness of the city. She was alone and she was helpless, wasn't she?

This gloomy reverie was interrupted by the ringing of her cell phone. She saw the glow of its green display on the floor by her feet and heard it vibrate as it received an incoming call.

It was Jack, she thought. It had to be Jack. He had gone to a bar to while away the time before she returned from work and had got absorbed in some ball game or boxing match being televised there. He did not know she had been sexually assaulted, made supine by a cocktail of sedatives administered without her knowledge. He did not know she had fought and wounded a madman who was now her prisoner.

He would know now, though, she thought, reaching for the phone, because she would tell him and he would return urgently with a posse of armed police officers and they would take Max off to Bellevue buckled into restraints with a rubber clamp in that grinning mouth. And he would never do again to anyone what he had done to her because there would be no end to his incarceration, other than death in his cell endured staring out at a barred window.

And that was the fate he fucking deserved.

The call ended as her fingers reached around the phone. She groaned inwardly.

'Hello?' she said it anyway, desperate not just for rescue but to alleviate her solitude. She craved a human voice. 'Hello?'

But there was only silence because the instrument was dead in her hand.

She did not sense a presence in the room with her until it was too late. Probably that was the drug from the wine, dulling her instincts, swamping her natural alertness. She was only aware that Max had returned when she felt the grip of his hand around her throat. How the fuck had he got out of the wine closet?

His free hand found her mouth, stifling her scream of fear and rage. He stared at her. There was desire in his eyes and the set of his mouth. Incredibly, there was also what she figured must pass in his incomplete mind for love. She was scared to death, but the air had an erotic charge around the two of them she could almost hear the crackle of.

If she wanted to survive this, she had to play along. The old cliché had it that only when you were close to death did you really appreciate life. Juliet felt that cliché intensely; at the moment she wanted to live more than she ever had before.

She reached out and touched Max's face. The effect was immediate on him. His eyes softened and his mouth puckered coyly like an adolescent boy's. He melted under her touch. Certain that she had never caressed anything quite so loathsome, she cocked her head and smiled at him, inviting him with her eyes. He touched her slowly, tenderly now, the tears trickling down his cheeks, the simpering expression on his face that of someone fulfilling his life's most precious dream.

The carving knife lay on the bed next to her. His blood was congealing on the blade, but Max seemed unaware of the weapon or its proximity. Her free hand moved towards it as Max leaned in to kiss her. Incrementally, her hand got closer and closer to the hilt of the knife. And then she had it and gripped and raised it high.

With no hesitation at all, Max raised his own hand and grabbed her by the wrist.

'Stop. Making. Me. Hurt. You,' he said again. It was a promise, not a threat.

She broke free of his grip on her by clawing at his eyes with the hand not holding the knife. He punched her hard on the mouth and again with a dull thud of his knuckles juddering against her right cheekbone. She fell off the bed onto her face, but managed to scramble up and into the bathroom before he could grab her securely again. She slammed the door closed, locked it and cowered in the corner furthest away from it, gasping for breath.

Forty-one

Max hammered on the door. It shook on its hinges with the pulverising force of him, but seemed solid and held. After a while, he stopped and there was silence.

She needed a weapon. She had dropped the carving knife in the bedroom struggle. *Think, girl,* she said to herself. *Come on Juliet, you can't give up now. You can't let that bastard get you. You can't. You have too much going for you, too much to live for. You can't let a miserable pervert like this guy deprive you of your future. You can't. Not in these horrible circumstances, not in this sordid way.*

She felt more alert. That was something. The caffeine and pseudoephedrine she had ingested were working against the drug he had given her. Unless it was the adrenalin. Whatever was doing it, she was escaping the narcotic swamp that had threatened to submerge her. Her brain felt more alert and her body more responsive.

She was pretty badly beaten up. Her vision was blurred in her left eye and it was swelling painfully. In a minute, she would examine the damage in the bathroom mirror. First, though, she really had to improvise a weapon of some sort. She had inflicted two puncture wounds to his shoulder and sliced deeply into the meat of his forearm. But he had not been bleeding excessively on the bed and he still possessed his strength and agility. She had hurt him, but she had not severed an artery or damaged any of his vital organs. The significant and depressing fact was that she had not hurt him seriously enough to really slow him down.

She put on the light and looked around. There was a stool in the bathroom, but it was too heavy to wield effectively as a club. There was the shower curtain rod, but that was a puny length of aluminium. She was so desperate, she thought about smashing the mirror above the sink and improvising a towel handle around a jagged shard of glass. Doing so would arm her with a primitive dagger.

Her eyes descended to the sink. There was a hairpin resting there. It was an antique one she had bought the previous year in a flea market. Juliet picked it up, unlatching the sharp silver needle that would secure it to her hair. It was steel and it was about four inches long. She could conceal it. It was not ideal, but it was better than being totally unarmed.

She stared at the bathroom door. She knew that Max was on the other side of it. She knew he would try to get in eventually, but the apartment was totally silent out there. She was quite surprised he had not rushed at the door and tried to batter it down with his shoulder. Then she remembered that one of his shoulders would be very sore from the puncture wounds inflicted by the paring knife.

She moved towards the door and listened intently. There was still nothing. She got down on her hands and knees and lowered her bruised face to the floor. She tried to look under it. As she did so, she caught the flit of a shadow cast just for a fraction of a second by something moving out there.

She stood. She would use this brief period of respite to examine her hurt eye. She approached the bathroom's full-length mirror to do so. She leaned in towards the mirror, a few inches from the glass to get a really good look.

The white of her eye was bloodied by a network of broken blood vessels. There was blood in a purple swelling underneath the eye and the lid too was swollen and bruising quite badly. She thought that she looked like someone who hadn't worn their seatbelt in an auto collision.

Or, she thought grimly, she looked like the victim of a particularly savage incidence of domestic violence. Either way, the bloodied and battered face staring back at her now was one she had seen on countless occasions in the ER. She had never in her worst nightmares imagined she might see it reflected back at her from a mirror.

She was examining a bloody cloud around her iris when the mirror glass exploded outwards in front of her face and Max's lunging arm reached through the jagged hole he had punched through it and grabbed her around the neck.

She screamed. Shock and outrage forced a shrill moan out of her that emptied her lungs and assaulted the air and reminded her she was still alive. She wrestled desperately. She so desperately wanted to survive this.

But he was stronger than she was and his grip on her was the iron grip of insanity and she could not shake free of it and after a few seconds of frantic struggle, he was able to haul her through the shattered glass.

He flung her to the ground. She landed as limply as a rag doll on some rusted old water pipes. She could smell the rust. There was light, but it was feeble. She seemed to be in some sort of tunnel, or passageway, she thought, but guided by the strong and savage instinct for survival she fumbled open the antique pin and plunged it into the meat of Max's thigh before fleeing into the gloom beyond him.

Juliet knew that he would follow. She was at a disadvantage: he knew the way around the hellish place he had dragged her into. He would navigate the passageways skilfully, where she merely fled in the full-pelt rush of total panic. This was his world.

Rats scurried and fled as her feet beat their desperate tattoo on the floor. Pipes rattled. Light came and went in dim yellow swatches from the rooms she ran parallel with. She sought only escape. She was fit and quick and she could run for ever and, if necessary, she thought that she would do exactly that.

She never saw the wall she hit. The denser darkness of the brick obstruction might have registered had both of her eyes been functioning properly, had her pursuer not drugged her, had she possessed even a modicum of composure in her attempt to get away.

She had hit the wall with a sickening impact and sank to her knees as her legs buckled under her. She could hear him approaching. She could hear the whisper of his feet growing louder as they covered what she knew to him must be familiar ground. She could see him, blurry at the edges, faceless in the darkness, hulking and indistinct and, as Juliet Devereau finally lost the fight to retain her consciousness, looking exactly like the bogeyman she had feared as a child.

Forty-two

Juliet had lost consciousness for an instant. She opened her eyes again. She realised that his progress in pursuit of her was not as implacable as she had supposed. Her flight had been random rather than planned. It had been that way out of necessity. She did not know her way around the vile labyrinth it was evident to her Max had cruelly used. He was walking in her direction, though. The whisper of his feet was a murmur now as he got closer to where she lay.

She struggled to get up. It was dark ahead and she rose shakily and put out her hands to guard against obstacles, feeling small and futile and impossibly trapped. She fought her way through some broken window panes and saw a light coming from above. A tunnel led to the light. It was human instinct to seek light in darkness and Juliet felt the tug of that illuminated place. It might provide a refuge for her. It could be no lonelier or desolate than the dark passageway in which she stood.

At first, she assumed the room in which she found herself that of some reclusive and elderly woman. Ancient dresses mouldered on hangers heavy with beads, swagged with detail picked out in brocade and black lace. An open jewellery box glimmered with heavy silver rings and bracelets and a rope of pearls coiled beside it like an opalescent snake. There was the musty smell of perfume long grown stale. There was a collection of crystal in a heavy display case full of faceted windows, still with the ornate key in the lock. There were ormolu clocks and veined marble vases and a book of pressed flowers, water-stained, smelling subtly of age and decay.

And then she saw the photographs. The boy between the parents in them had not changed so radically over the years that she did not recognise him. The room belonged to Max, she realised, with dawning horror. Just when she thought she might have crawled to safety, she was in Max's room. And it was a morbid shrine to his dead mother.

She tried to find her way out, frantically opening closets, pulling at the locked door, desperate for release from this horrible confinement and the threat it posed. There had to be a way out, didn't there? There had to be. Perhaps there would be a spare key. There was a bureau. She opened its drawers. Lying in one of them was a newspaper clipping. It was yellow and faded and its banner headline screamed: Husband kills wife. Then shoots self.

She found the keys to her own front door in the bureau. She took them. Then, sensing she was no longer alone in the room, she turned around. Max was there. He was standing right in front of her. He was staring at her, but he seemed miles away, somewhere else entirely. But he was very close. She could smell the harsh odour of his breath.

He said, 'I saw the whole thing. I was six years old.'

'You told me. You told me on the way back from your grandfather's funeral.'

He smiled. The smile was horrible, a grim contortion, a ghastly parody of good humour. 'When you were still responding sympathetically,' he said. 'Before the unfortunate change in you occurred.'

'You killed August. It was why you asked those questions. You killed him and it made you feel like God.'

'It was his time,' Max said, with a sigh. 'And I did it for you.'

He was blocking her way. She could only get out the way she had come in. It was a dreadful, defeating prospect, but she thought it was better than whatever he had planned for her. While she was alive there was hope, however slender that hope might be.

Max said, 'My father caught my mother cheating on him. I blamed him at the time. I sided with my mother. I've continued to blame him, down through the years. But that was before I discovered what women were capable of.' The look in his eyes clarified. Juliet was their focus now. 'That was before I met you,' he said, his face twisting into a snarl, raising his hands to attack.

She grabbed the lamp she had been planning to use since she first turned and saw him there. It was an old-fashioned oil lamp with a heavy brass base. It stood on an ornamental pillar to her right, against the wall. It was the same height as her shoulder and easy to reach for and swing. She smashed it hard into his temple and felt the judder of impact go through her arm before dropping it and running past him for the passages.

Staircases led this way and that, up as well as down. But the routes to the eighth-floor had all been blocked off. Heavy coils of barbed wire ferocious with steel thorns obstructed the way.

She ran with her arms outstretched, like someone in a sleeping nightmare, becoming familiar with the routes as she was forced to double-back like someone trapped in the bewildering turns of a maze.

He was pursuing her. He was not running. He did not need to, she realised with dismay. He could dictate her route and confine and cut her off in a dead-end as cramped and inescapable as a tomb. Still she ran. If there was no hope, there was at least defiance. She would not surrender herself to him. She would never do that so long as there was a single breath remaining in her body.

Forty-three

Juliet's capacity for violence astounded Max and he found her cruelty breathtaking. She was a doctor. She had sworn an oath to heal to the best of her ability. She was supposed to be compassionate by nature, wasn't she? It was a vocation, after all, not simply a career path. She wasn't a plastic surgeon or one of those society doctors out to wring what profit they could from a patient list of wealthy hypo-chondriacs. She worked in ER. She saved the poor and the ramshackle and the accident prone and the hapless victims of crime. Yet look what she had done to him.

His shoulder throbbed from where she had twice stabbed him. Each time his heart beat the puncture wounds there hurt like hammer blows. She had slashed at his forearm in the way a drunken butcher might. The blade had actually cut to the bone and he was only grateful it was muscle she had sliced through and not an artery.

She had tried to drive the carving knife through his chest on the bed, luring him with a leer of seduction he had thankfully seen through. And then she had tried to kill him yet again, tried to fracture his skull with the lamp August had bought as a present for his daughter and son-in-law.

The last blow had hurt him the most. Not because of the physical pain inflicted, but because of the timing of it. He had just confided in her his most painful secret in the hope that it would create some intimacy between them. But it had done no good. She was too callous and uncaring even to notice the precious, private nature of what he had revealed to her. She was one of those women, he had discovered too late, who cares only for themselves.

When he had still cherished dreams of their intimacy he had planned to ask Juliet to wear one of his mother's dresses. He had hoped that she might do it as a birthday treat for him or when they had been together for a while. It would have been a nice anniversary gesture.

She could have dabbed on a splash of his mother's perfume. She could have pulled on a pair of her Sunday gloves and carried her best handbag. She could have worn her shoes; the two women were around the same size, as far as he could remember. She could have had her hair done the way his mother did it, not to be morbid or ghoulish, just as a one-off treat for the man she loved.

That would not happen now, he thought bitterly, the throbbing of his stabbed shoulder a painful reminder of just how duplicitous Juliet had turned out to be. The possibility of her doing things to please him willingly had not just gone. It had never been there, had it? The Juliet he had hoped for had been just his romantic projection. Life was not a puppet theatre, you could not determine how people behaved. It had transpired that Juliet was vicious, manipulative, disloyal and insincere.

She would still wear his mother's clothes, though. He was determined about that. She would do it when she was dead. He would have to clean her up, apply a little make-up and dress her hair himself. But he would enjoy that. It was something, he thought as he closed in on her in the passageways, that he could look forward to. It would be a pleasant and absorbing diversion that would take his mind completely off his pain.

Shafts of light crisscrossed the section of passageway Juliet had found herself in. She no longer had to walk with her hands in front of her face. Holes had been bored at head-height in the right-hand wall of the passageway. It was from these that the light she could see by was cast. The illumination was steady and strong. She looked through one of the holes. It offered a perfect view of her own living room.

Realisation fully hit her then, with a sensation that felt like her stomach was being physically scraped out of her. Her skin crawled and she was wracked with a convulsive shivering. She walked to the next of the peepholes. It offered a more or less complete view of her ruined bathroom.

She ran. She did so out of blind instinct. She knew that he was stalking her, ever closer through this claustrophobic nightmare world he had put together. She had no choice but to run; going nowhere like a rodent in a maze or on a wheel in a cage.

She tripped and when she put her hands out to shield

her already battered face, something gave slightly in front of her and she saw a rectangle of light outlining a panel. She pushed through it. She blundered into her own recently reclaimed wine cellar. She had hardly recognised this fact, when a huge weight tumbled stiffly down on top of her, tipped by the concealed door she was coming through,.

She screamed with shock at first. But then again with sheer horror as she realised what had fallen on her. It was Jack. She had known in her heart he was dead since seeing the half-unpacked grocery bag in the kitchen on arriving home. Whimpering she heaved his stiffening weight off her. There was no time for grief. But she was sick and shaking as she looked at the man she loved. His flesh was cold and his face was ghastly in the grinning rictus of death. In her terror and pain she screamed again. She gave in to despair and the sound was shrill and loud and it reverberated through the labyrinth from which she had emerged. She knew that he would hear it and know its source and swiftly locate her, now. Dully, almost stubbornly, her brain insisted that she needed a weapon to fight him with. She supposed it was the instinct for survival. She sighed at its exasperating strength.

She saw the nail gun. It had slipped from its shelf, brought down by Jack's shoulder or one of his dead, flailing arms. It was lying beside her on the floor, bright and new and lethal.

She struggled to open the barricaded closet door until finally she managed to shove the fridge aside. Picking up the nail gun, she emerged into the kitchen. It was empty, and so was her living room. She emerged into the hallway and her door was still locked. After everything she had seen in the meantime, it no longer seemed surprising that he had contrived a way to lock her door from the outside. The entire apartment had been contrived. It was a cage and a trap and a stage. He had made it into those things.

She moved through her bedroom and into her bathroom. She looked at the broken pipes in the passageway beyond the shattered mirror. Shards of glass littered what she could see of the floor of that gloomy space. There was blood spattered and congealed there from their earlier struggle. A faucet dripped monotonously behind her.

I will have to alert the building's maintenance man to that, she thought, almost giggling at the notion. She was close to tripping into hysteria. She could not allow herself that refuge. She had to go back into the labyrinth. She had no other prospect of escape. She hefted the makeshift weapon in her hand. She did not feel much of a warrior.

She stepped into the passageway and he hit her in the gloom with a blow to the face that sent her crashing to the floor. She lay there in blood and leaking water and dust amid the broken metal pipes.

She lay there in shadow. Max was illuminated, as he sank to his haunches over her, by the light that bathed him from the bathroom. He had wrapped the hand he had hit her with in barbed wire, and the blood dripped from it onto the floor beside her. She supposed he was beyond feeling physical pain. She was not. He had gouged her cheek with the blow and the flesh there felt as though it was on fire.

He unwrapped the barbed wire from his fist. He leaned further over her. He said, 'You kissed me, and I thought, you could pull me out of these walls. I was never going to hurt you. That was never my intention. I swear to you it wasn't. But you betrayed me.'

He reached out for her. He moved his hands towards her neck. She lifted her arm and pressed the nail gun she had taken from the wine closet hard into his chest and triggered it with three explosive whumps.

He stood. He looked at the object Juliet held in her hand. His expression was incredulous. It did not change when he looked down at his chest and saw the three nail heads from the driven metal deeply puncturing him there. Blood blossomed from the wounds, across his chest, drenching his shirt in a sudden flood. He staggered then, and sank to the floor on his back.

Juliet was first and foremost a doctor. Instinct, raw and desperate, governed her response to the dying man on the floor beside her. She pumped his chest. She gave him mouth to mouth, willing her victim to live. Only when his gore had drenched them both and all hope was extinguished did she stop toiling over Max. Only when the life had clearly gone from him did she pause in her efforts and then, finally, stop.

She got to her feet. Tiny fragments of glass had become embedded in the skin of her knees. Blood was congealing in her hair and drying tightly across her face. She could only see out of one eye and it was likely that the earlier impact of her collision with the wall had broken her nose. The side of her face throbbed from the gash inflicted by the swiping barbed wire punch. Her clothes were rags, her senses pulverised by the drugs her central nervous system was struggling to resist.

She had won, but she felt no triumph. She had killed, but she felt no remorse. She had done only what she had needed to in order to survive an assault she had done nothing to provoke or justify. And she would have saved her attacker had it been within her power to do so.

She stifled a sob. She could not lose her composure now. She needed to find her cell phone and try to get a signal from it and call the police. She was still trapped in this bleak and alien place and they would liberate her from it and she would have her various wounds cleaned and dressed and the long journey to normality would begin.

There were practicalities to accomplish before she could allow herself to grieve for Jack. She had lost him. She was alone in the world again and soon, if she was not strong and determined, loss and grief would seem all the world had to offer her.

Forty-four

Holstrom suggested a three-month leave of absence from the hospital. She considered the offer compassionate and generous, characteristic of the man who had made it. But it was the last thing she actually needed.

'Grief needs to be confronted, not suppressed,' he said.

'I know that.'

'The ER is not a place for coming to terms with the loss of someone you loved.'

'I know that too.'

'Knowing and believing are not quite the same thing.'

'Work is therapeutic. I really do not want to have the time to dwell on what has happened.'

'You must take a break, Juliet. I insist upon it.'

They compromised on six weeks. The problem for Juliet was that it was her job that defined her. It was who she was. That was even more the case in the permanent absence of Jack from her life. Without the routine of work she barely knew who it was she was supposed to be.

Her physical injuries healed rapidly. Her nose was badly bruised rather than broken. Her damaged eye had suffered no permanent loss of vision. The gash on her cheek was deep and clean and was so skilfully sutured that she was told it would not leave a permanent scar. It had seemed strange to be treated as a patient at the hospital. It made her touchingly aware of how genuinely her colleagues actually cared for her.

She did not sign up for trauma counselling. She couldn't bear to talk about what had been done to her, couldn't stand to replay those last awful moments of Max's life, nor bring herself to think about Jack's. The images of Max bending over her, violating her, and the feel of the nails pumping into his chest were replayed endlessly when she tried to sleep. But it was the memory of the weight of Jack's dead body as it dropped onto her that made her wake, screaming, in the night.

Jack had died by strangulation. He had fought desperately hard to overcome his attacker, the pathologist said, despite the damage that had been inflicted when he was pushed down the steps of the subway station. The hospital had missed a fractured rib in the list of injuries from that earlier attack.

It must have made walking painful, with his burden of a full grocery bag. Even breathing normally would have been uncomfortable. But he had wanted more than anything to try to win her back and so he had ignored his own pain and discomfort to come over and cook her a meal. It had been a last, fatal gesture of the gallantry and love which had won her heart in the first place.

Jack had fought hard but Max had been stronger and had been armed with the ligature he carried in his pocket. It was a yard-long length of electrical cable tied between two clothes pegs, a makeshift garrotte, the weapon favoured by the Brooklyn killer Giuseppe Forno all those years ago. The police said he had probably improvised it on seeing his victim enter the building. Max was not a prolific killer, but he had shown a talent for it.

Max's death had given her as much closure as she could ever hope to have, and the rest she would deal with in her own way. It was a relief to discover that Max had not given her an STD, nor had he left her pregnant. Though by the time this was confirmed she already knew both were unlikely. The forensic experts had discovered a dress of hers in one of Max's drawers. It was the one she had wanted to wear but couldn't find on the long ago night of her house-warming dinner with Sydney and Mike.

It was caked in layers of dried semen. The camera angle had not allowed her to see what he was doing when he bucked naked above her unconscious body, but he had not been penetrating her. He had been masturbating above her into the satin folds of the stolen dress. She could not imagine what might have possessed his mind when he performed this perverse act. Nor did she really want to. She just wanted to put her life back together and try to move on from the experience.

With Jack dead, she was suddenly wealthy. Jack had left her everything. His father was dead, his mother had lost her mind to dementia and was well taken care of and would remain blessedly oblivious to the fact that her son had been murdered. Juliet was to profit from the royalties, Jack's lawyer Philip Beal told her, of the books she had never bothered to read.

She sold the house without ever being able to bear going back and seeing it again. They'd been happy there in the earlier part of their marriage, but she was done with the suburbs. And her last, enduring memory of the place was the one she most wanted to forget.

'I got it wrong,' she said to Sydney, over coffee one aimless morning a week into her enforced idleness.

'He was the one who was unfaithful, hon. You're going to tell me you drove him into her arms? Remembering the good times with Jack is fine. It doesn't qualify him for sainthood. Or you for martyrdom.'

'We both got it wrong. We were both to blame. But the marriage could have been saved. We were getting back on track and would have been happy together.'

'Happy ever after? Like in a story? Life isn't a fairy tale, Jules.'

'Yours seems to be.'

'From the outside, maybe. But we work at it and I was lucky to meet Mike and I'm thankful for that luck every day and believe me, so is he.'

'I thought I'd been given a second chance to get it right. I'd given Jack a chance to make amends. I was on the way to doing so anyway. And wholeheartedly.' She could feel herself tearing up.

'He's gone, Jules,' Sydney said, gently, taking and squeezing her hand. 'He was taken from you and he lost his life and it was tragic and shocking but he's gone. You need to accept that.'

'I do.'

*

The Tennis Club Blonde turned up at Jack's funeral. She was almost impossibly stylish in a black calf-length cashmere coat Juliet thought that had probably been bought for the occasion. She introduced herself as Celia Grey and without make up, her hair demurely pinned back under a black pill box hat, Juliet thought she looked very beautiful.

The time for acrimony had gone. Juliet would have thought that even had she not observed that Celia Grey's pale blue eyes were raw with grief.

'He loved you,' Celia said, simply.

'I loved him.'

'You were his world. He didn't know that, until he'd lost it.'

'He would have got it back,' Juliet said.

Sydney gave birth to a baby girl whom they named Sarah. Juliet was asked to be godmother, and it was the one bright spot in her life. She would take the responsibility seriously, she decided, be a proper presence in her life. She never wanted Sarah to feel as alone as she herself now felt.

On the day of the christening party, just three months after Jack's death, Juliet was astonished to find herself being asked out by Mike's brother, Rick. To any other single woman, he would have been a catch: funny, cute, a smart dresser and a lawyer, but the thought of being with another man, being touched by another man, was too horrendous to even contemplate, so she sat outside the restaurant where the christening party was being held trying to put her thoughts in order. She supposed that she must look normal, but if Rick could have seen the turmoil that went on inside, he wouldn't have come within a mile of her.

She said as much to Sydney who came out to join her, rocking Sarah in her arms.

'You know, Syd, it's ridiculous for me to go out with anyone. I don't think I could cope. I don't think they could cope. And I'm homeless again. And we all know what happened last time I was in this situation; it couldn't have ended worse.'

'I know.' Sydney sat down beside her, handing Sarah over, as if the sweet, solid weight of the baby could soothe her godmother. 'You're not going to find it easy for a while, but even though we have Sarah now, you can still come and live with us. We could do with a babysitter.'

Juliet smiled. 'Lovely as that offer is, you'll have enough disturbance being woken by Sarah's screams in the night. You really don't want to add mine to that list.'

'You still have nightmares?'

Juliet rubbed her eyes wearily. 'I can't see how they'll ever go. I try and put it behind me but it all comes creeping back while I'm asleep. Anyway, once I'm settled, Sarah can come for sleepovers with her auntie Juliet, and when she's older I'll feed her nothing but pizza and ice cream when she comes to stay and she'll never want to leave.'

'I can't wait, believe me. Once she's bigger me and Mike will be itching for a bit of down time. Now come on, come back in and I promise Rick won't make any more inappropriate proposals. Life will settle again,

Jules. It won't ever be the same, but it'll become normal for you, you'll see.'

'I know, Syd. That's what I'm afraid of.' But she got up, clasping Sarah to her, and returned to the party.

Forty-five

Juliet was house-sitting for one of the surgical residents at the hospital while the resident was on government secondment. It was a nice apartment. But it was temporary and the anxiety of not having a permanent home was a worry to Juliet that she had not the will or the energy to properly confront.

A week from the end of her temporary let, she received a letter. It arrived on embossed notepaper. It came from a Mr de Silva.

'I've remembered who he is. He's the guy who tried to rent me the place that was haunted,' she told Sydney over the phone.

'It wasn't exactly haunted,' Sydney said. 'There wasn't a ghost. Things didn't exactly go bump in the night.'

Juliet closed her eyes. She knew all about things going bump in the night. Ghosts were not required for that to happen. Monsters could do it just as effectively. 'What do you think he wants?'

'I have absolutely no idea,' Sydney said. 'Go see him. Find out what it is he wants. What have you got to lose?'

'You're right; I've already lost it all.'

She remembered that Mr de Silva was a dapper, middle-aged man who wore oil on his hair and a yellow rose in the buttonhole of his lapel. She could not imagine what he could want with her but she remembered him as so courteous in his manners he was almost stately. She could see no harm in going to meet and talk with him.

She met him in the lobby of the Carlyle. She supposed he had chosen it because it was a public space and she would likely feel safer there. And also because he was known there. As she walked into the hotel she noticed that the staff were solicitous in passing him, nodding and saying his name with little salutes. She gathered that he was probably a lavish tipper. It occurred to her that he might be wealthy in that unostentatious way people are when they have had money all their lives.

Mr de Silva rose to greet her. He had on an immaculate three-piece pinstripe suit with a gold watch-chain looped in thick links across his waistcoat. She saw his cufflinks when he sat back down and linked his fingers, resting his hands on his knees. The links were gold, with rubies mounted at their centre.

'I'm very grateful that you came.'

'I was intrigued,' she said. She sipped at the coffee he had ordered for her. The Carlyle did an excellent brew.

'I read the story in the newspapers. A lurid tale, Dr Devereau. Lies and exaggeration?'

'No. On the contrary, almost everything that got printed was true.'

He nodded. He was silent for a moment. Then he said, 'I feel partially responsible.'

'I can't imagine why.'

'You sensed a spectral presence in the apartment I showed you around. You knew there was a ghost. That was how, in the ninth floor apartment at the Brooklyn Bridge building, you knew there wasn't a ghost. Am I right?'

'I suppose so.' Juliet could not predict where this was leading.

'You knew the place wasn't haunted, because you'd been somewhere that was. So you found mundane excuses to justify the weird goings-on. You ignored the danger signs until it was too late.'

'You're right, Mr de Silva. That's essentially what I did.'

'Without your experience in my building, you would have become scared and suspicious a lot sooner.'

'Perhaps that's true. There's nothing that can be done about it now, though.'

'I feel culpable,' de Silva said. 'I want to make amends. I have a place you might like to move into. The rent is very reasonable.'

She thought that she would be taking her second cab ride in a day. But when he escorted her outside, the doorman gave a signal and a limousine pulled up with a liveried chauffeur at the wheel. The interior smelled of leather. When they had settled in their seats and were on their way, he smiled at her.

She said, 'Did you ever let your haunted apartment?'

He shook his head. 'Your visit was the decider. The

building is to be demolished. The city of New York has bought the property at a price most advantageous to me. They will build a new police headquarters there.'

They reached their destination. The building was so new that there was still the adhesive paper that protects the glass in transit on most of the windows. They took the express lift twenty floors up to the penthouse. It was a vast space, laid out like a loft, with pillars supporting the roof in the absence of interior walls.

Mr de Silva tapped at one of the pillars. They were thin, with a metallic lustre. 'Titanium,' he said. He held his arms wide. 'No neighbours. You have the whole floor to yourself.'

She looked at the ceiling. 'And above?'

'A garden,' he said. 'Your garden. You can grow anything you like there. I have every confidence that your garden will flourish.'

'I can't afford this place,' Juliet said.

'Oh, but you can,' Mr de Silva said.

'It's totally out of my league.'

'You can afford it,' he repeated. 'Trust me, Dr Devereau. You can.'

The rent was four thousand dollars a month and was fixed for a five-year term. Five years sounded to Juliet like a reasonable time in which to construct a new life for herself. Her god-daughter Sarah would be reading books by then. What she herself would be doing was far less easy to predict. This apartment would be a good place from which to start. In fact, Juliet thought, it would be perfect.

'You will need to buy furniture, of course,' Mr de Silva said. 'You will need to buy a bed.'

'A futon, I think,' Juliet said.

Mr de Silva frowned. 'A futon?'

She smiled at him. 'A bed where the mattress lies flat on the floor.'

HAMMER

Hammer has been synonymous with legendary British horror films for over half a century. With iconic characters ranging from Quatermass and Van Helsing to Frankenstein, Dracula, and now the Woman in Black, Hammer's productions have been terrifying and thrilling audiences worldwide for generations. And there is more to come.

Leading actors including Daniel Radcliffe, Hilary Swank and Chloe Moretz are now following in the footsteps of Hammer legends Sir Christopher Lee, Peter Cushing and Bette Davis through their involvement in new Hammer films.

Hammer's literary legacy is also being revived through its new Partnership with Arrow Books. This series will feature original tales by some of today's most celebrated authors, as well as classic stories from more than five decades of production.

Hammer is back, and its new incarnation is the home of smart horror – cool, stylish and provocative stories which aim to push audiences out of their comfort zones.

For more information on Hammer,
including details of official merchandise, visit:
www.hammerfilms.com